Vermont Bound

By Walter Luce

Oak Tree Press   Taylorville, IL

VERMONT BOUND, Copyright 2012, by Walter Luce, All Rights Reserved. Printed in the United States of America. No part of this book may be used or reproduced in any manner whatsoever without written permission except in the case of brief quotations used in critical articles and reviews. For information, address Oak Tree Press, 140 E. Palmer St., Taylorville, IL 62568.

Oak Tree Press books may be purchased for educational, business or sales promotional purposes. Contact Publisher for quantity discounts

First Edition, July 2012

ISBN 978-1-61009-201-2
LCCN 2012937977

To my wife Bonnie...
for giving me her valuable input,
support and encouragement to write ...

and to my editor Arlene Uslander
for her expert help, input and patience.

CHAPTER—1

Nickolas J. Pappas, known by his associates as Niko, successfully appealed his pornography conviction. The authorities had yet to connect him with the murder of a fellow competitor. In a matter of hours, he would be released from prison on five-hundred thousand dollars bail. Niko, confined to a wheelchair, waited for his driver and bodyguard, Deon Gates, to transport him from the Atlanta Penitentiary to freedom.

Two years earlier, he was run off a cliff by a white Chevy Van while riding his Harley. Ironic in a way. In 1972, Niko's recording studio produced "Chevy Van", a song written and sung by Sammy John, a popular '70s rock n' roll singer. While waiting for Deon, Niko relived that day, the attempt on his life. He would soon be free to seek his revenge.

* * *

It had been a beautiful Sunday, and Niko had one of those rare epiphanies in which a person recognizes the peak of life. He had everything, and here he was, sitting on the world's best motorcycle, watching the Annual Chattahoochee Raft Race, down the rough, steep bank in the river around which Atlanta,

Georgia, had grown, and which General Sherman couldn't burn. He, Nickolas J. Pappas, was part of this city. Why couldn't they let him...*give him*...that last thing, respect? He was going legit as soon as possible, using the many talents God gave him, and the money he'd made in ways that he'd confessed, trying to keep his soul. Billy Graham wanted to meet him. Yes, there was that spiritual side to resolve, and good works weren't enough, too easy. He knew that. He'd do what it took.

Beautiful drunk and sober girls were shedding their tops, a ritual by now for the cameramen along the outer banks of the Chattahoochee. They were beautiful. They teased, stirred men's blood. The men were handsome, too. Now there was talk of a *Playgirl* magazine. Niko had published theological articles, written his own book about the war in Vietnam. His break came with a directory of nudist camps, U.S.A., with not a photo in it, much less a nude; only a woman's navel on the cover. They kept busting him for selling *Playboy* magazine when you could buy outrageous pornography in most other U.S. cities.

Nickolas J. Pappas had his pride. Yes, that was what stuck. He would have to deal with that if he was to be free. He didn't like being pushed around. He wanted the power he saw other less gifted Atlantans enjoying. That young reporter who'd come to the mansion was surprised to see the books he'd written, his serious books, including the one about his struggle with the priesthood, the Vietnam critique, Altizer's theological bomb about the death of God, which everybody misunderstood. Niko didn't want inherited wealth and station; only what he'd worked for.

But why spoil a day like this, honeysuckle with the pine pollen, beautiful bodies that sometimes looked less so as they bent over their raft's edge, vomiting? That was life, good and bad. Why couldn't others understand? *He* needed forgiveness, too. He needed self-forgiveness, but he still depended too much on old-money Atlanta for approval.

That was what his wife, Kate...what the hell, was.

Jesus! No time to jump, even move! It was a big white Chevy Van, coming fast, and it hit him solidly before turning back onto the road. Niko was airborne for such a merciless short time before he hit the retaining-walls constructed of sections of concrete and steel-reinforcing rods that lined the embankment. The retaining-walls were there to keep the soil from washing away. That Sunday, they nearly tore the life from Nickolas J. Pappas. He could feel his bones break as he bounced from one retaining-wall to another down the side of the hill. He was lucky not to be speared by a piece of steel. Hearing the bike crashing down behind him, he hoped it wouldn't land on top of him. Before he lost consciousness, he thought he knew clearly who was responsible.

* * *

After three months, Niko insisted that he be discharged from the hospital. His hip was gone, but they told him it could be replaced. His pelvis was crushed, and would take a series of operations and years of rehabilitation. He probably wouldn't ever walk again.

Despite the hip and pending pornography charges, Niko, wheelchair bound was getting around these days, socializing with people in legitimate businesses. Cory Doran, his assistant, was handling his day-to-day operations. Cory was loyal to a fault, and doing a good job keeping Niko's businesses operating smoothly and profitably with the exception of their real estate division. They both were waiting to move into their new headquarters building that Turk Donatelli was close to finishing.

Turk Donatelli's first association with Niko was quite by accident. Turk had inherited the management of Niko's extensive legitimate real estate portfolio when Bill Wilson, Turk's former boss, was caught diverting funds from Niko's projects to build a mansion for himself and his girlfriend in North Atlanta.

Four years earlier, Turk, had worked for Bill, as his Regional Manager for his Florida Real Estate Development Company, building office buildings, hotels, and apartment projects. Bill was behind schedule and way over-budgets on Niko's Atlanta projects. Niko gave Bill an ultimatum: "Hire someone to straighten out my projects or be carried out of Atlanta in a box!" Bill, fearing for his life, contacted the only person he knew who could do that, Turk Donatelli. He convinced Turk that he would make it worth his while if he would come to Atlanta, from St. Pete, Florida, where he lived, and work for him. He never revealed to Turk who his partner was. After months of Bill's broken promises to pay him for his efforts, Turk insisted on an introduction to his silent partner, Nickolas J. Pappas.

* * *

Turk and Bill waited for about twenty minutes, when a very large man with a wide forehead, dressed in black, strode into the reception area and asked in a raspy voice, "Turk Donatelli?"

Observing this giant of a man with curiosity, Turk stood, and said, "Yes, I'm Turk."

The man growled, "Follow me, Donatelli." Turning toward Bill, he said, "Wilson, Niko doesn't want to see you. His lawyer will be in touch. You're lucky you're still upright. Now get the hell out of here!"

Turk started to protest, but was transfixed and unable to say anything. He thought about bolting for the exit right behind

Bill. Instead, he said, "Lead the way. Bill, I guess I'll see you later." Turk's need for money overcame his fears.

White as a sheet, Bill stammered, "Turk...tell... tell Niko I'll sign over my house. Tell him...I'll sign over my business. I just...all I want...is to be left alone."

"I have no idea what you've gotten me into, Bill, but you deceived me and evidently, you've screwed the wrong man this time. If I get out of here, you're on your own."

The other man said, "You coming or not, Donatelli? We don't have all day."

The hair stood up on Turk's neck. He said, "Let's go. Goodbye, Bill."

They went down a flight of stairs, which opened up on to a large conference room. Turk wondered why it was built underground. Security, he surmised. This made him even more uncomfortable than he already felt. Another man, larger than the first, stood near a door and said, "Wait here. I'll see if Mr. Pappas is ready to see you."

Turk was nervous; he realized that the two guys looked like bodyguards. He was thinking, *What the hell have I gotten myself into?* He thought he'd left the cloak-and-dagger shit behind him in Miami.

One of the men, said, "Mr. Pappas is ready to see you."

Turk followed him down another set of stairs, built deeper in the ground into another room, larger than the one they had just left. Sitting at the far end was a small-framed, balding man, in his mid-forties, Turk guessed. He had black deep set eyes, a dark-black pointed goatee and moustache, giving him the look of the devil. He was sitting slumped over behind an enormous desk.

On the other side of the room sat two other men to whom he wasn't introduced. And to his right, sitting at a small desk, was a gorgeous redhead. She looked to be in her early twenties, hair to her shoulders, bright green eyes, wearing a low-cut blouse.

Pappas didn't stand. He didn't extend his hand. He said, "Niko is the name. I don't shake hands. Germs, you know. My assistant tells me you insisted on seeing me. What do you want?"

"I'm here to discuss additional funding for Park Place and the Willow Crest apartments."

"I've been paying your draw request. What else do you want?" Niko asked coarsely, as though Turk were wasting his time.

"The subs and suppliers need to be paid what was owed them prior to me coming on the job. A promise Bill made to them."

"Why doesn't that surprise me?" he mocked. "How much would that be?" Handing him the accounts payable sheets he had prepared, Turk said, "The past-due amounts owed are shown on these sheets, Mr. Pappas."

Gesturing to the redhead, Niko handed the accounting to her, and said to Turk, "I'll look into it and get back to you. What else?"

"I need to be paid. Bill has only paid me a portion of what he owes me. I've been here for six months. I've showed you what I can do. It's time I'm paid."

"Another shit deal of Bill's," he mumbled. "I advanced him your draw."

"Well, I never got it!"

"Suppose I take care of that. What else do you want from me?"

"I need money for expenses and another fifty thousand for overheard on a monthly basis. I've inserted those amounts on the draw schedules I just gave you."

"You have, huh? Are the budgets padded?" he asked, looking Turk up and down.

"What do you mean, padded?" Turk asked, holding eye contact.

"We discovered Bill always inflated the amounts. Did you?"

Each man was feeling the other out, with their eye contact showdown. Turk softened his stare. Taking a minute to respond, he said, "Mr. Pappas, I don't operate that way. If I tell you something or I promise you something, you can literally take it to the bank. The budgets I've submitted are real. Trust me. I'm a man of my word."

Easing his eye contact, too, and looking to one side toward the redhead and smiling, he said, "I told you Niko is the name. Trust is something that's earned. I hope you're true to your word." The redhead whispered something to him. He looked up and said, "I'm told it will take some time to analyze these budgets you've submitted. As I said, I'll get back to you."

Turk was now impatient; he was growing accustomed to the big men around him and to Pappas' quirky ways and said, using his first name for the first time, "Niko, I need a commitment before I leave. I've shown you what I can do. I now need to see what you can do. You either trust me or you don't."

Pausing for a moment, Niko said, "What are you going to do if I don't fund your request?"

Hesitating while collecting his thoughts, he answered, "Mr. Pappas," deliberately addressing him by his last name, "anything I might say would sound like an ultimatum. I'm sure you're the kind of man who wouldn't appreciate that, but to answer your question, I'd probably continue to fund my own expenses and work like hell to meet our existing contractual arrangement, which Bill Wilson negotiated on my behalf. I always live up to my commitments. I would finish your projects, try to collect the two-hundred-grand you promised, and then go home."

Shaking his head up and down, and pursing his lips, Niko said, "Right answer, Turk." He reached into his desk drawer, pulled out three bundles of cash, and said, "Here's thirty thousand for you personally. I'll have a check made out for fifty-thousand made payable to Park Place Apartments. You open a new checking account. Drop off the signature cards for my accountant to sign. I expect you to supply me with an accounting and I'll replenish it on a monthly basis. What else do we need to discuss?"

"What role will Bill play in your operation?"

"He's done. My lawyers will deal with him. You're in charge."

"Bill asked me to relay to you that he would sign over his house, and his business. He just wants to be left alone." Turk felt relieved. Any obligation he felt toward Bill Wilson was now satisfied. He liked the feeling; with Bill out of the way, he would be calling the shots.

"Look, Turk, you don't need to be worrying about that weasel. Take care of my real estate projects; that's all you need to do."

"I can do that. Just keep paying me." He was now doing this for the money and money alone. He'd bail out as soon as he had enough to fund his own Florida real estate developments.

Niko stood, signaling to Turk that this meeting was over and said, "I like the job you're doing. Let me warn you, though, don't betray my trust. If you do, you won't get off as lightly as Bill." Bill had cost Niko millions of dollars in cost overruns. In six month's time, Turk had shown Niko he was more than qualified to manage his real estate portfolio.

"No need to warn me, Niko. I repeat, I'll do what I say I'm

going to do. I expect you to do the same. Good day," Turk said as he tried to find a place to conceal thirty-thousand dollars in cash. On his way out, the redhead followed him and handed him a fifty-thousand dollar check made payable to Park Place Apartments.

Accepting the check, he said, "Thank you, Miss. Please forgive me; I didn't get your name."

Looking him directly in the eyes, she said, "I'm Cory Doran, Niko's personal assistant. You'll report to me on a weekly basis. Be sure to account for this money. I'll be watching you." She turned as fast as she had appeared. Turk watched her go. The cheeks of her rear were tight. She walked with a sense of authority. She was truly beautiful. He couldn't help but think, *Niko, your lady is fine.*

CHAPTER—2

Niko liked this man, this Deon Gates, a former Navy SEAL, and tough as they came. He'd been tested twice already as his bodyguard. The evening outside the closed-circuit broadcast of the Ali-Foreman fight, Deon had done a cartwheel over the hood of Niko's limo and put two guys threatening Niko away like a couple of empty grocery bags the wind was blowing around. Unfortunately, he'd done the same thing with several friends who approached Niko too quickly in public to embrace him, and gotten hammered by Deon instead. Deon was straight ahead, listed as a record company executive. He said he viewed personal protection in the framework of ethical work. He claimed a samurai ethic. He would protect Niko with the sacrifice of his own life, but he wouldn't kill whoever tried to kill Niko, and he knew the offer would be coming.

It was clear to Niko that our government had made a big mistake, and lost the war. Many of our troops had passed the courage test, including Deon himself. What if he did beat up a few friends? He was articulate and sincere in his apologies. Niko figured he had the best bodyguard in the world, even if he wouldn't exact revenge for him. Niko might have to do that himself.

Niko wished he'd had a chance for that kind of training. Could he have done it? He thought he could have, but he'd never know now. He needed to concentrate his energies on going legitimate and shedding his massive pornography business, or he'd be going to prison for a long time.

As Niko reminisced, he turned to Deon who was there to pick him up from prison, and said, "Free at last! Free at last! Get me out of here and home." His freedom gained, he forgot about his disabilities for a moment.

Deon had purchased a van and had it retrofitted to accommodate a wheelchair; Niko refused to ride up on the lift. He motioned for Deon to help him into the front seat. Deon loaded the chair in the rear.

"Your wife and kids will be happy to see you," Deon said, as he fired up the van.

"I hope so. Prison changes you, Deon," Niko said as he soaked up the sights. After eighteen months in prison, everything looked good.

"How's that, Mr. Pappas?"

"You realize what you took for granted. You appreciate things more. Kind of like what being 'born again' must feel like."

"You want to stop along the way or do you want to go straight to the mansion?"

"I'd like to stop at the office and see Cory, but my wife would be pissed if I did." Cory Doran was Niko's personal assistant and one of his lovers. Cory ran Niko's operation while he was incarcerated. She started working for Niko when she was eighteen, inventorying books and adult films in his downtown Atlanta warehouse. She was a tall redhead with long flowing hair, small pert breasts, shapely legs, green eyes, and a terrific smile. Niko had noticed her on one of his visits. He promoted her to his office as a receptionist. Two years later, she was his right hand and worked directly out of his office. He trusted her with his life. She did a good job running his affairs while he was in prison. Nobody screwed around with Cory. She was a bright, fearless woman.

Several minutes passed as they sped their way down Peachtree Street toward Powers Ferry Road where Niko's mansion was located. Niko turned to Deon and said, "You know what? I've changed my mind. Let's stop at the office so I can see what's going on. Cory should be there, don't you think?"

"You know she is. She's been waiting for you since this morning."

"She visited me three, four times a week. The prison authorities thought I was running my business through her and my lawyers."

"You were, weren't you?"

"Yes, but they weren't smart enough to figure out how. Some of those prison guards were industrious. I slipped them a few bucks when I could. I was the only one in there along with a few of my cellmates who ate steaks once a week." He felt money was the best equalizer. Niko grew up poor.

* * *

Nickolas J. Pappas' great wealth came mostly from his adult book business. He was born right after the depression, and raised by his Greek immigrant grandparents in Scarborough, North Carolina. Niko was an altar boy in the Greek Orthodox Church for fourteen years. He even had desires of becoming a priest, but he liked women and money too much. He was ambitious and enjoyed living on the edge.

In 1951, in the pursuit of easy money, he was convicted of breaking and entering. The sentence of four years was suspended and he didn't go to prison. Instead, he came to Atlanta after dropping out of high school. Broke and only seventeen, Niko rolled into Atlanta on the back of a truck traveling from central Florida to deliver fruit to the Farmers Market. He stayed and enrolled himself in a Roman Catholic school.

After receiving his diploma, he registered at Georgia Technical College studying textile engineering while working nights at the *Global News*, in underground Atlanta for fifty-dollars a week. He worked there for two years and then purchased a newsstand of his own. He soon owned and operated four, adding a shoeshine parlor to each. They were attractive structures, carrying greeting cards, magazines like *Mademoiselle, Life* and *Time*, in addition to a complete newspaper line.

Then when *Playboy* came out, Niko realized that ninety-percent of his sales were coming from ten percent of his display. The display was sex-oriented, so he threw out everything else and opened his first "adult book stand."

Nickolas J. Pappas was labeled the "pornography king" when he helped form an association of adult book store sellers and publishers. The group wasn't able to find a national director, so he volunteered. Niko made several speeches all around the country. At each and every one of these gatherings, he took a real stab at the government about what freedoms he thought the public was entitled to. He believed that a person should be able to buy anything they wanted to read; that the government had no right to dictate what they bought.

He went further and claimed that the Nixon administration

was using the "adult" field as a scapegoat to hide its own shortcomings, and take people's minds off issues like Vietnam, hunger, and world events. Niko was rationalizing selling pornography in his adult book stores.

In 1970, Pappas' various businesses had been linked to organized crime by the FBI. While attending a pornography convention held in Las Vegas in 1969, Pappas bragged about owning ninety-percent of the sex film-vending machines in the United States. This didn't sit well with the mob. In attendance was a member of the DeCavalcante family. They made it clear to Niko that he might manage the machines, but "the family" managed him. Niko still denied any connection to the Mafia family or to any other element of organized crime.

The previous year, 1970, a competitor's adult book store in Louisville, Kentucky, was destroyed by fire. Niko was indicted by the grand jury for conspiracy in connection with that burning. At first, he pleaded "not guilty," and then changed his plea to "no contest," on the advice of his attorneys. Niko's lawyers plea-bargained for probation only. The FBI orchestrated the probation plea, knowing full well Niko would violate it. Then they would be able to put him behind bars for an extended period of time. The authorities were closing in on Nickolas J. Pappas.

CHAPTER—3

Deon parked in the front of Niko's ten-story office building. He made sure the way was clear. Niko didn't take his security as seriously as Deon did. He helped Niko into the wheelchair and pushed him into the lobby to a private elevator. A guard employed by Deon stood rigid, ready to frisk and question anyone before allowing access to Niko's suite of offices, which occupied the entire tenth floor.

Cory was waiting for him. Her greeting was business-like. They never showed any affection for each other in public. "It's nice to have you back in the office, Mr. Pappas."

Cory dismissed Deon and wheeled Niko into his office. The view of the Atlanta skyline from Niko's office was breathtaking. He looked around. Other than being ten stories in the air instead of two stories underground, not much had changed. His large walk-in safe, where he housed his considerable cash from his adult store business was to the left of his desk. Cory's office was still to his right, and the large conference room was right in front of his desk. The offices were decorated in contemporary black leather, and stainless steel furnishings, surrounded by large glass windows on three sides viewing downtown Atlanta.

Turning to Cory, Niko asked, "Other than my legal problems, what's the most pressing thing we need to deal with?"

Taking a minute to answer, as tough as Cory seemed, she would have liked a personal greeting; after all, they were supposedly in love. Shrugging off the feeling, she answered, "Our real estate projects are sucking our cash dry. We can't get a loan and the Decker's, our consulting firm, is demanding more cash on a weekly basis to keep their bills paid than we can provide."

Taking Cory's hand and drawing her closer to him, Niko said, "I got ahead of myself. I've missed you terribly, Cory."

Delighted by the comment, but not showing it, Cory said, "Niko, we've got some pressing issues to discuss. You and I can get together later, but thanks for the kind words. I've missed you, too."

Squeezing, and then releasing her hand, Niko said, "The only time our real estate operation has been trouble-free and making money is when Donatelli was running it. Is he in Florida caring for that sick wife of his?"

"Last I knew he was still in St. Petersburg."

"Can't we get him back here?" Niko asked earnestly while drinking in the Atlanta skyline.

"I don't know. Turk was pretty serious about taking care of his wife and raising their son. The FBI and the GBI were all over his ass because of his association with us."

"I know that, but Turk isn't the scaring-off kind. He's still the guarantor signed personally on my construction loans, isn't he?"

"He is. Every time the Decker Group wants to draw down any of our construction loans, Turk flies in here to insure the work is done." When Turk left Atlanta, Niko, hired the Decker Group to handle his real estate development.

"Then why in hell can't the bank fund our projects? Why do we have to use *our* cash?"

"Donatelli won't sign off on the Decker Group's draws. He claims they're ripping you off and he won't have any part of it."

Agitated, Niko slammed his fist down on top of his desk and said, "Well, then we have to get rid of the Decker Group, don't we?"

"It's not that easy. We have a long-term contract for them to provide the management of our real estate operation. We don't know anything about these real estate projects. Who would manage them? We've been so tied up with getting you out of prison that part of our business has suffered a great deal."

"If Donatelli says Decker is screwing us, then by God, they must be. I'll give Turk a call. He has to come back. I'll see to it. What else do we need to discuss?"

Not letting the subject go, Cory said, "Turk might be very difficult to persuade."

"Why's that?"

"Don't you remember? Over a year ago, a few months before you went to prison, your partner, Cliff Overton, along with his so-called assistant, Ross Naylor, went to his house and beat the hell out of Turk.

"Turk knew I didn't have anything to do with that beating. That was all Overton's doing. Didn't Turk and his partner what's his name, Digger, return the beating and then some?"

"He did. They put Overton and Naylor in the hospital."

"What's the story on Turk's guy, Digger?" Niko asked.

"Digger almost killed Deon." Cory reminded Niko.

"What was that all about?"

Cory went on to explain, "Digger served one tour in Vietnam

with Deon. When Digger got back stateside, he was stationed in Fort Bragg, North Carolina, with Deon. The story goes that Deon was dating an Army sergeant's wife. The sergeant came back from his tour in Vietnam and found out Deon had been screwing her. There was a confrontation in a bar and Deon literally beat the sergeant to death in front of his wife. And what made matters worse, the sergeant's wife happened to be Digger's high school sweetheart."

"Who told you this?" Niko asked.

"Turk related the story to me."

"Refresh my memory. What did Digger do to Deon? You say he almost killed him." Niko had been so tied up in trying to stay out of prison that he had paid little attention to issues that didn't directly involve him. He was comfortable letting Cory deal with them.

"From what I learned from Deon and Turk, one night Digger and Deon agreed to meet on Cold River Road. It's a desolate stretch of road located about a mile from our condo project."

"Yeah, I know the spot. Get on with the story." Niko really didn't give a shit about either one of them.

Cory continued, "Deon got the worst of the confrontation. Digger transported Deon to the Grady Memorial Hospital emergency room and pushed him through the automatic sliding doors in a wheelchair and left him. Deon spent four weeks there recuperating. I understand through Turk that Digger was out of commission for three weeks as well."

"Well then, it sounds to me like the score is even all around," Niko said.

"I think it goes deeper than that. Turk is a changed man. He quit drinking and gambling. He claims to maintain a monogamous relationship. He's concerned about going to jail because of his association with you. But I will say this: he's been tight-lipped and he's never waivered in his support for you. He likes you, Niko. He thinks you got a raw deal going to prison for selling adult books."

"Turk has always done exactly as he said he would. I'm going to call him."

"What do we do about the Decker Group?"

"Hold them off. I'll see if I can get Turk to come back here and then I'll let him deal with the Decker Group."

"Good idea. I sure hope he comes back. We need him right now. Are you going home?" Cory had feelings for Turk; feelings she had yet to define.

"I am. I'll see you first thing in the morning. We'll have dinner and spend tomorrow night together."

"In the shape you're in, Niko. Are you sure?"

Damn right I'm sure. I might not be able to walk, but I can still make love. I'll see you in the morning."

Laughing, Cory pushed Niko to the elevator where Deon was waiting and said, "Mr. Pappas is ready to go home."

CHAPTER—4

Niko's 16,500 square-foot house was built by Turk Donatelli three years earlier on thirty acres, located on Powers Ferry Road, one of the most exclusive areas in Atlanta. The architecture was Old English. Niko liked the Royal Coach Hotel's English architecture, and wanted his house designed like it. The mansion had nine bedrooms, ten baths, three offices, two studies, a film room, library, a four-lane bowling alley, tennis courts, and two swimming pools. The grounds housed riding stables, a guest house, and an eight-car garage, with a garret.

The English Manor-house sat in the middle of the thirty acres, with a long, narrow, twisting driveway leading to it, lined with mature pink and white dogwoods. A ten-foot-high wrought-iron fence was installed around the perimeter, equipped with the latest security devices available. A guard-house was built at the entry, along with four out-posts located at the corners, so that the perimeter could be observed from all angles.

Niko's neighbors included some of the wealthiest, most powerful, politically-connected people in the city of Atlanta.

They were adamantly against him and his family living on their street. They did everything possible to dissuade him from building a house there. They tried to block his building permits, which Turk overcame. He was handsomely paid, and praised by Niko for that feat. The group lobbied the banks to insure that Niko couldn't secure a loan to build his house. Niko built it with cash, pulling the plug on their efforts.

The neighbors even conspired to have him arrested for selling pornography, which only made Niko more determined to win in court. His position was that it was his right, as it was every citizen's right, to sell or buy any type of magazine he or she desired. He would simply post bail, hire the best defense lawyers in Atlanta, and continue to promote his business. To date, Niko had won every case filed against him, except for the New Orleans obscenity charge, which was now on appeal, based on his right of free expression.

Niko was proud of his prestigious address. Anybody who was anybody in Atlanta lived on Powers Ferry Road. Deon pulled into the entry. The guard bent down and said something to him, and then waved them through.

"What was that all about?" Niko asked.

"He informed me that the FBI just left."

"I wish to hell they'd leave my family alone for a while," Niko mumbled.

By the time they reached the massive circular driveway, Niko's wife, Kate, and his two boys were waiting for him under the portico. Kate had visited Niko a few times while he was in prison, but Noll, eight and Ben, ten, hadn't seen their father since he was incarcerated. They were jumping up and down. They helped Deon retrieve the wheelchair. The younger one, Noll, jumped into it and was pushed around by Ben. Niko, standing braced up against the door of the van, managed a smile.

"Come on, boys, your dad needs that chair. Wheel it on over here and stop horsing around," Kate said while embracing Niko. Their relationship was one born out of need; Kate needed money, and Niko needed someone to raise his sons. The spark for Niko had gone out of their relationship years ago.

"What took you so long, Nickolas? We expected you earlier." Kate always addressed him as Nickolas. She despised the nickname Niko.

"I stopped off at the office to take care of some pressing business."

With a heavy sigh, Kate said, "Some things never change, do they, Nickolas?"

"Come on, Kate. Let's not go there. I hurt, I'm hungry, and I'm tired."

"Don't you have any pain pills?"

"They don't give you enough pain pills in prison. They're afraid you'll sell them. I've got some being delivered."

"Good. Dinner is ready. The boy's are hungry, too," Kate said, as she wheeled Niko around and headed toward the house.

Niko turned to Deon and said, "Pick me up in the morning at six."

"I'll be here." Deon was still concerned for his boss's safety. There were some former associates who were trying to muscle in on his adult bookstore business of whom Niko needed to be aware. Deon would brief him tomorrow.

Niko didn't eat very much; food wasn't a priority to him. He spent some time with his two boys; then Kate ushered them off to bed, while Niko retired to his large den. With the fireplace crackling and a glass of wine, Niko lay back in his easy chair and quietly rejoiced in his worldly comforts, vowing to do whatever he had to, to stay out of prison. Kate poured herself a glass of wine and joined him.

"Honey, was prison as bad as I think it was?" she asked sincerely, while taking a seat next to Niko and cradling his hand in hers. Kate had met Niko in college. They were married shortly after they graduated. Kate always thought Niko would be an engineer. She had no idea he would become "the porno-king of the southeast." She'd given in to the money and power which came with being his wife. She was still in love with him, and it hurt knowing that Niko wasn't in love with her, only himself.

"Kate, the hardest thing for me was the constant pain I was in. I'd had what, ten surgeries before I was sent to prison? The authorities went out of their way to insure that my pain medication never got to me. They sabotaged my rehabilitation. They seemed to like seeing me suffer. The pain was excruciating, awful."

"What do you feel your chances are on appeal?"

"My lawyers tell me I should get off. Let's talk about something else, Kate. How are the boys doing?" Niko didn't want to cause Kate any more concern than she already had, and besides, he never discussed those types of things with her. He wasn't about to start now.

"Okay, have it your way. The boys are doing fine considering they don't have a father around much." She couldn't help but dig at him. Niko never shared anything with her anymore, not even her bed.

"Cut that out. You and the boys have more than I ever had. You seem to like our lifestyle." Niko knew he wasn't the best dad in the world, but his family certainly had everything they could ever want or need. Seeking money and power was what used to occupy his every thought; now it was how to settle a score and stay out of prison. The warmth of the fire and the wine felt good. He fell asleep thinking about the next day. Kate went to bed lonely like she had every night for eighteen months, loving a man who had become much too distant.

CHAPTER—5

Turk Donatelli was having a difficult time paying the interest on his real estate debt. The real estate market in the tri-city area of Tampa, St. Pete, and Clearwater was dismal. Interest rates were rising again and credit was nearly impossible to obtain for home buyers. The Savings and Loans were experiencing a huge loss of deposits and non-earning assets were on the rise. Turk's lines-of-credit were exhausted and his cash reserves almost gone.

Because of the downturn in the real estate market, his investors weren't willing to invest more money into Turk's many projects, which included a large golf course development, a five-story office building and several residential communities. Turk spent most of his days seeking loans and trying to raise money to keep his projects going. He figured at the rate he was using his cash reserves, he had about three months before he would have to declare bankruptcy.

* * *

Turk had married Karen Hill and adopted her son, Jason, then six years old, in 1975, three years earlier. They owned a luxury two-story condominium on St. Pete beach in Florida. Turk had modified his behavior by abstaining from drinking, smoking, and chasing skirts to being a monogamous husband and a good father to Jason.

Two years before, Karen was diagnosed with a mild case of multiple sclerosis (MS). Recently, the diagnosis was upgraded to Progressive MS, which meant the disease was invading her entire body. There were days when her vision was clouded. Some days she had a difficult time walking. Then, just as suddenly, her condition would improve and the MS would go into remission. The one constant was that the MS was acting up more frequently of late.

Turk was still able to afford a housekeeper. He was searching for a part-time live-in woman to help Karen in the house and to tend to Jason on occasions when the MS showed its ugly head. Karen's care was the most important thing to Turk. Next most important was Karen's son, Jason.

Turk had spent a considerable amount of his wealth chasing cures for Karen's MS. He had built and financed hyperbaric clinics. He built and funded four before he realized they weren't doing Karen any good. The pursuit of a cure for the woman he truly loved and respected blinded Turk's business sense. He'd bought a farm, stocked it with cows to produce colostrum, which was supposed to help alleviate the debilitating effects of MS. He commissioned experts in the field who researched multiple sclerosis, burning through many thousands of dollars. This was the first thing in Turk's life he couldn't control or fix. He was now caring for a very frightened wife and he was raising a ten-year-old son. Turk's past had prepared him for just about any kind of hardship, but being a caregiver wasn't one of them. He would soon have to learn how to be one.

* * *

Turk, the oldest of eight, was born poor, on a farm in rural Vermont. Exposed to a neighbor's wealth early in life, he vowed to become a rich man. During the Vietnam conflict, he was drafted into the Army. Honorably discharged, he worked as a carpenter on a large Miami apartment project. He was quickly promoted to Project Manager. Turk formed a construction company, awarded millions of dollars worth of construction contracts to his own company, assuring huge profits, neglecting the obvious conflict of interest.

He managed to build a multi-million dollar real estate portfolio, and in spite of physical and personal attacks, refused to join the union, until the Mob gave him an ultimatum: join, or be killed. At that point, he negotiated the sale of his business to the Mob, and safe passage out of town. He left his true love and Miami with his first wife, both committed to their marriage, to start over in Ocala, Florida.

In Ocala, Turk formed another construction company and really tried to straighten out his life. He quit drinking, quit gambling, and he worked hard to be a good husband, but he just couldn't do it. He let himself be seduced by the mayor's wife. He built a bar featuring beautiful, scantily-clad hostesses and was drawn into drinking, and chasing skirts again.

His wife, Darcy, a beautiful, recently retired Eastern Airline stewardess, wanted a family and Turk thought he did, too. After many late nights and a hot and heavy relationship with the mayor's wife, guilt overtook Turk, and he asked Darcy for a divorce. Darcy hired the mayor as her divorce attorney. Turk had earlier transferred a good portion of his assets to Darcy because of a pending IRS claim, and the court awarded her most of his wealth. Having no one to turn to, Turk chose to exit Ocala.

Turk and an associate, China Jon, left for Europe. The two

traveled around Europe for six-months in order for Turk to *find himself*. Finally feeling that he had, they returned to Florida and he was able to get a job building apartments. He met Karen and Jason in St. Pete, Florida, the three became very close, and eventually, they moved to the beach. Once again, Turk formed his own real estate company, and was soon making money again.

 Turk had been sober for over two years. He maintained a monogamous relationship. He was a good father to Jason. His worst fear was letting Karen and Jason down. He had to find a way to cure Karen's MS and to raise more money to continue her treatments and his real estate projects. He was a man on a mission, and if anyone could do it, Turk Donatelli could.

* * *

 Turk wheeled Karen out on the second floor balcony of their beach-front home. Not much was said; Karen had to be lifted and placed into the wheelchair. If she had her way, she would have stayed in bed, but Turk was insistent that they try to live as normal a life as they could. Ever since they had moved to the beach, they would sit, drink in hand, waiting for the sun to set over the ocean. The sunset never got old to them.

 "Would you like me to mix you a drink, Karen?"

 "I don't want a drink…I want a joint. Marijuana is the only thing that seems to ease my pain. Do we have any?"

 "We do. I'll roll you a joint." Turk hadn't smoked since his trip to Europe, nor would he now, but he didn't protest Karen's desire; he'd seen the effect marijuana had on her symptoms. It relaxed her and helped her blurred vision.

 Turk went to the bedroom and brought out a bag of grass he'd recently purchased for her. He was getting proficient at rolling joints. He really didn't mind; it seemed to help her a lot. He just hoped this wouldn't become a habit and a problem in the future. He went back out to the patio, placed the joint between her lips, and flicked on a disposable lighter. Karen took a drag and inhaled deeply.

"Does this stuff really help you?"

"You keep asking me the same question. You know damn well it helps me. My doctor even says it helps, and he approves. The government should legalize it for medical use...they should."

"Okay, I just don't want it to become a problem, that's all."

"What difference does it make anyway? My life is over," she stated as she slumped down into her wheelchair.

"Aw, come on, Karen, you know better. We'll find a cure. You've got to keep a positive attitude."

"This disease is shit. That's what it is. I really don't give a damn anymore. I might as well be dead," Karen said, as she started to cry. The doctors had informed Turk that depression and crying were a part of the process of trying to cope with MS.

"Come on, baby, be strong," he cajoled as he put the joint to her lips again. She inhaled deeply and exhaled slowly.

"I'm not as strong as you, Turk. Why? I ask you...why me?"

Drying her eyes, Turk said, "Drink your wine and let's enjoy the sunset."

"I'm sorry, Turk. I'm just so scared."

Putting his arms around her and drawing her close, he whispered, "Baby, we're in this together. Don't worry, I'll never abandon you. I love you so much." He could feel her relax. The tears stopped rolling down her cheeks.

Looking up at Turk, she said, "You promise, Turk? You promise?"

"I promise, Karen. I'll do whatever I have to, to take care of you and Jason. I promise." Turk never broke a promise. He hoped he could live up to this one.

"I know you will, Turk. I think I hear the phone ringing. Do you?"

Feeling sorry for Karen and really not wanting to answer the telephone, he said, "Whoever it is can call back."

"It might be Jason. Please answer it." Jason was spending the night with his grandmother.

Turk rushed to the phone. "Turk Donatelli here."

"It's been a long time since I've talked to you, Turk. How are you doing?"

Not in a very good mood and irritated because they were interrupted, Turk said, "Who's asking? I really don't have time for idle chit-chat." He didn't recognize the voice.

"Hey, Turk, don't get testy. This is Niko in Atlanta. I need to talk to you. Is this a bad time?"

"I'll be damned, Niko! You're the last person I expected to hear from. Are you still in prison?"

"Nope, I got out on appeal a few days ago."

"I'm happy for you. Give me a number and I'll call you back. I'm in the middle of something. I need fifteen minutes."

"I really don't know what the number is here. I'll call *you* back."

"That will work." Turk knew that Niko knew the number he was calling from. He was probably concerned about the FBI listening in. He couldn't help but wonder what Niko wanted. He figured it would have to be his real estate projects; they were screwed up again. Turk smiled and said to himself, *This might be the answer to my money problems.* Getting involved again with this element wasn't what Turk really wanted to do, *but would it be so bad?*

"Who was that, honey?" Karen asked.

"It was a call from an old friend in Atlanta. He's going to call back in a few minutes. Can I get you another drink?"

"No, but I'd like another hit off that joint."

"You got it. Beautiful sunset, isn't it?"

"I love it here, Turk, don't you?"

A twinge of guilt struck him. *A move back to Atlanta might do Karen in*, he shuddered to think. "I do, Karen." he answered absently, thinking about the phone call he was about to receive.

"Is the sunset in Vermont this pretty, Turk.?" Karen was born in Florida and had never visited New England. But Turk often mentioned how quaint, how tranquil his home state was.

"It's different. The mountains swallow the sun instead of the ocean. But it's beautiful."

"How would you compare Vermont to Florida? From what I've read, Vermont is beautiful...the Green Mountain State, if I recall."

"That's a tough one. There are more people in Tampa than there are in the whole state of Vermont."

"You know what I'd like...what I dream about sometimes?" Karen said, as she looked out over the Gulf of Mexico, her stare transfixed.

"No, what do you dream about, honey?" She looked relaxed for the first time in a long time.

"Living out my final days in a little farm house in the mountains of Vermont."

Caught totally off guard, Turk had no clue that Karen even liked the idea of going to Vermont, much less wanting to live there. "Baby, I didn't realize you even thought about Vermont, and besides you're no where near your final days."

She seemed not to hear Turk. "Jason could ride horses. He could attend a small country school...or I could home school him...I am a certified teacher, you know."

Turk thought this might be the marijuana talking. "Would you really like moving to Vermont? What about the winters?

They can be brutal."

"Oh, I hadn't thought about that."

"I'll tell you what, Karen. I just might make that dream come true. But do me a favor, stop talking abut your final days...we have a lot of days left."

Squeezing Turks hand, tears in her eyes, she looked up at Turk and said, "I'd have a garden, too."

"I'd help you plant it, baby." Turk wiped away her tears.

Hours passed and still no phone call; Turk was beginning to wonder why Niko didn't call back. He knew that the conversation would be about him taking over Niko's real estate division once more. When Turk told Niko he was leaving Atlanta, their construction projects were on schedule and on budget. To take Turk's place, Niko awarded the Decker Group a management contract to complete and continue their real estate projects. The success of the projects was secondary to the Decker Group; fleecing Niko was first. They felt Niko would be an easy mark with him in prison for many years. They failed to consider Turk's vigilance over the projects, and Niko being released early on bail.

Turk helped Karen to bed. He rolled her another joint, helped her take a few hits, pulled the cover up, and kissed her good night. He went downstairs to his study. Then he poured himself a glass of Perrier, squeezed a piece of lime into it, and reached for the biography of Papa Hemmingway. Turk's preferred reading was biographies.

CHAPTER—6

Turk, quickly grabbing the ringing telephone, hoping not to awaken Karen, he answered, "Good evening."

"Sorry I'm late returning this call. I had some pressing business to attend to."

"No problem, Niko. What can I do for you?"

"I don't want to get into a bunch of details over the phone, Turk, but you know damn well what I want to talk to you about. Will you come to Atlanta so we can discuss the management of my real estate projects?"

"I'm pretty comfortable here in Tampa."

"Turk, you're not into playing games, nor am I. My sources have you looking for money all over the place. Get your ass up here so we can talk. We need each other."

"I forgot about your resources, Niko. I'll see you the day after tomorrow. Does that work for you?"

"I'll have Jimmy pick you up at the airport. Bye." Jimmy West was one of Turk's drivers when he was in Atlanta. No response required, Turk hung up the phone.

He had a hard time sleeping that night. Under no

circumstances would he consider going back to work for Niko unless Karen and Jason moved to Atlanta. He had no idea how she felt about Pappas now. The last time in Atlanta, she had shown a little sympathy for Niko's plight. Being an educated woman who taught college journalism, she felt folks should be able to buy whatever they wanted to read. She didn't necessarily agree with or condone pornography, but what she did believe in strongly was the First Amendment. Karen felt that the religious right and the government were after Niko and his operation, and she didn't want Turk involved. He finally fell asleep. He would confront Karen in the morning.

* * *

Jason arrived home early that Sunday morning. Turk was grilling pancakes, sipping his third cup of coffee, and preparing a breakfast tray for Karen.

"What are you doing today, Jason?"

"I'm going to play volleyball."

"Let me ask you, did you like Atlanta?"

"Sure. I still have friends there."

"What if we moved back there for a while? How would you feel about that?"

"I don't know. I like it here a lot." Jason said, as he gobbled down the first batch of pancakes and drained a large glass of milk.

"I can see you're in a hurry. Get out of here and go play. Be sure to check in at noon."

Hurrying around the table, he kissed Turk and said, "Bye. What's for lunch?" Turk didn't have time to answer. Jason was out the door and running down the beach barefooted. The boy hated to wear shoes.

Turk put a cup of coffee on the tray next to a plate on which there was two slices of toast, an egg, two slices of bacon, and a glass of ice-cold colostrum. Was the colostrum doing any good? Probably not, but at least it was something. The only thing so far that had any positive effect on MS was an illegal weed.

Turk mounted the stairs slowly. He wasn't anxious to break the news to Karen that he would be going to Atlanta to meet with Nickolas J. Pappas the following day.

"How are you feeling this morning, honey?" Turk asked as he set down the tray.

"I feel a lot better."

"Hungry?"

"I'm famished. Looks good, Turk, thanks," she said as she bit into a slice of toast.

"After you eat your breakfast I need to talk to you."

"Talk to me about what?"

"We need to discuss our finances, and stuff. Call me when you're finished. I'll go clean up the kitchen."

Karen had an idea that Turk was having financial difficulties though he never talked about any of his business-related problems. She knew the real estate market was suffering high interest rates. She'd heard Turk on the phone late at night talking to his investors trying to raise funds. She hoped Turk was okay. She wouldn't mind having to give up their opulent lifestyle. Turk was a good husband and father; that's really all she cared about.

She finished her breakfast and called out to Turk, "Honey, I'm finished."

"I'll be right up. Do you need anything else?"

"No, breakfast was good, thanks."

Slowly climbing the stairs Turk wasn't in a hurry to break the news to Karen about going to Atlanta. As he reached for the breakfast tray, he said, "Baby, Pappas called me last night. He's asked me if I would fly to Atlanta and meet with him."

Karen quickly looked up at Turk. She could see the worry written on his face. She was concerned for him for the first time since they had left Atlanta. She'd thought Atlanta was behind them. She took a minute to answer, and then bringing her true feelings under control, she asked, "What does he want, Turk?"

"He didn't get specific on the phone. I can speculate, though. He probably wants me to come back to Atlanta and get his real estate projects back on track. It couldn't be anything else that I know of."

"How do you feel about that?" This was Karen's way of getting Turk's feelings first and then, and only then, would she voice hers.

"My first reaction is not to get involved. That would probably be best for everyone concerned."

"Then what is it you want from me?"

"I haven't said anything, but I'm in a world of crap right now. Our cash reserves are about gone and you know what condition the real estate market is in. I need money and I need it fast. Niko would be a good place to start."

"But, at what price, Turk, and I don't mean interest rates?"

"I know what you mean. I'm still signed personally on all of the real estate loans. The Decker Group Niko hired never secured any permanent loans, so I'm still on the hook for those."

"You've been inspecting those projects on a monthly basis, haven't you?"

"I have."

"What condition are they in?"

"Bad."

"Can you clean them up?"

"Yes, I can. I've made sure there's enough money left in the construction loans to finish each project."

"So you figure Pappas is going to ask you to move back to Atlanta and take over where you left off running his real estate division. Is that right?" Karen was a quick study. She knew what was coming next.

"That's the way I've got it figured."

"Just assume for a moment that's the case. Will you be safe? Will the FBI and the GBI leave you alone?"

"I'd bring Digger with me for protection. The FBI and the GBI will monitor and harass anyone associated with Niko, I'm sure."

"Will a deal with Niko solve your financial worries?"

"I think it will."

"Again I ask...what do you want from me?"

"I wouldn't even think about making a deal unless you and Jason moved to Atlanta with me."

Karen wasn't going to answer Turk right now. Instead she, asked, "When were you planning on going to Atlanta to meet Niko?"

"Tomorrow."

"That soon? Look, you don't know if that is what Niko wants you to do or not. Why don't you go to Atlanta and see what he has to offer and then we'll talk about this some more."

"So you're okay with this?"

"I didn't say that. I'm okay with you going to Atlanta and meeting with Niko to see what he wants. All we're doing is speculating right now." Karen was very bright. She had an IQ of 170. She knew how to handle Turk. She was really concerned about this endeavor. She hoped with all her heart that Turk wouldn't get involved again with Nickolas J. Papas.

CHAPTER—7

It was a smooth flight into Atlanta International Airport. Jimmy had been waiting for his old boss for an hour. He knew better than to be late; Turk wouldn't tolerate it. Jimmy could see Turk coming down the exit ramp.

"Hi, Mr. Donatelli, it's been a while. It's nice to see you."

"Good to see you too, Jimmy. Are things going okay for you?"

"Things are good. Got any luggage?"

"Nope, I'm not going to be here that long."

"Mr. Pappas instructed me to bring you to the office as soon as you got here. That okay with you?"

"Fine, Jimmy. Where are you parked?"

"Right out in front of Eastern Airlines."

"Let's go."

Turk threw his overnight bag into the back seat. Climbed into the front and buckled his seat belt. This surprised Jimmy. Turk always sat in the back seat and never buckled his seat belt.

"All right, Jimmy, what's been going on with Niko's business since I left Atlanta?"

"What do you mean going on?" Jimmy asked nervously.

"Come on, Jimmy, you know damn well what I'm talking about. For starters, where are Overton and Naylor?"

Cliff Overton was an associate of Niko's. They had met in the early '70s after Niko discovered some book store operators were stealing proceeds from his peep machines. Cliff was a petty thief and an underling in the New York mob. He was an expert locksmith, just what Niko needed to secure his money. Cliff modified the peep-machines so that the operators couldn't get at the quarters. Niko and Cliff ultimately became partners in a few adult bookstores.

Cliff was a burley man, medium height, with a barrel chest, protruding waist, long arms and stubby legs. He had long brown curly hair, with a receding hairline. A scar ran from his left eye brow to his lower cheek. He had dark brown eyes, which were set wide apart, under an extended brow, separated by a large cauliflower nose, all plastered on a leathered face. Cliff was a scary looking guy.

Ross Naylor was a tall good looking man with a very low IQ. He was Overton's sidekick. Ross would do just about anything Cliff asked him to do. He mostly got in the way, but Overton needed a driver and a yes-man around to sooth his ego. Ross fit the bill.

The last time Turk had seen either of them was outside of a bar they frequented, The Wolfs Den. Turk beat Naylor with a baseball bat and Digger beat Overton with his fist. They beat them so badly; they both were hospitalized for weeks. Turk wanted to know where they were, so if he ran into them on this trip he would be prepared.

Interrupting Turk's thoughts, Jimmy answered, "As far as I know, Niko sent them to the West Coast."

"To do what, oversee his adult bookstores?"

"I would assume so. I don't really know. They've been gone for a year. I mostly drove Cory around until Niko got out of prison. Now I work in the warehouse for Ms. Staidly." Jimmy made it a point not to know too much or talk about it if he did know; that's how he kept his job as a driver and a gofer. Turk was aware of how Jimmy operated.

* * *

Vera Staidly managed Niko's trucking, warehouse and adult bookstores. Turk remembered the first time he met her. She was a big woman, not fat, but big. She wore a red-checkered flannel shirt, tucked in at the waist, faded blue jeans, fashioned with a wide black leather belt. She wore steel-toed construction boots. Her gait was manly and her hair was combed back in a DA, Elvis Presley style. Her office at the time was sparsely furnished, but neat and orderly. Vera was gay. Standing at attention next to her large desk was a very pretty young woman with blonde hair, big blue eyes, and large breasts. She was a knock-out. He recalled he could hardly take his eyes off her.

Vera operated Niko's warehouses that supplied his network of adult bookstores from the East to the West coast. She was Niko's most trusted employee and confidant. Niko was in the process of transferring ownership of his adult bookstores over to her, as he was claiming to the authorities he was getting out of the pornography business. The FBI knew it was a sham on Niko's part, but the public really thought Pappas was going legit and that's just what Niko wanted the public to think.

Vera and Turk really didn't like each other, but they did trust each other. They both had Niko's interest at heart. Vera, like Turk, never took advantage of their close relationship with Niko.

* * *

Jimmy pulled up in front of the office building and asked,

"Mr. Donatelli, do you want me to wait for you?"

"Please. I shouldn't be long."

Turk entered the lobby and headed for the private elevator that was used exclusively for tenth floor access to Niko's suite of offices. One giant security guard stood next to the elevator and another guard was manning a nondescript office to the right. Turk was familiar; he'd built the building and he'd been through this process a number of times. "Hi, guys, tenth floor please." He thought he might get a chuckle; none ensued.

"Who are you?" the giant security guard asked.

"I'm Turk Donatelli...here to see Mr. Pappas."

"We're expecting you. I have to ask you to go over there and check in please." He pointed to the small out of the way office.

Turk knew the drill. He would be checked for weapons when he got on the elevator and again when he got off. He hoped that when he got to the tenth floor, Deon Gates wouldn't be there. He didn't want to have to face him just yet.

Getting off the elevator, Turk was met by another security guard, larger than the one downstairs. The guard rang Cory's extension. She came right out.

"Hi Turk, it's been a while since I've seen you. It's good to have you back." Cory had more than a passing interest in Turk. She looked him up and down, and smiled.

Turk could feel Cory's stare, returning the compliment, he said, "I'm not back yet, Cory. But I have to admit you're still easy on the eyes. It's good to see you, too."

"He needs your help, Turk," she said, as she escorted him in to see Pappas.

CHAPTER—8

The morning mail had arrived and Niko was counting the cash he'd received from all over the country. This was a morning ritual, a ritual Turk had witnessed before.

Niko's X-rated bookstores had been in operation for seven years. The real money was made from his peep-show machines. People deposited eight quarters and they got a two-minute show; if they kept pumping in the quarters, they continued being entertained. Niko had thousands of peep-show machines located throughout the United States, including Alaska. Adult bookstore owners would lease the machines from Niko and the proceeds were split fifty-fifty.

The pornography industry had grown bolder in its merchandising as the '70s approached. Rubber sex organs were making their way into Niko's gaudily-painted adult book stores. Fifteen-minute films of couples engaged in intercourse were selling rapidly. But nothing could compete with the profit potential of the peep-show machines.

Soon, Pappas was manufacturing fifty machines a week at his Atlanta warehouse under the charge of Vera Staidly. The country at that time was so wide open to marketing pornography it was like the development of the West. They couldn't make the machines fast enough to satisfy the demand.

Pappas already had a distribution empire in place distributing sexual aids, books, phonograph records, films, to his adult book stores. That was what really made the peep-show business successful. He had over 4,000 machines leased out at one time; his revenue tripled. Each machine conservatively produced $125.00 per week. When split, Pappas would net $250,000 a week, which amounted to twenty-five-million a year. From out of town, the proceeds...quarters changed into dollars...would arrive each morning by registered mail, which Niko would open himself. From news accounts, his estimated wealth was pegged at one-hundred million.

* * *

"I see some things never change. It's good to see you again, Niko." Niko pushed the cash to one side, backed up his wheel chair and motioned for Turk to sit at the conference table. Cory joined them.

"You're looking fit, Turk."

"I wish I could say the same for you. How are you feeling?" Niko was thin. A partial body cast from the waist down restricted his movement.

"I just had a hip replaced. I'll be in this half-assed body cast for another six weeks. Maybe after this operation, with some rehabilitation, I'll be able to walk at least that's what the doctors tell me."

"Are you in pain?"

"I'm in pain all the time. But you learn to live with it. That's enough about me. What about you? I understand you've put yourself through some kind of personal transformation. Is there any truth to that?"

Smiling, Turk admitted, "If you mean quitting drinking, and chasing women, yeah, I've transformed, as you say." Turk knew this was the end of the small-talk. Niko didn't engage in much small-talk.

Shifting in his wheel chair and leaning toward Turk, Niko said, "What's it going to take to get you back to Atlanta and straighten out our real estate division again?"

Turk paused for a moment, carefully thinking how he should answer, and said, "Money and a number of assurances."

Leaning back in his chair and locking eyes with Turk, Niko said, "Money won't be a problem. Let's talk about assurances first. Start in the order of importance."

"The first one would be keeping me out of prison."

"Why in hell would you go to prison? You would be handling my real estate division; they can't put you in prison for that."

"Under the RICO Act, they can if the money we use isn't legit."

"You know I'm going legit. I don't want to go back to prison, either. Look, Turk, I can't guarantee you won't be questioned by the goddamn GBI or the FBI, but I can assure you I'll provide the best lawyers money can buy. I'll also not ask you to get involved in anything that isn't totally above board. That's about as good as I can do. What other assurances are you looking for?"

"I don't want anything to do with Cliff Overton and Ross Naylor. Overton will screw you big-time if he hasn't already. I don't trust him at all."

"Overton and that halfwit, Naylor are on the West Coast. They get to Atlanta once a month. After what you and your sidekick did to them, I figured you evened the score. I'll keep them out of your way. What else."

"I'll only answer to you and Cory."

"Okay, go on."

"I want Digger to be my driver."

"Shit, Turk, after what he did to Deon? How do you suppose we keep those two apart?"

"Simple, you tell Deon, and I'll tell Digger to declare a truce."

"This is a lot of assurances. Christ, I'll have to write them down. Is there anything else before we talk money?"

"Last but not least, I don't want my office in this building. I'll want an office in one of our office buildings at the airport."

"That's fine. You'll be spending most of your time out there anyway. What's the price tag for your services?"

"That depends on my ownership once I finish these projects. Permanent loans are going to have to be put in place paying off the construction loans that I'm now signed on personally. Right now, legally, I own these projects. You're not even on the deeds. How do you see us dealing with that?"

"That's a tough one, Turk. The Decker Group couldn't secure any permanent loans. I don't think they even tried. You'll probably have to stay on the notes. You have my word when we get to that point, I'll be fair."

"Niko, no disrespect, but what if you're incarcerated? I want it to be clear to both of us as to my role, and my ownership, should that happen."

"Look, we'll work that out over the next few weeks. What kind of draw are you looking for?" Niko backed up his wheel chair and wheeled himself over to the huge picture window overlooking the Atlanta skyline.

Following him, Turk said, "Same as before. One hundred-thousand a month and you pick up my expenses, including ten-thousand a month for Digger."

"Where will you live?"

"I'll rent a house in Dunwoody."

"How long will it take you to get here?"

"That will depend on my wife, if she'll move back to Atlanta, two weeks."

"You drive a hard bargain, Turk. What will you do about the Decker Group? They claim I owe them over a million dollars in fees." Niko knew that would get to Turk. He wheeled his chair around and looked up at Turk.

"Wow! Those bastards have billed you over a million dollars...for what?" Turk's blood was boiling. They were ripping Niko off just like he had predicted.

"They claim management fees. Cory will give you copies of their invoices. The Decker Group has stopped construction until they get paid."

"You didn't tell me that, Niko. The banks will stop funding and they might even call the loans due if we stop construction."

"I know. Construction *has* stopped." Niko knew Turk was back now. He would do almost anything to protect his credit and banking sources.

"Damn! That means I'll have to deal with Decker before I go back to Florida. I wish you'd told me this before I got here. We can't have all of those projects stopped."

Turk was deep in thought when Niko said, "We got a deal. Get with Cory and go to work. I've got a lot to do today." He knew Turk was capable of cleaning up their real estate operation. He needed to turn his attention to staying out of prison.

"Niko, let me be very clear. The only reason I'm back on board is because I have my name on those construction loans. As soon as I get those cleared up and these projects back on track, I'm out of here." Turk wished he hadn't come to Atlanta. He could feel himself being dragged back into a mess and possible legal issues, too.

"And I thought it was because you loved me, Turk." He knew Turk's name was on the line and he needed money to keep his Florida operation afloat. He also knew that Turk liked the challenge, but he'd never admit it.

"Take care of yourself, Niko. I have a lot to do. Do I use the same law firm to reduce our arrangement to a written agreement?"

"No, I've commissioned a new law firm. Cory will give you the details. Oh, by the way, Turk...thanks." Niko was appreciative of Turk's help and jealous of his integrity.

Niko went back to counting his money. Cory and Turk spent a few minutes together discussing lawyers and how they would communicate. Walking Turk back to the elevator, she gently squeezed his arm, and said, "Turk, thanks for coming to Niko's rescue. I know the Decker Group has been taking advantage of us. I couldn't do anything about it because I was so tied up with getting Niko out of prison. I owe you one."

"Cory, I'll pull his real estate projects out of a hole, but do this for me...keep Overton and Naylor away from me."

"You can count on that. Where are you staying tonight?"

"I have a ticket back to Florida this evening. I'll cancel that flight and book the rest of the week at the Royal Coach. I've got to deal with the Decker Group before I can go back anyway."

"Do you think you can? I don't think the Decker Group will be too easy to deal with. They feel they have a solid contract and are owed the management fees."

"I'll take care of it, rest assured. Bye, Cory, and by the way, it *was* nice seeing you again. You look good," he said as the elevator door closed. He needed to keep his feelings for her under control. Messing with Niko's woman wouldn't be healthy.

CHAPTER—9

Jimmy, Turk's driver while in Atlanta, was waiting for him in the lobby. Jimmy West was twenty-two. He had shoulder-length brown, wavy hair, and long sideburns. His bright blue eyes set in an angular face, made him look almost pretty. He was colorfully dressed in blue bell-bottom pants, a flowered long-sleeved silk shit, and platform shoes. Around his neck hung a string of beads, and he wore a bracelet around both wrists. His petite hands were graced with two rings each. Turk never remembered seeing him without a can of Pepsi.

"Jimmy, I need to check into the Royal Coach. Then we need to inspect our projects. I think there's enough time to do that before dark. What do you think?"

"Let's catch the Fox Theater on the way to the hotel. That will save us a bunch of time."

"I forgot about that project." Niko had bought and was remodeling that historic building. "Is he still going to donate the Fox Theater to the city's Fine Arts department?"

"That's what I read in the papers."

The Fox Theater was a beautiful historic building. AT&T had

purchased it and was going to tear it down and build an office building. The theater could actually be seen from Niko's office. The local folks wanted to restore it. They felt it should remain a part of Atlanta's history, but the opposition was so fierce that AT&T figured, and rightly so, they would never be able to get a permit to build an office building on that site. A group calling themselves "Save the Fox" approached Pappas and asked if he would purchase the Fox from AT&T and preserve it. It was obvious to Turk that Niko's generosity was self-served. He didn't want to go to prison and this was his way of saying to the courts and the citizens of Atlanta, "I'm legitimate."

Niko and Jimmy toured the Fox Theater. Not much was going on. It looked like the Decker Group had stopped construction. The renovation was close to being finished. It wouldn't take Turk long to complete this project.

Jimmy pulled up in front of the Royal Coach. Turk went to the front desk and checked in. He didn't recognize anyone even though he had stayed there many times over the years. He went over to the bank of payphones and called Digger, hoping he would be there.

Digger, like Deon, was a retired Navy Seal. He'd served three tours in Viet Nam. Turk met Digger when Turk worked in Army Finance. Turk paid him his "hazard duty pay." Digger trained Navy Seals underwater demolition while stationed in Key West, Florida. Digger had beaten up more airmen than Germans during WWII. It was his drinking that made him wild. Turk hired him on the condition that he didn't drink, to handle security for his many real estate projects, and eventually, for his personal well-being. He became Turk's bodyguard and best friend.

Digger was six-feet tall, weighed about 220 pounds, dark complexion, long apelike arms and huge hands, gnarled and calloused. His face was large; eyebrows ran the width of his forehead, nostrils flared beneath a flattened nose. His square jaw against a pockmarked background all combined to make him a scary looking guy.

"Digger, how long will it take you to get your affairs in order and join me in Atlanta?"

"Not any longer than it will take me to get to the airport." Digger was very glad to hear from his friend.

"I'm staying at the Royal Coach. I'll make a reservation for you. I'm going to inspect our projects this afternoon. I'll meet you for breakfast at eight. Call me if you're delayed."

"Keep the coffee hot. I'll be there." It had been eighteen months since they were in Atlanta together. Goosebumps covered Digger as he thought back to their Atlanta exit.

* * *

The two had waited across the street from the Wolf's Den, a bar that Cliff Overton and Ross Naylor, who both worked for Niko Pappas, frequented. This was their second night of observing the two men coming and going. They knew that the Georgia Bureau of Investigation (GBI) detectives were watching *them* watch the two men.

"When do you think we can hit these guys, boss?" Digger had asked.

"I wonder if the GBI will give a shit if we beat these two up. They might enjoy it. What do you think?"

"I don't know. Want me to ask them?"

Laughing, Turk said, "And how would you do that?"

Just as serious as Digger could be, he said, "I'll get out of this car, walk over there, and tell them to disappear for an hour or two. We have a score to settle."

"Just like that? You've got to be kidding me."

"I'm not kidding, Turk. I don't think the GBI like these guys any more than we do. They wouldn't want us to kill them, but beating them up might just be what the doctor ordered. I think those red-neck detectives would love it."

"Oh, what the hell, you got balls enough to ask them? When would you do it?"

"Those two bastards will be coming out of that bar in an hour or so. The two detectives are parked right over there. I'll go right now."

Turk thought this was the craziest idea he'd ever heard, but said, "Go ahead and ask away, Digger. I've got bail money with me. Good luck."

The detectives were aware that Digger and Turk knew they were being watched. Digger skillfully approached their vehicle and rapped on their window. They talked for quite a while. Turk began to worry that Digger would be arrested when the Ford the detectives were driving sped off.

Digger slid back into the seat next to Turk with a huge smile on his face and said, "I told you they wouldn't give a shit, Turk."

"I can't believe it! What did they say? Better yet, what did you say to them?"

"I told them the truth. I said, we've got a score to settle with a couple of guys, and we'd like for them to leave for a few hours."

Turk, all excited, asked, "How'd they react?"

"They asked me if I planned on killing them. I told them we were just going to bust them up a little."

Turk could hardly believe Digger could pull this off, and exclaimed, "No way you said that! What did they say then?"

"The tall one, the driver, asked me if I knew that one of these guys is a pretty good boxer. I told him I did know Overton was a boxer, and I didn't give a shit. They both laughed and his partner said, "Let them at it. We couldn't care less who wins, as long as they don't kill each other.'"

"The driver, still smiling, said, 'We don't know nothing,' started the car, and drove off."

"I'll be goddamned! I hope they don't come back and arrest us."

Very sure of himself, Digger said, "They won't, boss, they won't. Now let's get ready for these bastards."

Turk reached around to the back seat, grabbed his Atlanta Braves baseball bat, and said, "I think I'm ready, but I'm nervous as hell. It's been a while since I've done anything like this." His palms were sweating.

"Be careful where you hit that asshole. You might kill him with that bat. I don't want you to end up being Niko's cellmate."

"I'll be careful. What are you going to use for protection? You know Overton will be carrying some kind of weapon."

"I don't need anything. I can handle him; just make sure you keep Naylor busy. I don't want him coming up behind me while I'm taking care of Overton."

"Don't worry, I've got him covered. Let's get into position. They'll be coming out of the bar any time now if they stick to their old habits. I hope those goddamn detectives weren't blowing smoke up your ass, Digger."

"I doubt it, but so what if they were? All we're doing is fighting outside a bar. They can't put us away for mixing it up, can they?"

"No, I guess not. Damn, I'm pumped up. Let's go!"

Naylor always parked in the rear of The Wolf's Den. Turk took his position behind a trash dumpster. Digger stood with his back to the wall, just outside the covered rear entrance. They must have waited thirty minutes, though it seemed longer to Turk. He was about to give up on this outing just as he saw Overton and Naylor coming out.

Despite his large size, Digger moved like a cat. He hit Overton so hard, he was slammed up against the wall. At the same time, Turk came out from behind the dumpster with his bat over his head and struck Naylor across the chest, knocking him to the ground. Just as he turned, he saw a flash of metal coming from Overton's hand as he drew a revolver from his jacket. Turk whirled and struck Overton's wrist before Digger could get to him. Overton screamed in pain as he dropped the pistol and grabbed his shattered wrist.

Digger rushed over and drop-kicked Overton in the chest before he could recover. Simultaneously, Turk turned and kicked Naylor in the face as he was trying to get up, knocking him against the dumpster. Turk was right on top of him, pounding him for all he was worth. Feeling Naylor's body go limp, he stopped and turned to see Digger pounding Overton's face. Overton was still conscious as Turk pulled Digger aside and got down and said to Overton, "Remember me, you worthless piece of shit?" At the same time, he raised the bat and brought it down as hard as he could on his shin bone. He heard it break and Overton's scream.

"Let's get out of here, Digger."

"You got it, boss; good job!"

They were both pumped so full of adrenalin it was hard for them to calmly walk away like they'd planned. Back at the car, they were both still trembling with excitement. Overton was slowly getting up; Naylor was squirming around on the ground, trying to get up. Turk and Digger looked at each other, smiled, and Turk said, "Our job is done!"

"I believe it is and a job done well, boss. You surprised me. You're pretty damn good with those hands."

"It's been a while since I've had to use my fists. I hope it will be a long time before I have to use them again," Turk said, taking one last look at their victims holding on to each other, struggling to their car. With Niko in prison and revenge gained, Turk felt he could finally exit Atlanta.

"What now, boss?"

"Let's get to the airport. I'll be on my way to St. Pete before midnight. I've got a sick wife and a young son waiting for me," Turk said.

"I wish I had someone waiting for me. I'll be in Miami if you need me. You know how to contact me."

"Hey, Digger, you know I'm always there for you if you need me."

After a quick, but strong hug, they went their separate ways.

CHAPTER—10

With Digger on his way back to Atlanta, Turk felt more comfortable. Now he needed to inspect the rest of the projects.

Jimmy was waiting for Turk right outside the entrance. Their next stop was Peachtree Industrial Park, which was a very large development, including warehouses, commercial space, office buildings, and a retail shopping mall located right next to the Atlanta International Airport. They were trying to complete them before the Summer Olympics. The exposure to the corporate world during those games would prove invaluable.

Pulling up in front of the Industrial Park large barricades blocked their entry. Jimmy asked, "What now, boss?"

"Pull over to the curb. I'll investigate. You stay in the car." Turk noted two uniformed security guards policing the entry.

Approaching the barricades, one of the guards challenged Turk. "Sir, this site has been locked down. For your own safety, we must ask you to stay on the sidewalk."

Eying the guard's name-tag, Turk said, "Dan, I'm one of the owners. I'm here to inspect the property."

"I'm sorry, sir, we have orders not to let anyone onto the property. You'll have to get permission from the Decker Group."

Not wanting to start an argument and needing a little more information, Turk asked, "Dan, who in the Decker Group do I need to get permission from?"

"Saul Decker. Want his number?"

"I do. Is the entire job stopped?"

Handing Turk a card with Saul's name and address on it, he said, "Yep, the whole project."

"How long has it been shut down?"

"I don't know for sure...maybe a week or so."

Turk glanced at the card. The Decker Group was still located on Piedmont Road in the same office building where Turk had met Saul when he left Atlanta eighteen months before. Knowing that trying to gain entry now would be futile, Turk said, "Thanks, Dan, I'll see you later."

"Can I have your name please? I have to keep track of any visitors, you know."

"I tell you what, Dan. I'll be in Decker's office before they can see any list of visitors." Turk instructed Jimmy to go to Piedmont Road to visit Saul.

Jimmy knew where the Decker's group office was; he'd been there many times. After observing Turk in his rearview mirror, he wouldn't want to be in Saul Decker's shoes. Jimmy had seen that look before, Turk meant business.

* * *

"I'm here to see Saul Decker."

"I remember you," the cute receptionist said. "You stood us up. You were supposed to meet us for a drink at Harrisons, remember?"

"Something must have come up. You're way too pretty to

stand up. Is Saul in?"

"Turk Donatelli isn't it?" she asked with a sexy smile.

"You have a good memory," Turk said, as she lifted the phone and announced him.

Saul Decker came rushing out of his office to greet Turk. "Good to see you, Turk. Come on in. Grab a seat."

Saul used a conference room as his office. Turk remembered it well. It was decked out in a gaudy red motif. A large, dark-mahogany, red leather inlaid conference table with ten uncomfortable high-backed, red felt-covered chairs surrounding it, sat in the middle of the room. Saul's files were neatly stacked at one end of the table. Turk took a seat next to those.

"How can I help you, Turk?" Saul asked, as he leaned back in his chair, crossing his arms.

"I'm not going to sugar-coat why I'm here. I'm here to take back the management and completion of Niko's projects, that simple."

"Not quite that simple, Turk. I'm owed a lot of money. I'm not turning those projects loose until I'm paid, and paid in full."

Hesitating as though contemplating, looking directly at Saul, Turk said very quietly, "I think you've been paid a lot more than you're worth."

"What do you mean by that? Ever since you left, some eighteen months ago, I've busted my ass for Pappas. He owes me in excess of a million dollars. He's damn lucky I didn't just take over his projects."

"Saul, I think you're damn lucky you're still in one piece. If he knew what I know, you probably wouldn't still be here."

Saul stood up straight, and said, "Are you *threatening* me? With the trouble Pappas has been in and just getting out of prison, I'm sure the GBI wouldn't allow him to threaten me. I'll have him thrown back in jail."

"If I were you, Saul, I would sit down and listen to what I have to say, or you might be the one going to jail."

Leaning forward and placing both hands on the table, Saul looked down at Turk, and hissed, "Just what the hell are you talking about? I haven't done anything wrong."

Turk stood and said, "Saul, sit down and listen before I knock you on your ass."

Saul didn't like being threatened, but the look on Turk's face intimidated him. He would sit and hear him out. "Okay, look, let's talk this through."

Sitting back down, Turk said, "That's better." Saul eased back into his comfortable perch. "When you took over our projects, your contract stated cost-plus, which Niko agreed to. It didn't say anything about allowing you to take kick-backs from your suppliers, and sub-contractors, now did it?"

"Are you accusing me of stealing?"

"I am."

"Prove it!"

"I can. Do you really want me to?"

"You've got nothing on me. You've been gone for eighteen months. What do you know?"

"Don't sell me short, Decker. You replaced every sub and supplier I had working on our jobs. When I turned over the management to you, the jobs were on budget and on schedule; they aren't now. In fact, you've run them into the ground intentionally."

"What do you mean intentionally? Why would I do that?" He was clearly nervous.

"To collect more fees from the porno-king who was in prison, with his partner, me, in Florida. You got greedy, Saul, real greedy."

Clearly disheveled, Saul began to stutter. "You...you can't prove any of this. Get out of my office before I call the cops."

"You do that and it will be the first nail in your coffin." Turk felt Saul was on the run and he wasn't about to leave until Saul came around.

"Now you're threatening to have me killed?"

"No, no, I'm not. That's just an expression, Saul. I figure you ripped off Niko for about a million or more, if I had to guess."

"How do you figure?"

"You inflated contracts to garner more fees. You over-billed for what you called extras because the blueprints weren't right. You're as big a crook as they come. Now I want you to call off your security guards today. If you don't, I will subpoena your records, and cancelled checks. Our lawyers will interview every supplier and sub-contractor you've placed on our jobs. You know damn well what you've done. When I'm finished with you, you may be writing Pappas a check for more than you've claimed he owes you."

Absorbing Turk's points, Saul replied, "I need time to think about it. I'll let you know my position by the end of next week. I suggest you get out of here."

Saul was sweating. Turk knew he had him on the ropes. He had an idea Saul was in bed with his subs and suppliers; he had no proof, but when they started changing all the capable subs and suppliers, Turk knew something was up. "Saul, I'm giving you until tomorrow morning. When I go to inspect Peachtree Industrial Park, I don't want to see a guard. Oh, and one more thing. I'm staying at the Royal Coach and I'm having breakfast at eight with an associate. I expect my server to hand me a sealed envelope with your resignation in it. In that letter, you will acknowledge you've been handsomely compensated and no monies are due your firm. Close it out wishing us nothing but success."

"I have to weigh my options, Donatelli. Now get the hell out of here!" He knew then that Turk had his number. His firm had skimmed millions from Niko's projects.

Standing up and walking around behind Saul, Turk put his hands on Saul's shoulders; he could feel him tighten up, and said, "Think hard and fast, Saul. I don't want Pappas to get wind of your indiscretions, if you know what I mean." Turk walked out. Saul didn't say a word.

CHAPTER—11

Digger couldn't get a flight out of Miami to Atlanta at that time of night. He boarded a flight to Jacksonville, Florida. An hour later, he rented a car, and drove the rest of the way into Atlanta. He checked into the Royal Coach around three that morning. The six years he'd worked in some capacity for Turk, there was never a dull moment. He would do anything for Turk, anything. He loved the intrigue that seemed to follow Turk; it reminded him of his Navy Seal days.

Digger was sitting near an exit in the dining room twenty minutes early when Turk entered. Turk knew Digger would be there come hell or high water. He also knew he would be sitting next to an exit. Digger was very cautious. He'd been Turk's bodyguard off and on for six years.

"Hi, Digger, it's good to see you again."

Standing up, and moving toward Turk with open arms, they embraced. "Nice to see you, too, boss. I guess we're back in business, huh?"

"I think we are, Digger. I think we are."

"Where do we start?"

"Let's start by ordering breakfast. I'm expecting a letter to be delivered. If not we'll be paying Saul Decker a visit."

"I remember him. He took over the real estate operation when we left Atlanta a while back, didn't he?"

"He did. I've cut a new deal with Pappas. We need to get these real estate projects back on budget and on schedule."

"I know you can do that. What do you want me to do?"

"Before I get into that, Digger, I need your assurance that you and Deon won't mix it up again."

With a smirk on his face, Digger asked, "Is he still around?"

"He is. He's still working security for Niko."

"I'm okay with that, but what about him?" About two years ago Digger had severely beaten Deon. He drove him to the Grady Hospital, strapped him into a wheel chair pushed him through the emergency room doors, and left him.

"Niko says he'll insure us that Deon won't start any trouble."

"Okay then, it's settled. But as one retired Navy Seal to another, the relationship will be tenuous at best between us. He won't forget what I did to him. He will seek revenge; that's just the way we Navy Seals are."

"I know that. It should only take us ten months to a year to get these projects finished. Then I'm done with Niko's organization."

Smiling, Digger said, "Seems like I've heard that before."

Smiling in return, Turk said, "I'm a changed person, Digger."

Suddenly, Digger sprang to his feet, jumped in front of the man approaching Turk from behind, and said, "Whoa, can I help you, sir?"

"Hold your horses, big fella. I'm just a messenger. I have a delivery for Mr. Donatelli. Are you him?"

"No, I'm not, but I'll see to it he gets it."

"I can't do that. I have to deliver it to him personally; those are my instructions."

By this time, Turk was out of his chair, facing the intruder. "I'm Donatelli."

Trying to identify Turk, and ignoring Digger, the deliveryman said, "You fit the description." He handed Turk a sealed envelop. "Good day." He turned and was out of there as quickly as he had appeared.

Wondering if his bluff had worked, Turk sliced open the envelope with his breakfast knife, while Digger ordered more coffee. The letter read:

To whom it may concern,

As of this day October 5th, 1974, the Decker Group respectfully resigns their position as the management company for the real estate projects listed on the attached.

In consideration of our resignation, we consider all fees owed us paid in full and that both parties are no longer obligated in any way to each other contractually.

We wish State Industries success.

Sincerely,

Saul Decker, President and CEO

"Well, Digger, it looks like we *are* back in business. On our way to Peachtree Industrial Park, I'll brief you on what comes next."

Springing gracefully from his chair, Digger said, "I've parked the rental car right out front."

"I'm going to need a strong construction team to take on these projects. Some folks we can trust and who know how to get a job done. Got anyone in mind?"

"We need China Jon. He'd be the one."

China Jon was Turk's projects manager in Miami and Ocala. The last time Turk had seen CJ was when they got back from Europe before Turk had met Karen, after a bitter divorce. They had traveled for six-months all through Europe and the northern half of Africa. They also had roomed together when Turk was in the Army and they had worked as laborers on construction sites while Turk was in college. China Jon was a Chinese linguist while he served in the Air Force. He was teaching school when Turk met him.

Taking a moment to consider the suggestion, Turk said, "I doubt if he would come to Atlanta to work. The last time we talked, he claimed he wanted to live an easier life and was ditching the construction business."

"Do you know where he is?"

"I think he's still in Frederick, Maryland, where he was born."

"Suppose I pay CJ a visit and see if he won't join us."

"That might be a good idea. If he says no, do you have any other ideas?"

"I do. What about contacting Terry O'Neil?"

"Wow! Wouldn't it be great if we could convince both of them to come to Atlanta? We could finish these projects in a hurry." Turk was excited by the idea of working with his two best construction guys again.

"Is Terry still in the worm business in Florida?"

"He is, with his brother I believe."

"Why don't I pay him a visit as well?"

"We probably can't convince them over the phone, can we?"

"I don't think so. They owe you big time, Turk. I think if I contact them personally, and look them square in the eye, I can convince them to come. It's too easy to say *no* over the phone."

"I think you're right. How long will that take? I don't want to run into Overton and Naylor without you around."

"I'll get it done while you're in Florida getting ready to move back to Atlanta. I should be able to make contact in a few days and have an answer from them in a week."

"That won't work. The Decker Group has pulled off all of the projects. I can have Jimmy help me, but I'll need to be here while you go see CJ and Terry."

"If you think you'll be all right until I get back, I'll get on the road right now."

"I should be fine. I'll make arrangements to stay here for another week. Get it done as quickly as you can."

"I will."

"Call me if you need help. Thanks for coming to my rescue, Digger. I'll call Jimmy and have him pick me up."

"You got it, boss. See you in a few days."

CHAPTER—12

While Turk waited for Jimmy, he called Karen, "Honey, you okay?"

"I'm good...Turk. How's it going in Atlanta?"

"Complicated, that's why I called. I was scheduled to be home tonight but I've been delayed." Turk didn't want to tell her that he'd made a deal with Pappas just yet.

"What do you mean?" Karen was expecting this call. She knew his trip wouldn't be as simple as Turk had tried to make out.

"The Decker Group walked off the jobs. I need to stay here until I get some supervision in place."

"How long will that be?"

"I figure a week or so."

"You didn't pack enough to stay a week. What are you going to do for clothes?" Karen wanted to make light of the fact that Turk was going to be gone. She knew he had work to do and didn't want him to be concerned about her and Jason.

"I'll buy some. Are you and Jason going to be okay?"

"Sure we'll be okay. Get what you have to get done and let

me know when you'll be coming home."

"How are you feeling?" This was easier than he expected it to be.

"I'm feeling fine right now. I'll be okay. Don't worry about me. Do what you have to do. I'll see you in a few days. I love you."

"I love you, too. Give Jason a hug for me. I'll call you tomorrow, honey. Bye."

Jimmy was waiting in front of the hotel. Turk, consumed in thought, got into the back seat and said, "Let's pick up where we left off. I need to inspect the projects."

Digger was already on his way to the airport; destination: Frederick, Maryland.

"Same order as yesterday, boss?"

"Yes."

Decker's security guards had been pulled off the Peachtree Industrial Park project. Turk and Jimmy went straight to the construction office. The offices had been vacated.

Jimmy busted the lock to gain entry. Papers were strewn all over the place. Copy machines, typewriters, adding machines and any other equipment an office needs to function were gone. The Decker Group had cleaned them out.

Turk lifted a phone and was surprised to hear a dial tone. The first thing he needed to do was contact his bankers and give them assurance that he was on the job and that everything would be back to normal by the end of the week. The next thing would be to start calling the subcontractors and suppliers and get them back to work.

"Jimmy, I'm going to stay here and make some calls. You need to get on over to our Cobb County apartment project and then onto our office complex in Douglas County. Call me from each place and let me know if anyone is working and what kind of shape they're in."

"Okay, boss. I'll call you as soon as I get there."

"Jimmy, plan on working long hours the rest of the week. We've got a lot of work to do."

Turk called all three lenders. The banks had done a considerable amount of business with him and they were relieved that he was back on the job. He assured them that things would be back to normal shortly. He also informed them that he would be making substantial draw requests over the next few weeks. His banking ties placated, now, he had to turn his attention to getting his subs back to work. But first he felt he should call Cory and give her an update.

"Hi, Cory. I'm out at our Industrial Park. The phones are still working."

"How are things there?" Cory knew that the jobs had been stopped. She had expected a lot of opposition from the Decker Group.

"The construction office here is pretty torn up, but the projects are fine. There's just no activity, but I can fix that."

"What about the Decker Group? What are you going to do about them?"

"They're done. I have a letter of resignation signed by Saul Decker."

"What about the money we owe them?"

"That's taken care of. We don't owe them any money. I have it in writing. I'll drop off the letter tomorrow."

"You've got to be kidding me, Turk. What did you do to them to get them to leave peacefully and forgive over a million dollars in fees?"

"Let's just say they got caught with their hands in the cookie jar at Niko's expense. I don't want to get into that right now. I called to tell you I've taken over. I'll be in town for a week or so before I go back to Florida and make arrangements to move my family back to Atlanta. You can contact me here or at the hotel. I've got to go now, Cory. I have a lot of calls to make...so long for now."

Cory whispered a goodbye, still holding the phone. She couldn't believe Turk had gotten that done as fast as he did. She relayed the good news to Niko.

"Cory, I told you he would do it! I knew he could. His signature is on those loans. What choice did he have?" Niko was coming across as though Turk was at his mercy.

"Niko, Turk could have stayed in Florida. He probably knows we would have come up with the cash. Give him credit. He's one of the few people around us we can totally count on and trust." Cory was put out by Niko's attitude. She had more than friendly feelings for Turk Donatelli.

"You're right. We need more associates like Turk. I'll fix that Decker Group for ripping me off. I will." Niko had grown even more callous than he was before he went to prison. He expected people to do his bidding.

* * *

"Turk, I just arrived at the apartment site. What do you want me to do now?" Jimmy asked.

"Is there any construction activity there?"

"Not much. There's a few subs milling around looking for some money they say the Decker Group owes them, that's all."

"Tell them I'll be at that site tomorrow morning and to come back and see me around ten."

"I'll do that."

"Jimmy, call Pop's Security. Instruct them to deploy a security team over here and to the other two sites. Tell them I want our projects secured by this evening. Can you do that?"

"Yes, I've dealt with Pop before."

"As soon as you know they've dispatched a security team to that site, go to the office building and call me from there."

"I got it. Consider it done." Jimmy was glad to be working for Turk again. No bullshit with him.

Turk found a Rolodex file on one of the desks that housed the subs' and suppliers' telephone numbers. He already had a list he used when he did his monthly inspections. He was familiar with most of them. He didn't want them to go right back to work. He wanted to find out how much money they had kicked back to the Decker Group. And if they did, he was going to require that they pay back the money and he was going to replace them. In three hours, he had called fifteen subcontractors and set up appointments every thirty minutes, starting at eight the next morning.

He requested that each subcontractor to bring a copy of his contract, the amount of money he had drawn to-date and the amount of money he felt he needed to be paid in order to go back to work. Turk scheduled them in order of importance: the major trades like the electrical, plumbing, carpentry, mechanical, and roofing, along with the major suppliers of lumber, concrete, cabinets, and finish-trim material. Most, if not all, of the trades he contacted, worked on all three projects so Turk figured he should be able to get them up and running in less time.

The next order of business would be to contact the subs and suppliers that were on the job when he left Atlanta, advising them to be prepared to come back to work for him on very little notice.

"Boss, I've been trying to get through to you. The line has been busy every time I called. I'm at our office building site now. Security is in place at both of these sites. What about yours?" Jimmy asked.

Before Turk could answer, in walked Pop, the owner of the security company. "What's the number there, Jimmy? I'll call you right back. Pop just walked in."

"The phones have been disconnected. I'm calling from a payphone down the street."

"Never mind, then. Come on back and pick me up. This has been a long day." Turk didn't wait for an answer. He got up and shook Pop's hand.

"It's been a while, Pop. How are you doing?"

"Better now that you're back. Good to see you again, Mr. Donatelli."

"Likewise. What do I owe this personal visit to, Pop?"

"I wanted to be sure you were here. Jimmy West called me and said you authorized all this security and I wanted to be sure it was true. Rumor has it that Pappas guy didn't pay his bills while he was in prison. Is that true?"

"That might be, Pop; no fault of his, though. I just got here. It will take me a few days to get my arms around these projects."

"I got your word I'll be paid?"

"You got it."

"That's good enough for me. I dispatched a total of twelve guards today. It will take another ten or so to do the job right. You okay with that?"

"Fine."

"Got lists of folks you want me to let in or keep out?"

"Work with Jimmy on that...he'll know. Digger will be back in a few days. You've worked with him before?"

"Yes. I like hm. And it sure feels good to be working for you again, Mr. Donatelli. I did get a call from Digger. I posted my best security officer outside. He'll be with you until Digger gets back. Goodbye." Pop was a very big man, almost as big as

Digger. He looked like a policeman with the .357 pistol he wore at his side. Turk had set Pop up in the security business three years before. Most of his personnel were trained by Digger. Turk was comfortable now knowing Pop had secured his jobs.

Jimmy arrived to pick up Turk. "I need to stop off and buy some clothes."

"Where do you want to go?"

"Moss Brothers will do. I haven't been to Lenox Square since I left Atlanta, two years ago. Why don't we go shopping there and get a bite to eat."

"We'll be there in thirty minutes."

Turk bought three pair of slacks, some underwear and socks, sport shirts, two suits, a few ties, six dress shirts, a pair of brown loafers, and a pair of steel-toed boots for walking the job sites. The total bill was over fifteen-hundred dollars. He would present that to Cory for reimbursement as soon as he met with her. They had a quick meal at Friday's, and Turk returned to the hotel. Jimmy's instructions were to pick up Turk at eight the next morning.

* * *

Turk grabbed an *Atlanta Journal* on his way through the lobby to breakfast. The hostess asked, "Sir, table for one?"

Unfolding the newspaper, Turk said, "Yes, just one this morning, thanks."

"Follow me please. Coffee?"

"Yes, please, black."

"Your waitress will be right with you."

As he waited for his coffee, he noticed the headlines glaring at him. "Piedmont office building burnt to the ground last night. Arson suspected." It was the Decker Group's office building. He almost knocked over his coffee as he as he rushed out of the coffee shop to a phone in the lobby.

"Cory, what's going on?"

"What do you mean, Turk?"

"Have you seen today's paper?"

"No, I haven't had time yet."

"Is Niko in the office?"

"No, I expect him in about half an hour. What's the matter? Is there something wrong?"

"Get a newspaper and see for yourself. Tell Niko I'm on my way to see him." As soon as he hung up, he called Jimmy.

"Jimmy, don't bother to pick me up this morning. Go out to the job site and meet with the subs I've got appointments with. Take the information we requested and tell them I'll get back to them."

"Okay. Where will you be?"

"I've got an appointment with Niko this morning. I'll take a cab to his office and call you from there."

"Whatever you say, boss. Consider it done." Jimmy knew what was wrong. He'd already read the morning *Journal*.

Getting off the elevator, Turk was met by Deon. "I heard the likes of you were back in town, Donatelli. I've been told to stay out of your way and Digger's, too," Deon said as he frisked him.

"Treat me with respect and I'll treat you the same way, Deon. Digger and you need to control yourselves." Deon's coal-black eyes matched his boss's, Niko Pappas. If looks could kill, that would have been the end of Turk.

"Yeah, right. For now anyway. I'll get Cory."

"Come on in, Turk. Niko still isn't here. He'll be here in ten minutes."

"Cory, I haven't been in town two days and Niko is already getting me in trouble. What is wrong with that man? I thought he was going legit for crissakes."

"You don't know that Niko had anything to do with Decker's

building burning down."

"Come on, Cory. You know damn well he had something to do with it. The GBI will figure it out, too. They probably already have."

"They've got to prove it."

"That's not it, Cory. The GBI don't give a hoot about the Decker Group. All they care about is Niko. He should know better than to get them on his case, especially if he's trying to stay out of prison."

"How will this affect you, Turk? You didn't have anything to do with it, did you?"

"Cory, you know damn well I don't operate that way. How will it affect me, you ask? I'll tell you how. The GBI and probably the FBI will be in my office before the week is out. They know I'm back in town. They will know that we replaced the Decker Group."

"You've got nothing to worry about. You didn't do anything, right?" Cory was always making excuses and standing up for Niko. She was troubled with this as much as Turk, but she couldn't vent her frustration like Turk could.

"I hear you want to see me, Turk," Niko interrupted as he wheeled his way to his desk.

"You're damn right I do, Niko."

"What about?" he asked nonchalantly.

"Did you see the lead story in the *Journal* this morning?"

"I did. The bastard had it coming, stealing from me like he did."

"You do know that the GBI and the FBI will be on our asses, don't you?"

"They can't prove anything and they're on my ass anyway. What difference does that make?"

His indifference was troubling Turk. "I came back to Atlanta to save your real estate investments, not to have to deal with the GBI and the FBI again. That's why I left in the first place. Why did you have to stir them up?"

"Awe stop bullshitting me, Turk. You came back here to save your ass. You're signed personally on those construction loans. Don't try this good-guy-bad-guy shit with me."

"You ungrateful bastard! You really think that? I'm one of the few who has looked out for you. What did prison do to you? Don't you have a moral fiber left in that wrecked body?"

"Calm down, Turk, calm down. You got nothing to worry about. So they question you. What do you care?"

"You just don't get it, Niko. You think everybody is out to screw you. You're blind to your friends. I'll finish these projects for the reason you just stated. My name is on the line. My association with you could do me more harm than walking away from these projects. But I'm a real estate developer who can't operate without banks. So you're right, I'm screwed." Turk turned and left his office, slamming the door. Cory was right behind him.

"Turk, wait a minute. I need to talk to you," she pleaded.

"I'm done talking, Cory. I can take care of this mess. Just make sure Niko lives up to his end of our deal. I'm not one of his lackeys like this guy," he said, pointing to Deon.

Dismissing Deon, Cory said, "Look, Turk, Niko is in a foul mood. He was served yesterday with a warrant for his arrest on murder charges."

"Murder charges!" Turk exclaimed.

"Yes, murder charges. It took the lawyers all day to get him out on bail."

"I didn't think you could get out on bail this quick if you were accused of murder."

"The incident took place many years ago. He was charged

with accessory to murder. The FBI is coming at Niko pretty hard. So give him some slack, will you?"

"I've given Niko all the slack I'm going to. I'll finish these projects, and then I'm done."

"Okay, that's enough for today. Keep me apprised of what's going on, will you?"

"I will, Cory, but tell Niko he better treat me right. I own every piece of real estate he thinks he controls. See you."

CHAPTER – 13

After landing at the Washington DC airport, Digger rented a car and got directions via the beltway to Frederick, Maryland. He'd called China Jon's folks, the last known number for CJ, and left a message that he was on his way to see him.

Three hours later, Digger parked across the street from their house. He waited thirty minutes to see if CJ would show himself. He didn't want to involve his parents if he could help it. A white Ford station wagon pulled up and a short, rotund, bespectacled man rolled out of the driver seat. Digger thought that might be his dad. CJ always joked about how much his dad liked to eat.

Knocking lightly on the door, Digger didn't know what to expect. A very pretty petite lady, about sixty answered, and said, "Can I help you, young man?"

"Yes, ma'am, my name is Digger. I'm a friend of China Jon's. By chance is he in?"

"I don't know any China Jon. If you mean Johnny, he has his own place." She'd heard her son called China Jon a few times, and didn't like the name. To her, he had always been Johnny.

"Shirley, who's that at the door?" Herb Garber shouted.

"It's someone wanting to see Johnny, Herb."

Digger saw Herb approaching over Mrs. Garber's shoulder. "Folks, I'm an old friend of your son's. I wanted to talk to him about a job, that's all," said Digger.

"What did you say your name was?" Herb asked.

"My name is Digger."

"I heard about you. A tough Navy Seal, right?"

"I don't know about tough, but I am a retired Navy Seal."

"My son speaks highly of you. You have anything to do with that Donatelli guy?"

"I do. I work for him."

"You say you got a job for my son?"

"I do, if he'll take it."

"Well, he sure needs one. He's been living in a cabin he built up in the mountains ever since his divorce."

Mrs. Garber had stepped aside and Herb reached out to shake Digger's hand, and said, "Come on in. We were just sitting down for tea and cookies. Would you care to join us?"

"I'd like that, Mr. Garber; it's been a long drive."

The interior of the house was typical '50s décor. It was pleasant, but dark. Plastic covers on the furniture. Small rooms, high ceilings, walls still covered with lead paint. Mr. Garber and Digger sat on a couch and Mrs. Garber sat in a rocking chair. The cookies were homemade, oatmeal with raisins. The tea was strong and hot. The silence was hard to bear.

"Thanks, the cookies are delicious," Digger said, trying to start a conversation. They both just stared at Digger as though he had arrived from another planet.

"Why thank you, sir," Mrs. Garber said.

"What kind of job?" Herb asked.

"You mean for your son?"

"Yes."

"The same thing he used to do for Turk."

"You mean construction management?"

"Yes. Is it all right with Jon that we talk about his business, Herb?" Digger asked.

"Probably not. You ready to go for a ride, Digger?"

"Where to?"

"Where he lives. He doesn't have a phone and he's lucky he's got electricity."

"Are you going to take me there?"

"No, I want you to follow me. You'll never find his place by yourself. Johnny and I aren't talking all that much."

"May I ask why?"

"It's just that our son is so damn smart: IQ of 175-plus. He's our only child. We expected more from him than what he's doing, working as a carpenter, and living in the woods. Maybe you can wake him up. Drink your tea and let's go."

Traveling on a dirt road, twenty minutes later Herb pulled up short of a long, winding, rutted dirt driveway. He stopped, walked over to Digger's car, and said, "He's there now."

"How do you know? I don't see a car."

"He doesn't have a car. He rides a bicycle. See it leaning up against the cabin?"

"Yes, I do." Digger was now curious as to what was going on with his good friend, China Jon.

"Tell him I said hello. Good luck." Herb turned around and headed back down the road, leaving Digger pondering what to do next. The driveway looked pretty rough so he walked to the cabin.

From the outside, the cabin looked more like a deer camp. It had wood shingles and a felt-tar roof. Smoke was streaming from a chimney. There were no windows in the front and only one window on the side. The entry door was solid wood. The cabin, which had not been painted, was built on six cinder-block columns about a foot off the ground. The earth around the cabin was recently disturbed, indicating to Digger the cabin hadn't been there long.

Not much made Digger nervous, but approaching the front door, he was visibly concerned for his friend. He knocked lightly.

"Door's open, come on in." China Jon said.

There, next to the pot belly stove, sat his friend, China Jon, drinking a Busch beer, and smoking a Salem cigarette. Digger didn't recognize him. He sported a full beard and his hair was shoulder-length. His clothes were frayed and worn. His steel-toed work boots rested on a small wooden box. A knotted red bandana was tied around his neck. Without getting up, China Jon said, "Well, I'll be damned! You're the last person I thought I'd ever see here."

"CJ, I'm glad to see you, too. Got any soda?"

"There should be some Coca Cola left in that cooler. Grab one," he said, still not moving.

Digger pulled a Coke out of the cooler, looked around for a place to sit, and said, "What can I say? I never expected to see you living like this. What's going on with you, CJ?"

"Everything is good, Digger. Are things good with you?"

"I'm doing okay."

"What brings you to my humble abode?" CJ asked, as he reached for a bag of pot.

"I came to see if you would be willing to work for Turk in Atlanta for a few months, cleaning up some real estate projects."

Expertly rolling a joint, CJ said, "I'm done with the

construction management business; too much politics."

"By the looks of your clothes and that tool belt over in the corner, you haven't quit construction entirely."

"Well, that's another story. Let's smoke this joint or are you still on the wagon?"

"Go ahead, you know I can't." Digger had been sober for five years. One of the conditions of his employment was that he abstain from drink and drugs.

Inhaling deeply, CJ asked, "How's Turk doing? I haven't heard form him since we separated in Spain a couple of years ago. I've been meaning to look him up. He tried several times to contact me through my parents. I should have called him."

"He could be doing better. He's happily married to Karen, but she's not all that well. He adopted her son, Jason." Digger could tell by the look on CJ's face that he felt bad about not contacting Turk.

"That married business sure is tough. I married Cia as soon as I got back to the States. We've been divorced for six months. The marriage didn't last but a year."

"Why was that, CJ?" Digger wanted his friend to open up so he could figure out how to approach him with an employment opportunity.

"Cia was a great woman, but I was, and have always been in love with my first wife. You remember, Beth Peters. I married her three times. Can't get over her no matter how hard I try."

"What happened with you and Cia?"

"Not much really. She didn't want to live the simple life I aspire to. She wanted me to be an English professor at some fancy college. I wanted to be a carpenter with basically no responsibilities."

"Well, it looks like you've succeeded at that. Are you really happy living under these conditions?"

"I don't know for sure. I've only been here a few months. I built this cabin with my own hands. That felt pretty good. I don't have a lot of worries. But I don't have a lot of money, either."

"CJ, you're too damn bright to be living like this."

"That's what everyone preaches to me, Digger," he said, as he took another hit off his joint.

After two beers, and muddled conversation, Digger came to the realization that CJ just didn't have any motivation. He worked as a carpenter, drank beer, and smoked pot. That was it. "Where's the bathroom? I got to get rid of some of this pop."

"That's one of the modern conveniences I don't have. There's a latrine about fifty yards behind the cabin. You can't miss it. If you can't smell it, follow the path and you'll find it."

Laughing, Digger headed for the door, turned and said, "CJ, while I'm emptying my bladder, think about this. Come to Atlanta and help Turk out of a mess. The money is good and he'd really love to see you." CJ looked up quickly and started to say something, then fell silent.

Returning to the cabin after falling down twice trying to find the outhouse, he finally gave up and pissed on a tree. "Well, what do you think?"

"I'm okay here. I can't get involved with Turk again. I don't like most of the people he associates with...present company excluded."

"Thanks, but this trip isn't about you, CJ. I came here because Turk needs your help and he needs it badly. You owe him."

"What do I owe him, Digger? What do I really owe him? I gave him four years and that was enough."

"I don't have to answer that. You know damn well what he did for you. He's given you, not loaned you, money when you needed it. He stood by you during your relationship with your first wife when she was only seventeen and her parents were trying to have you put in jail. Need I go on? Think hard, CJ, think hard. He needs you now. It's payback time."

"Come on, Digger; don't lay a goddamn guilt trip on me. I'm comfortable right here."

"*You* come on, CJ. You're drinking too much. You're smoking too much dope. You look like shit. You're feeling sorry for yourself. You think the world is wrong and you're right. You got a shit-load of problems. I can appreciate that, but this isn't about you. It's about Turk!"

China Jon was visibly upset. He'd been shirking his responsibility to society by blaming society. Digger was reminding him. He did owe Turk, but he just couldn't do it. "I'm sorry, Digger, I can't accept. It's best that you leave now."

Digger thought he could see tears. "CJ, you're stoned and half-drunk. I hope you can remember what I'm about to say." He took his wallet out and counted out ten one hundred dollar bills. "Here's a grand. I expect you to get a shave, a haircut, new clothes and an airline ticket to Atlanta. If you're not there in a week, consider this grand a parting gift of our friendship. Good luck, friend."

As soon as China Jon heard Digger's car start and head down the road, he burst into tears. Digger had opened sore wounds. CJ had escaped his responsibilities by drinking and smoking pot. His failures were his own doings. He couldn't sleep without some kind of self-medication. He only worked enough hours to buy his drugs and food. He did feel sorry for himself. He screamed out loud, "To hell with Digger...to hell with them all!" CJ's failed marriages and his genius contributed to his depressed state.

* * *

On his way back to the airport Digger couldn't help but feel sorry for his friend, China Jon. He hated to do what he had done, but he also knew CJ might come around. Right now, he needed to fly to Orlando and meet up with Terry O'Neil, the worm farmer.

It didn't take Digger long to find Terry's farm. There was a worm-stand right in front of his house. He pulled up and a young boy came running up to the car, and asked, "How many worms you want, mister? I just dug up a fresh batch."

Smiling, Digger said, "Are you one of Terry's boys?"

"Yes, I'm the youngest. I have two brothers. I'm ten. I know how to sell worms. You don't need my dad," the young boy spieled out.

"By the looks of it, I figure you can, son. I don't need any *fresh* worms right now, though. I'm here to see your dad. I'm an old friend. Do you know where I can find him?"

"Right over there," the boy said, pointing to an open field.

Terry was bending over a wheelbarrow, loading it with cornmeal when Digger finally spotted him next to a shed. "Hi, Terry...you've lost weight. You look good." Terry was always trying to lose weight.

Startled, Terry turned and faced Digger. A wide smile spread across his friendly face, "I'll be! It's been a long time, Digger," he said as he wiped off his hands and rushed to greet Digger opened-armed.

After a lengthy embrace, they stood, smiling, taking each other in, Terry said, "Come on, Digger. Let's get some lemonade. I made it this morning." Terry didn't drink and he knew Digger was on the wagon.

"I'd like that, Terry. It looks like you got quite an operation going. Has the worm business been good to you?" Turk financed the operation for him and his brother. Digger couldn't help but reminisce.

* * *

Turk was in the process of transferring his operation to Ocala and he wanted Terry to move there and continue doing what he was doing in Miami, supervising construction. He offered Terry the job, and Terry explained, "Well, thank you, that's very generous of you Turk, but if you do go to Ocala, I want to try something on my own. You'll laugh when I tell you what I want to do."

"Try me. I'm in no laughing mood." At the time, Turk, had been given an ultimatum by the Miami Beach mob, either sign with the union or be killed. Turk's company was non-union. Rather than join the mob, he decided to sell out to them and move to Ocala.

"Okay, I want to go into the worm business," Terri offered.

"Worm business? What the hell is that?" Turk asked him, laughing after all.

"See I told you, you'd laugh. My brother and I would like to try our hand at worm farming. There's a shortage of good worms," he explained seriously to Turk.

"I thought worms were worms."

"Me too, but that's not the case. Try to buy some; not many folks want to devote the time and money to raise worms for fishing. That is, good worms."

"How do you go about getting into the 'good worm' business?" Turk asked him.

"My farm has the right soil conditions. My brother will handle selling them. All I need to do now is complete the process I've started, but I need another $50,000 before I can."

"I can help you there. Consider your parting bonus $50,000, providing you stay on with me long enough to see this transfer to Ocala take place. Will you do that?"

"Yes, I absolutely will. That's a very generous offer."

"You've earned it. Good luck with the worm farming." Digger had heard Turk tell that story over and over. He was amazed that there even was such a thing as worm farming.

* * *

Snapping Digger out of his trip down memory lane, Terry answered, "More than I ever could have hoped for. My brother, God rests his soul, and I had the right idea at the right time. We were pioneers in the worm business and it paid off handsomely."

"What happened to your brother?"

"Something you read about, but you never think can happen to you. Tractor turned over on him; killed him instantly. We found him lying under it one afternoon about two months ago."

"Wow, I'm really sorry to hear that!" Digger felt bad for Terry, but he'd never known his brother.

"Thanks, what do I owe this visit to? I know you're not interested in the worm business."

"It's not important now, Terry. With your brother gone, I can see you have your hands full tending your worm business. I was here on Turk's behalf. He needs some help in Atlanta cleaning up some bad real estate deals. I thought if you could help him, he would be grateful."

"There's nothing I won't do for Turk. It was his gift of fifty thousand dollars that got me and my brother into the worm business. He's the most generous guy I've ever known. I wish I could help him. I really do."

"He'll understand your circumstances, Terry."

"What about China Jon? He'd be a better choice than me."

Digger briefed Terry on his trip to see CJ, and said, "I left him some money. I hope he takes Turk up on his offer, not so much for Turk's sake, but in China Jon's best interest. I think

CJ needs a break from the back woods, his drinking, and himself for that matter."

"CJ always was the rebel. I bet he comes and helps Turk. They were real close at one time, real close."

"I hope you're right, Terry. Look, I got to get back to the airport. It was good seeing you again."

"Likewise, Digger. Be sure to give Turk my sincere apologies. Take care, and have a safe flight back to Atlanta. Don't be a stranger. Goodbye."

CHAPTER – 14

In order for Turk to get his projects back on schedule and on budget he had to work fourteen-hour days. Three hours were spent traveling from one site to the other. In three days, he managed to get most of the subcontractors back on the job. He quickly hired two superintendants. He was in the process of rescheduling and revising budgets on all three projects.

All of this was running through Turk's mind when his new receptionist buzzed him, and announced that two GBI detectives were there to see him.

"Please send them in." Turk got up from his desk and moved toward the door in order to greet them upon entry.

"I didn't expect to see you this soon, Carl. It is Carl Pettit, right? And your partner, if I remember, is Donald Knight, I believe."

"You have a good memory, Donatelli," said Carl.

"What do I owe this visit to, gentlemen?"

"We heard you were back in town. We stopped by to see how you were doing. How *are* you doing, Turk?"

"I could be better. What can I do for you guys?"

"You read the papers. Do you know anything about the Decker's office building going up in flames?"

"No, I don't."

Gazing around the office, Carl said, "This used to be their construction office. Funny you come to town, take over their construction, and their place burns down. It doesn't figure, Donatelli."

"I didn't have anything to do with that, Carl, and you know it. That's not the way I operate."

"But your partner operates that way. He's out on appeal. What about him?"

"What about him? I don't keep track of what he does. You'll have to ask him."

"Let's start over, Donatelli. Tell me what you're doing back in Atlanta."

"That's simple, Carl. I have a personal interest in three rather large real estate projects. I'm here to get them back on schedule, and finished."

"So you're partners with Pappas again. Is that what you're telling me?" Carl asked as his partner, Donald, thumbed through some papers lying on top of a filing cabinet.

"I guess you'd call us partners, though I like to think I'm my own man. Hey, Donald, those papers interest you?"

Detective Knight didn't answer; he backed away and took a seat.

"Turk, I know you know more than you're going to tell us. Let me say this. The GBI and the FBI are going to do everything in their power to put Pappas away for good. I'm warning you. Don't get in so far that you end up in prison, too."

"Carl, I'm here to finish these projects and then I'm done."

"How long do you figure that will take?"

"Eighteen months to finish what's under construction.

There's enough land to continue building for another three years."

"Be careful, Turk. This guy is dangerous, very dangerous, and we're going to get him," Carl said as he nodded to his partner. "We'll be in touch."

The two GBI agents were on their way out as Turk's receptionist was on her way in. "Mr. Donatelli, a person by the name of China Jon, I think I got that right, is waiting at an airport payphone, and asked you to call him back," she said, handing him the message.

Turk's heart skipped a beat. It had been a few years since he'd had any contact with his old friend, China Jon. They had roomed together in college, traveled through Europe together, and fought the mob and the unions in Miami. He couldn't wait to see him.

"I'll call him. Have Jimmy bring the car around and tell him to hurry. We're going to the airport."

* * *

"Hey, CJ...welcome to Atlanta. I was beginning to think I'd never see you again. Where at the airport are you?"

"I'll be outside of Delta Airlines. Who are you sending to pick me up?" Chills went up his spine when he heard his old friend's voice. He'd forgotten how close they were and how much he had missed Turk's company.

"Are you kidding me? I'm coming to pick you up. Jimmy and I will be there in ten minutes. Our construction office is that close. Sit tight, we'll be right there."

China Jon had given this a lot of thought. In the beginning, when Digger offered him passage and a job in Atlanta, he didn't want anything to do with it. But when he tried to spend the thousand dollars, he couldn't do it with out feeling guilty. He needed the money, and he owed a dear friend, Turk. CJ asked himself what he could do with that money, if anything, and not feel obligated. How was he going to change his attitude? He figured if he started with a shave and a haircut, he wouldn't feel guilty about that.

The barber wheeled him around, holding up a mirror, asking CJ for approval. What the mirror reflected was a person CJ hadn't seen for a while. His face was clean-shaven, showing a white outline where his beard had been. His neck was white to his shoulders. He looked ten years younger and according to CJ, not bad looking at that.

As CJ stood and paid the barber, his entire frame came into view. His shirt was frayed at the collar and cuffs. His pants were stained and the make-shift patches he had stuck on were hanging. His barely distinguished brown boots were crumbled and worn. For the first time in a long time, CJ saw his old self. He liked what he saw.

Mounting his bicycle, he rode to the nearest men's store. Standing outside, trying to work up the courage to go in and buy a new wardrobe was daunting to him. He'd been so in love and he had hurt for so long, he just lost interest in living. The haircut and shave and the impression of what he saw in the mirror lifted his sprits.

"How can I help you, sir?" the salesman asked, as if he needed to.

"Kind of obvious, isn't it? I need a new wardrobe."

"What kind of look did you have in mind, sir?" The salesman had no idea where to start. He needed direction. He couldn't figure out whether this was a homeless man who had come into some money, or a construction worker who might have robbed a bank and gotten a haircut.

"To start with, I'd like a pair of dress slacks and a dress shirt. Then a couple pair of jeans and a couple of work shirts. I need a reversible belt, and a new pair of boots, just like the ones I have on, if you stock them," CJ said, pointing to his old boots. He was feeling better already. He felt like he was going places he'd not planned on going.

"What type of work do you do, sir?" He hoped this guy had some money. He didn't want to dress him and have him run out of the store with the new clothes on.

"Right now, I guess I'm headed to Atlanta to work in construction."

"What type of work?" he asked, thinking it had to be carpentry, laborer, or maybe a brick mason."

"Like I said, construction work; probably a project manager or superintendant."

"Oh, very well then, come with me." The salesman led CJ to a dressing area and asked him to have a seat; he would be right back. He told one of the other salesmen to keep an eye on the door in case his customer tried to run out.

China Jon sat in front of three floor-to-ceiling mirrors. He'd been so distraught over his lost loves and so into his drugs, he'd forgotten what real living was all about. He looked the part of a lost soul, and he was.

"Here you go; try these pants on for size. This shirt should go well with them," the salesman said, as he handed CJ a pair of dress slacks sized 32-inch waist and 32-inches long. CJ was thinner than he had ever been.

"Looking in the mirror, he felt a complete transformation. He'd been set free. Free of the shackles he had felt. All because of a debt he felt he owed Turk Donatelli. Once again, Turk had come to his rescue without him even knowing it.

"Very good, just the right fit," CJ said as he viewed a new man. The salesman had already laid out the other clothes for him to try on.

"What size boots, sir?"

"I used to wear a ten...ten should do it," CJ answered, looking down at his bare feet. "Better bring me some socks, too. While you're at it, I'll need some underwear."

"That will be $455.30 sir," The salesman said, still not sure CJ had any money.

"Here's five hundred. Keep the change. You were most helpful."

* * *

"Jimmy, you've never met China Jon. We all call him CJ." Turk commenced to brief Jimmy on his relationship with China Jon.

"So what you're saying, boss, is I'll be working for China Jon?"

"I hadn't thought about it that way, but yes, you will be working for CJ and me."

"I can do that. I like working for you, Mr. Donatelli."

"Why is that, Jimmy?" Turk was curious, but really didn't care. He was anxious to see his old friend.

"You know what you want and you know how to get things done. There's no bullshit with you, if you don't mind me saying so," Jimmy said, eying Turk in his rearview mirror. His boss looked happy for the first time since he'd been back.

"Thanks, that's the only way I know. CJ should be in front of Delta."

Turk spotted CJ a long time before CJ saw him. His friend looked considerably thinner. He could see the outline of a recent haircut and shave. It was obvious he had new clothes on and he was shuffling his feet, smoking a Salem, no doubt.

Jimmy pulled up to the curb. Turk jumped out and started toward CJ. CJ instantly recognized Turk. A big smile crossed his face, the first in quite a while. They embraced, not saying a word, just holding each other. Turk broke the embrace and holding CJ's shoulders, said, "I have missed your company so much. Why has it taken this long for us to get back together?"

Choking back tears of emotion, CJ said, "I have a lot of reasons and I'm sure you do, too. But let's get out of here and reacquaint ourselves. What do you say?"

"I think that's a great idea. Let's go."

They piled into the backseat. Turk introduced the two, and said, "Jimmy, head to the Royal Coach. Our receptionist, what's her name, should have CJ booked there already."

"Royal Coach it is. Her name is Brenda."

"Brenda, you say. I need to remember that."

"I can see not much has changed with you, Turk. You still have a driver and it looks like you still travel first-class. Not that there's anything wrong with that, you know."

"I don't know about that, CJ. You had me on a five dollar-a-day budget while we were traveling through Europe." CJ had given Turk a book by Arthur Fommer touting traveling through Europe on five dollars a day before he left Ocala. It was an experience Turk would never forget.

"I did, and you weren't really very good about maintaining it, if I remember correctly," CJ said, laughing and remembering Turk sneaking off to a Holiday Inn to get a steak and a proper shower.

"I don't think I did so badly. Digger tells me you're living in the mountains in a cabin you built with your own hands. That true?"

"Yeah, pretty much. Let's say I've been through a tough patch."

"Let me guess. You married Beth again and she broke your heart." Turk was familiar with their on-off-again relationship.

"You got it. But I also felt lousy about abandoning Cia."

"How's Cia doing?"

"She's okay. She went back to Ocala. She's living with her parents right now. She's still selling real estate."

"How'd you meet up with Beth again?"

"She contacted me through my parents. My marriage to Cia wasn't going well. She wanted me to be more than a carpenter. She thought I was wasting my life away. I kind of was. Beth came along and said she still loved me. I divorced Cia and married Beth for the third time. Her father died and she needed to move back to Coral Gables and handle some Coral Gables banking affairs. I wouldn't go, so we divorced again. You got the picture?"

"I got the picture. You can't stand that highfalutin life style, right?"

"Right, I bailed again. Just can't seem to get it right. What about you? I hear you're happily married, and don't drink anymore, that true?"

"Yes, that is true. I got a good woman and I love her son. The drinking and running around got old."

"I hear you. What have you got in store for me?" CJ asked, just as they pulled up to the hotel.

"I need you to help me get three very large projects back on track."

"Okay, I hope I still know how."

"It won't take you long. Hey, why don't you check in and get comfortable. I've got some business I need to attend to this afternoon. We'll meet for breakfast at eight, okay."

"Sure, it's been a while since I've stayed in luxury." CJ was feeling overwhelmed by the thought of being involved in this type of work again. He hoped Turk wouldn't notice.

"CJ, do you need any money?"

"I got a few bucks. Will I need a credit card for my room? All of mine have expired."

"Your room and expenses here at the hotel are taken care of. Just sign your name. Here are a few bucks to tide you over until pay day." Turk peeled off ten more one-hundred dollar bills and handed them to CJ. "We'll talk more over breakfast."

"Wow! Thanks, Turk. Just like old times, huh?"

"Not quite, CJ. Not quite."

CHAPTER – 15

"Cory, send in Overton. Tell his dumb-ass sidekick, Naylor, to wait until we're finished," Niko said, counting the last of his morning cash delivery.

"Niko, what's so damn urgent I had to fly in here from California?" asked a red-faced Overton. He drank a bottle of rum the night before, and also gave himself a shot of heroin and took several hits of speed. He was hooked on "Blacks," a black pill containing amphetamine.

"I got a job for you and your dumb-ass sidekick, that's what."

"What kind of job?"

"You remember Turk Donatelli?" Niko knew the mention of him would set off Overton.

"Do I remember him? You're fucking right I remember him. I find that bastard and I'll kill him."

"No, you won't do anything of the sort. I promised Donatelli you'd stay away from him."

"Since when do you make promises for me?" Overton was visibly agitated. He could hardly sit still. He got up and started to pace.

"Ever since I needed his help cleaning up the Decker group's mess, that's when. Why don't you sit down? What's the matter with you anyway? Are you still getting hopped up on speed?"

"So what if I am? I told you to stay out of the real estate business, I did."

"Look, Overton let's stop this quibbling. Like I said, I got a job for you."

"Let's hear it," he said, sitting back down. Overton twitched. He couldn't control his head from going back and forth. It irritated Niko.

"You've got to clean up your act. Ever since I sent you to California, you've been high on drugs. Pretty soon you won't be any good to me or yourself, for that matter."

"I didn't fly all the way to Atlanta to get a fucking lecture. What the fuck do you want me to do?"

"Lighten up, Overton. I'm not one of your lackeys! I want you to burn down my real estate projects."

"You mean the same real estate projects you hired Donatelli to clean up?"

"Those are the ones."

"Come on, Niko, that doesn't make any sense."

"I'm not going to get into the details as to why I want this done. I just want it done." Niko figured that the projects were in Turk's name and during their last meeting, he sensed that Turk was about to cut him out of any ownership. He wanted to collect the insurance money, rid himself of Turk, and the projects.

"You mean burn down all of those buildings?"

"That's what I mean. Can it be done?"

"Well, it's not like burning down an adult bookstore. But it probably can be done." Overton's only experience with burning down buildings was when he had partnered with Niko and they burned out a competitor's store and he didn't do a very good job at that.

"You screwed that job up, Overton. You can't, and I mean *can't* screw this one up. Donatelli has got some pretty smart people around him and the GBI are just looking for a reason to put me away. I took the rap for the job you did in Kentucky. I refuse to take responsibility for this one. If you can't handle it, just tell me, and I'll get someone else to do it."

"I can do it. When do you want it done?" Overton asked, as he thought back to the Kentucky burning of a competitor's adult book store.

* * *

It had been a Sunday night on the ugly side of Louisville, Kentucky; so late that even the nasty street traffic that fed this fringe neighborhood had slowed down. Even the sex deviates were home in some bed. Only a slow freight train seemed to move with purpose, behind some warehouses and project housing. The man in the Ford station wagon had been parked for four hours, waiting after a long drive from Atlanta. The younger and thinner man looked eagerly at his long-haired, burly boss.

"Not yet," said Cliff Overton. "This guy's been spooked. He may come back." Overton drove away and returned to another vantage point. Ross Naylor, his helper, was only twenty-five at the time, and proud to be working in what he called "the real world." He'd even met the boss, Niko Pappas, once. Right now he was getting on Overton's nerves.

"So this guy won't lease, and he wants to buy Niko's peep machines?" Naylor asked.

"Look, Naylor, you don't need to know nothin' about that shit. You just keep your eyes pealed for Ballard," Overton said, trying to control his temper.

"What if he comes back, boss?" Naylor sensed he'd better stop asking questions; they were there to do a job.

"If that ornery little fuck, Nat Ballard, comes back and we catch him, we may have to kill the bastard," Cliff said for effect. He wanted Naylor to respect him, maybe even fear him. He knew that Ballard had no protection from the local police, who'd be glad to see him gone, but murder was murder, and Cliff wasn't in the mood to take that step tonight.

"Look," he said to Naylor, "I told you this and you're makin' me repeat myself. This guy thinks he's a genius for usin' peep shows with sex. He's got his own machine that's about as up-to-date as those early nickelodeon guys in Atlantic City or them books you run the pages by fast and it's like a cartoon. You've seen the dirty ones—Popeye pokin' Olive Oyl and all. That's about how good his are."

Naylor had wanted Overton's approval and he remembered one thing. "You designed ours," he said, and it got a good reaction.

"Exactly. Mine don't stick and burn up the goddamn film, and you can't break the coin box with a goddamn atom bomb. One of Niko's guys comes by once a week or so and takes half, and the owner gets half. But this asshole thinks he's Edison or somethin'. Sold his to the guys on Times Square, so he's a pioneer. Half the time, you get some old black and white smoker movie made in Mexico in 1910, you lose your quarters, and you lose customers. This country's changing and we're state of the art. We've gone from belly buttons to split beavers in ten years; cum shots soon, the works."

Naylor seemed embarrassed, but nodded. He'd never seen their product and suddenly, it was all he could think of. He was risking his life for something he hadn't seen. Would they let him watch the movies being made, stand next to a naked woman while she waited for her cue? He had no idea how these films were made. He had an erection.

Overton broke the reverie.

"I don't like it that we gotta use that side door with the big light. Fucker's not stupid. Like a bunker...one door, no windows. Even the cops might check if that light's out."

"That's why I shoot it out with the pellet gun, right?" Naylor asked, eager to please.

"Change of plans. That's the most conspicuous thing we could do." He got out and walked around to Naylor's side. "Get out, numb-nuts, and drive."

When they were seated, Overton had said: "Drive me to that door, let me unload the gas bottles, and go park under that big tree a block away. I'll be in by the time you sneak back. Come in quiet, but say your name. Something goes wrong, I drive getaway or I holler "on foot" and we ditch the car and run for it, hide somewhere until morning, then call a cab and get a bus ticket home. Car's stolen, untraceable. Got it?"

Naylor nodded and drove slowly onto the two-lane, then into the "Pink Pussycat" parking lot and up to the door. Cliff took out the last gas bottle and Naylor drove away. This was the moment of greatest vulnerability, brightly lit with a set of lock picks and gas. "I got locked out of my shop, officer. There's a big lawnmower in there I'll need for summer. Want to get her tuned up. No, there's no grass here..."

Inside, Overton waited for his eyes to adjust. He had a penlight with a red cover and felt very professional. This wouldn't go out of control like the last job. He just barely managed to cover that. Something about the crime...it didn't bother you and you weren't nervous, exactly, but once you started, things could go wrong and then there you were doing something stupid. He saw the light at the door as Naylor entered and said, "It's Naylor."

"You just stand there and let your eyes adjust," Overton told him. "I'll get started." He emptied one can of gas on the cash register counter and the showcase that had the sex toys. He started throwing magazines and books into the middle of the shop. Ballard wouldn't keep any of his bookkeeping records here. He would have those at home or some place safer. He'd have a set for the Internal Revenue Service, and one for himself.

"God, it smells like a dirty bathroom," Naylor said before the gas fumes reached him. "What do these guys...?"

"Hey, shut it," Overton ordered. "They beat off in the booths, right? And I can't explain what these plastic dongs do, much less some of that other shit. This is my living, not my life. I stick my dick in a woman as often as I can and don't use appliances. You grab a can...no, two...and saturate those booths where the machines are. Don't like the smell? We're about to fix that." He checked behind in his waistband where he'd put the .38, under his windbreaker. He wished he could take off his jacket. He was sweating now. They kept working.

Overton blew out his first match. "I saw some paint cans over there," he said. "Dump 'em out here with the gas; use your screwdriver."

Naylor started to say something, but Overton cut him off. "Move!"

Naylor had gotten five of the cans open and dumped before Overton stopped him. He'd given in to his restlessness and put the penlight on one can. It was latex, water-soluble paint and might slow the fire. *This is what happens*, Cliff thought. *I know I'm smarter than that.* "Stop, enough," he told Naylor, who may have tried to tell him already that it was latex paint. Overton's ears were burning. "Torch time," he had said, in what he hoped was a confident voice. "Remember, throw your boots and gloves onto the fire, the screwdriver, and anything that you got gas on." He took off his windbreaker and tossed it onto the pile of cans and boxes of books, magazines, films. He poured the last can onto that, and then shed his gloves. "Go look outside. If it looks clear, come get me with the car. No screeching tires. Easy does it. You got rid of everything gassy?" Maybe he was *too* smart.

"Yeah," Naylor said, then peeked outside and slid through the door. Overton went to check it to make sure the dumb motherfucker hadn't locked him in, then came back and stood for a few moments, looking down at the mess in the dim light. He heard a car engine come near. He struck the match, backed away, and threw it. Flame-out. Fuck! Things go wrong! Second match did it. OK. He backed out fast, shucking his rain boots last at the door and tossing them back into the stinking dark room. The fire had faltered, but flared again. He figured it was on for the duration now; so much gas in there. He left the door open for ventilation, because otherwise, the place was a bunker—not even any windows except those little ones in the booths that showed you glimpses into human nature you wouldn't have thought existed.

It was the Ford wagon outside and nothing else. "Out," Overton said to Naylor. "I'm driving."

Forty miles south of Louisville, Naylor's knees were still jumping from adrenaline. Overton made himself laugh out loud. He stopped to change license plates, in case somebody had seen the first one. They weren't out of Kentucky yet. Maybe they should have gone west to Indiana or north to Ohio, but it was a waste of time, unless they got caught. "You know that latex paint?" he asked his jumpy partner. "I did that on purpose. Number one, it slows down the burning a little so we could get out. Two, it looks unprofessional; confuses the cops and firemen. Three, it does more smoke damage. Four, maybe the cops think it was amateurs…kids or citizen vigilantes," Cliff claimed, trying to justify his stupidity to Naylor. It didn't take much. Naylor wasn't the sharpest tool in the shed.

Naylor had been impressed. "How'd you get in so fast?"

"Don't you ever fucking listen?" Overton yelled. "I picked the lock. I'm a locksmith. That's why Niko hired me."

"Man, he's smart to think of that", Naylor said.

Overton had pulled the car off the road and stared at him. "Who designed the machine? Who just did this job? Me. This ain't an empire. I'm goin' up, too, kid. I'm goin' all the way, with or without Niko."

"You'd leave Niko?"

Overton paused. "Politics, it's all politics…Niko and I are partners. When I go on my own, it'll be because he has more than he can handle. I ask his blessing and we continue to cooperate. I studied Meyer Lansky and the Trafficantes in Tampa, and Carlos Marcello in New Orleans. They know the key. Show your boss respect when you tell him you want a bigger taste or you want to be a boss. Listen to his advice. Wait for the right time. If I didn't think Niko could do that, I wouldn't have partnered up with him. I'm not some bent-nose gunsel. I'm a businessman and craftsman."

Naylor nodded and didn't comment on Cliff's cauliflower nose, and Overton got the wagon moving again. "You think that Ballard guy will raise hell, do anything?" Naylor asked.

"This is your last question, 'cause after I answer it, you're going to drive all the way home while I sleep in the back."

"Hell, no. The law's happy to have somebody burn him out and he can't, and won't turn to the courts. If he tries, I'll personally take care of him. Will he come after us? He'd have to be crazy.

We're the guys who go all the way. We make lemonade out of lemons, like Niko says; only there's room for more than one lemonade stand. What there ain't room for, is Nate Ballard. He's a piss-ant and we just stomped him, and we won't see him anymore. I guarantee it."

* * *

Shaking Overton from his thoughts, Niko said, "The burnings need to take place during my trail. I want the public and the authorities to see me so they can't connect me to the fires."

"When is your trial scheduled?" Overton asked, thinking he'd like to see Niko go to prison so he would be the boss. He didn't like answering to Niko.

"Don't know for sure; probably six-months. You'll need a few months to plan the operation. As soon as the *Atlanta Journal* reports my trial dates, you'll know when to do it. We won't need to talk about it anymore. You keep an eye out for those reports."

"I'll get it done, partner. What else do we need to discuss?"

Niko didn't like Overton referring to him as partner. In no way was he his equal. "What makes you think you're my partner? For crissakes, we own two book stores together out of hundreds."

"Sorry about that, Niko." He knew better than to piss off Niko. He wanted out of there. He needed another hit of speed. He was getting jumpy.

"There is one other thing. The California cash account seems to be dropping. What's going on with that?"

"Yeah, I noticed that, too. There's more competition in California than there is here." Overton had been skimming money off the top to support his penchant for drugs and prostitutes. He didn't think Niko would notice.

"Maybe that's the answer. You better check our bookstore operators a little closer. If I find out someone is stealing from us, there will be hell to pay. I don't stand for that shit, you know."

"I know, Niko. I'll keep a close eye on the operators, trust me."

"I have to trust you, Overton. I don't have any choice. Just make damn sure I'm getting my cut." Niko couldn't see what was right in front of him. A little guy wanting power, hooked on drugs laying in wait for Niko to screw up. If only he knew.

"Good luck with the trial. I know you'll win," Overton said as he got up to leave, all the time hoping Niko would lose and go to prison. "I'll see you in a few months."

"Yeah, hopefully you'll see a free man."

CHAPTER – 16

Six months had passed and with China Jon's help, Turk brought Niko's projects back on schedule and on budget. Turk had managed to get the bankers to increase their loans to cover the cost overruns.

Turk, Karen, and Jason had rented a beautiful home in Dunwoody, a fashionable part of Atlanta. Jason was attending Sandy Springs Middle School and was doing well. He'd reacquainted himself with his old friends and made new ones. The move from St. Pete didn't seem to be as life-changing as Turk had felt it was going to be. Karen's MS was in remission and she was involved in Jason's school activities. She worked-out three times a week and worked part-time helping Turk with his apartment project.

China Jon or CJ, as Turk usually called him, had agreed to go to work for six-months as a favor to Turk. He would then make a decision as to whether or not he wanted to continue in the construction business. CJ had stopped drinking. He still smoked marijuana and Salem cigarettes. He wasn't dating. He was trying to get over his lost love. He was a natural organizer and a fast study. CJ was managing all three projects so well all Turk had to do was tend to the banking and the reporting to Cory and Niko.

Turk was to meet CJ for breakfast for his six-month review, and really hoped his friend would continue. It would be difficult to replace him.

* * *

CJ ordered scrambled eggs, toast, and coffee. Turk ordered a half a pink grapefruit and water. He was running five miles a day and was closely watching his food intake. He found that jogging helped relieve stress.

"So, CJ, it's been six months you've stayed on with me."

"Before I get into that Turk, I've heard a rumor you need to know about."

"Who'd you hear this rumor from, CJ?"

"Pop Hansen, the owner of Pops Security came by my office yesterday. One of his security guards was drinking at the Wolf's Den. Some guy by the name of Naylor was bragging he and his partner were going to burn down some buildings out near the airport. Pop thought you might need to know."

"I thought Naylor was in California. He used to drink at the Wolf's Den. In fact, Digger and I beat the shit out of him right behind it. Did Pop know what they planned on burning?"

"No, but the indication was it would happen soon."

"Okay, thanks CJ, I'll check it out. Now what about you? I need you for at least another six months. What do you say?"

"I still don't like the pressure of this business. I'll stay on for another six months if you promise to turn me loose after that."

"Okay, I promise. But let me ask you why you're so determined to get out of this business. You're making more money than you ever will pounding nails."

"Turk, let's just say I like the simple life; that's all there is to it."

"I'll give you that. Okay, I promise. CJ, when you get back to the office, call Pop and have him double up on the night security."

"He'll ask me, for how long?"

"Tell him until further notice. I need to investigate this burning business he heard about."

"You got it. By the way, my dislike of this business has nothing to do with you, Turk. I just don't like being around people anymore. I like my solitude, my pot, and my privacy, that's all."

"I think I understand. But you're damn good at this business; I hate to see you pass on this opportunity. But I'll agree not to ask you to stay on after the six months is up." Turk really didn't understand why CJ liked living the way he did. Right now, though, he needed to get with Digger.

Breakfast finished, CJ, left for his office and Turk called Digger.

* * *

"Digger, our friend Naylor is in town."

"Really, is Overton here, too?"

"Don't know. You need to find out, though." Turk briefed him on what CJ had just told him.

"Are you thinking they'll target our projects?"

"I sure am."

"Why would they want to go against Niko?"

"I think Niko is part of it."

"Why in hell would Niko want his own projects burned down?"

"I haven't got that figured out yet. I really don't know if he's involved in this or not. But I can't think of anything else Naylor would burn down other than a few book stores, which he's done before."

"How do you tie Niko into it?"

"I think he's aware I've had enough of his shit and I'm probably thinking about taking his projects, seeing they're in my name. If the projects were burned down, he'd get the insurance money and then he wouldn't rebuild. He'd still have the land and he figures I'd go back to Florida. Something like that. Anyway, I don't have it all figured out yet."

"Wow, Turk, what do you want me to do?"

"I've asked Pop to double security on our jobs. I want you to find Naylor and have him shadowed. Then fly to California and track Overton and see if you can find out more about their plans. Naylor isn't capable of doing anything without Overton. In the meantime, I'll confront Cory and see what kind of reaction I get from her."

"What if you're right in your assessment? What are we going to do about it?"

"We'll have to take out Overton and Naylor before they can execute their plans, whatever that may be."

"If Niko is part of this plot...if there is a plot... he'll just hire someone else to do the job and they might not be as easy to deal with as Overton and Naylor. They're basically idiots, if you know what I mean."

"I agree. Let's do our homework and discuss this further, but in the meantime, let's be sure we're on our toes. Burning down our buildings might be the best thing that could happen to us."

"You're kidding, right, Turk?"

"Not really. I'll see you when you get back. I'm on my way to see Cory."

* * *

"Cory, my sources tell me Naylor is in town. Is Overton here, too?"

"I don't believe so, Turk. Why do you ask?"

"Naylor was drinking at the Wolf's Den the other night."

"You'd think he'd stay away from there after what you did to him. Are you sure it was Naylor?"

"I am."

"I really don't know. I'll ask Niko when he gets in and let you know. They might be in town on other business, but you'd think I would know about it. Why does it worry you, Turk? Niko had a talk with them; they won't bother you."

"Okay, if you say so, Cory." Turk didn't want to show his hand just yet. He wanted to see what she would come back with after talking to Niko.

"Anything else we need to discuss?"

"When is Niko due in court?"

"His trial starts next week."

"How long do the lawyers think the trial will last?"

"They're not sure, probably six or eight weeks. Why?"

"Just curious that's all. Is there anything I can do for Niko in the meantime?"

"No, not right now. Thanks for asking, though. I'll let you know what he says about Naylor being in town. I've got to go now, Turk. I have a lot of work to do. See you."

* * *

Digger arrived at the Los Angles Airport about 9:00 a.m., noon east coast time. He rented a car and checked into the Royal Coach Inn. After unpacking his suitcase, he holstered his .22 Luger automatic to his ankle. The .22 isn't a very powerful weapon, but Digger was an expert shot and could place a shot that would maim or kill someone within fifty yards. He carried a large Special Forces knife strapped to the other ankle in case he needed an even quieter weapon. Digger had been trained in the art of self-defense as a Navy Seal.

He was also a master of disguise. In a small handbag was a collection of make-up, masks, mustaches, wigs, and hair dye. He didn't want to be recognized. His orders were to take out Overton if there was a plot to burn Niko's projects. Digger hoped he wouldn't have to kill Overton, but if he was forced to, he would. There was no love lost between the two.

Overton lived in a small apartment located on the second floor of the Pink Pussy Cat, a strip club. Digger was aware of the location. He wore jeans, a tight-fitting black shirt, steel-toed boots and a Dodgers' baseball cap. The bouncer looked Digger up and down and then said, "That'll be five bucks. Don't touch the girls. You can look, but don't touch. Got that, mister?"

"I got it," Digger said as he handed him five dollars.

The place was dark and smoky. There were three stages for the girls to dance on. If a patron wanted a pretty lady to dance on his table, he raised his hand and summoned her over. She would dance on his table top as long as he kept stuffing five dollar bills into a garter belt strapped around her thigh.

Digger sat at the bar. His eyes slowing adjusting, he looked around in the hope of seeing Overton there. It was still early and he didn't recognize anyone. He sipped a soda and water with a twist of lime and enjoyed the sights. The women were beautiful. The dancers were a mixture of wanna-be actresses, single moms with great bodies, motorcycle mamas, young drug addicted women working for their next fix, and some working their way through college. The hours were good and the money was more than they could earn working anywhere else. A good dancer could make over five hundred dollars a night, and a thousand a night on weekends.

Overton wasn't hard to spot. He came in through the rear door and took a seat at the end of the bar. It had been over a year since Digger had seen him. He'd lost weight, probably from the speed he was taking, Digger figured. He dressed better than Digger remembered, probably because of his position as Niko's right-hand man on the West Coast. Digger wasn't concerned about Overton recognizing him because of his disguise. He observed Overton for a while to try to find what he was up to, and to see where he would go from here.

So much for keeping your hands off the girl, Digger thought to himself. Overton had his hands all over a pretty young blonde woman. He was whispering something to her and she nodded after he handed her what looked like a hundred dollar bill. She went to the same door from which Overton had entered the club. Overton slid off the bar stool and followed her. Digger worked his way to the back and stood next to the door, hoping the rather large man who stood there would turn away long enough for him to gain entry.

Digger waited for about fifteen minutes, then decided he needed to find another way in. He went outside and surveyed the perimeter of the building. Overton's apartment was located on the corner of the second floor. There was a light on. The fire escape was just below his window. Digger moved the garbage dumpster beneath it and jumped up and grabbed the stairs, pulling them toward him. He gained easy access to Overton's bedroom window. So much for Overton's security, Digger thought.

Digger could hear muffled cries coming from the bedroom. He peered in just below a shade that had not been closed all the way. He could see Overton bending over the pretty little blonde, holding his penis in one hand and a drink in the other. He couldn't make out what Overton was saying, but the look on the girl's face was frightening. Then things went black.

"Well, well, pay back is a bitch, isn't it!" Overton spewed out.

These were the first words Digger heard since one of Overton's bodyguards had knocked him unconscious with a blunt instrument of some kind. Digger cussed himself for being so careless. He was so intent on what Overton was doing to the little blonde that he didn't hear the man sneak up behind him and knock him out.

"Overton, you're a fucking creep. Untie me and we'll see." Digger said as he tried to loosen his bonds.

Overton didn't say anything; he belted Digger across the face with a closed fist. He hit him so hard that the chair fell over.

Digger screamed, "Is that all you got, you faggot?"

Overton responded by kicking Digger in the face. He felt his front teeth come loose. Spitting blood, Digger said, "You fucking coward! Untie me, you bastard!"

All that did was make Overton angrier, "Call me a faggot, you fucking Navy Seal creep," he said, as he kicked Digger in the groin. "Take that, you patriotic bastard! You fucking Seals aren't so tough!"

The intentional diversion by Digger allowed him to slip his bonds. His arms were free, but his legs were still bound to the chair. Digger reached up, and grabbed Overton by the throat, pulling him to the floor. Still spitting blood, Digger said, "You little bastard, you're mine now."

Digger applied enough pressure until Overton passed out. He released his grip and untied his legs. Then he sat Overton in the same chair and bound him to it. Digger didn't know where his bodyguard was, but he thought he probably was standing guard just outside the front door. He was about to deal with that when he spit out two front teeth. He picked them up, put them into his pocket, and moved toward the door. He could see the shadow under the crack in the door so his suspicions were right. He called out, "Help!" The door flew open.

Digger said, "Surprise!" He hit the bodyguard square in the face, followed by a solid kick to the groin, causing him to bend over at the waist. As he bent over, Digger came down on his neck with both hands. The bodyguard piled up in a heap at Digger's feet. Digger bound him with duct tape and went to the bathroom to clean up. As he washed the blood from his hands and face, noticed that one side of his face was cut from his ear lobe to his chin, which he knew was Overton's way of marking his victims. The other side had been kicked so hard that Digger hardly recognized himself.

He could hear Overton calling out, "Help me! Someone help me!"

"I'll help you, you little fucking weasel!"

"Let me go, you prick!" Overton yelled. Digger was able to stand what Overton threw at him, but he knew damn well that Overton couldn't take the pain Digger was about to inflict on him.

"Oh, I'm not going to let you go until we have an understanding, Overton."

"What do you mean? What kind of understanding?"

"First, I want to see your skin crawl. You're hooked on drugs. When was your last fix, Overton? You'll need one soon, won't you?" Digger spotted his .22 and his knife on the kitchen counter.

"You better get out of here before my bodyguards come for me."

"I've taken care of the one at the door, Overton. I can handle any others that come."

"You're not supposed to touch me. Niko told me so."

"You started this, I didn't. I do plan on finishing it, though."

"What are you going to do to me?"

"I'm not going to kill you. But I am going to hurt you. I'm

going to hurt you bad." Digger was hungry. Taping Overton's mouth, he proceeded to the kitchen. He found some dated milk, eggs, and a bunch of beer and wine. The eggs looked okay so he scrambled up half a dozen. He located some bread and a toaster. Every bite was painful, but it did take the edge off. He'd been in much greater pain before. Digger knew how to handle pain.

It had been about two hours and Overton began to sweat. As Digger ripped the duct tape from his mouth, he said, "Need a fix, old boy?"

"I'll get you for this, you bastard."

"Now, now Overton, don't get nasty. You want a fix? Where are your drugs? I might just give you one."

"Like, I'm going to tell you where they are." This was all Digger needed to hear; he now knew there were some drugs in the apartment. He could find them. It didn't take him long. He found them in a plastic bag inside the water closet tank. Not too smart; that was the first place any cop would look. Dangling the drugs in front of Overton, he said, "Wouldn't you like one of these? Or would you rather have a shot of this?" He pointed at the black tar in the same bag as the speed. Digger had seen a lot of heroin while he was in Nam. He'd used it on occasion to ward off sleep while in long, drawn-out fights with the North Viet Cong.

Overton said nothing, his eyes just got bigger and he began to sweat even more. Digger went to the kitchen, got a spoon, put a small amount of black tar into the spoon, pulled a lighter from Overton's pocket and began to heat the tar into a liquid. He found a needle in the night-stand next to the bed and sucked up the potion. All the while, Overton was licking his lips. His mouth was dry, and he was having stomach cramps. It had been over four hours since his last fix and he was starting to hallucinate. "Come on, Digger, let me go." His plea was weak.

"Tell me what Naylor is doing in Atlanta."

"I don't know."

"Bullshit! Naylor doesn't do a damn thing without you knowing about it. What's going on, Overton?"

"Nothing, I tell you, nothing. He's just there on book store business, that's all."

"Okay," holding the needle up. "Maybe in an hour or so, your memory will get better." Digger turned his attention to the bodyguard lying on the floor. He loosened the tape around his nose so he wouldn't suffocate, and left him there. He wasn't going anywhere.

Digger once again covered Overton's mouth and turned on the TV. He didn't pay any attention to what was playing. He was concerned about his teeth. He wondered if a dentist could put them back in place. He was still in a great deal of pain. He wanted to get this over with and catch a plane back to Atlanta.

Three more hours had passed and Digger knew that Overton would do anything for a fix. He once again pulled the tape off Overton's mouth. Gagging on his puke, Overton sputtered, "Look, what you want from me...I'll do anything...I'm hurting and you know it." He continued to gag and throw up.

"I'll ask you one more time. What is Naylor doing in Atlanta?"

"I told you, he's there on business...Niko's and my business."

"I'm going to make this easier for you, Overton. I know he's there to burn down some buildings, which you two aren't very good at. Now tell me whose buildings and why?"

"Come on, Digger, you know I can't tell you that. Niko will kill me."

This gave Digger the information he was looking for. Now he

wanted the details. "OK, you see, that wasn't so hard, was it?"

"What do you mean? I didn't tell you nothing."

"So Niko is in on this. Turk was right. He's planning to burn down his own buildings."

"I ain't saying."

"Oh, you're going to tell me. Here's the deal. You tell me what I need to know. Then I'll give you a fix and I'll let you live; that simple."

"Okay, okay, but you can't let Niko know, you can't. It will ruin me, it will ruin me." Overton was a defeated man. The lack of drugs made him weak and he was weeping.

"Go on," Digger said, holding the needle up so Overton could see it.

"Niko wants us to burn down his buildings during his trial. That way, no one can accuse him of doing it for the insurance money."

"There's more to it than that, Overton. What is it?"

"He wants Turk out of Atlanta. He's afraid Turk will take his projects."

"Is that it?"

"That's it, believe me. Give me a shot, Digger. I need a fix. I'm dying here."

"I'll give you a shot. That should last you until someone finds you. I'll give your bodyguard one, too."

"Hurry, I'm in pain, please hurry."

Digger took Overton's left arm and slid the needle into his vein and pushed. In a matter of moments, Overton's breathing was normal, and he stopped sweating. He fixed another needle and shot the big bodyguard in the arm, too.

"I'm letting you go this time, Overton, but if I hear of you coming to Atlanta, or I see you in Atlanta, I'll track you down and cut your throat."

"Aren't you going to untie me?"

"No, someone will find you. I'll make sure of that. One other thing, Overton: I don't know what you're going to tell Niko, but if I were you I wouldn't tell him about this. I would find an excuse to get out of your assignment…like maybe your old man died or something, if you don't, I'll have to kill both of you. Goodbye."

"Wait, wait, untie me, you bastard," Overton pleaded, just as Digger slid the knife alongside the scar already running down the side of Overton's face. Blood started dripping from his chin onto his shoulder. He started screaming. Digger stuffed the bread wrapper into his mouth and said, "Overton, I hope for your sake this is the last time we meet. If I have to deal with you again in any manner, I'll kill you. You're nothing but a parasite on society."

Digger went back to the hotel, cleaned up the best he could, put bandages on his face, secured his luggage, packed his pistol and knife, and hailed a cab to the airport. His flight back to Atlanta was scheduled in an hour. Just before he boarded, he called the Pink Pussy Cat from a payphone and told the person who answered that Overton needed some assistance. After explaining his wounds to the flight attendant, he boarded. He said he'd been in a car accident.

CHAPTER—17

"Wow! It looks like you ran into a buzz saw, Digger. What the hell happened to you?" Turk said, as soon as Digger sat down.

"You should see the other guy." Digger said, with a smile on what was left of his face.

"You know Digger, you and I seem to get into more shit. What did we do to deserve this?"

"The way I got it figured, boss, the action always seems to be where the money is. There's lots of money in construction and the pornography industry draws all the crooks."

"Does that make us crooks, too, Digger?"

"In a way, it probably does. Anyway, let me brief you on what went on in California. You were right; Niko is behind this burning business." Digger went on to explain what he'd discovered.

"Man, that's some trip. Do you think Overton will back off?"

"No, he'll huddle with Niko, and probably already has."

"What do you think we should do?"

"We can take Overton out."

"We can't do that, Digger. The law will be on our asses. We have to do this legally. Niko is going on trial this week. He doesn't need or want any publicity. Maybe I should just confront him and see if I can come to some kind of peaceful settlement of affairs."

"Maybe that approach will work. I don't think they'll try anything for a while. It will take them a little time to regroup. In the meantime, I'll beef up security for you and our projects, just in case."

"Sounds like a plan. I'll set up a meeting with Niko. You need to take care of that face of yours. What's under that bandage?"

"Overton's trademark."

"How deep did he cut you?"

"A little more than a surface cut. I'll be okay, though. The scar ought to add to my good looks, don't you think, Turk?"

"Yeah, Rock Hudson you ain't." Only Digger could joke about his face being sliced up.

"On your way out, tell Jimmy to get ready to take me to Niko's office. Be sure to take care of that handsome puss of yours."

* * *

"What do you mean he's too busy to see me?" Turk said to Cory.

"Niko is with his lawyers; they're preparing him for his trial."

"I need to see him. It will only take a few minutes," Turk said, as he headed for the door to Niko's office.

"Whoa, big boy," Deon said, as he stepped in front of Turk. "You heard Cory. Niko is busy." Deon had no use for Turk, probably stemming from his association with Digger.

"Get the hell out of my way, Deon. I'm going in there and see Niko." Turk tried to push Deon aside. He stood fast.

"Hold on, guys. I'll see if Niko can break away. Stay put!" Both Deon and Turk pulled back. Cory could be damn convincing when she was aggravated.

"Give him fifteen minutes and he'll see you, Turk." Cory said on her return. "Deon, go back to your desk. Turk, come into my office. Niko will meet you there."

Deon backed away, expressing his displeasure. "Donatelli, you're more trouble than you're worth."

"Fuck off Deon. You're an asshole."

"All right, you guys. Enough of this shit. You both work for Niko. We got enough problems without you two continuing your feud. Now quit it!" Cory retorted, her hands on her hips. Both men knew they needed to back off.

Niko closed the door behind him. Cory left them alone. "What's so urgent, Turk?"

"You know damn well what's so urgent. I'm sure you've talked to Overton."

"I have. The little prick probably got what he deserved. Now what do you want, Turk? I've got a trial to get ready for."

"Don't play dumb with me, Niko. You instructed Overton and Naylor to burn down your buildings to collect the insurance and get rid of me. First, they're idiots and you should know better than to give them an assignment to burn anything. Remember, you took the wrap for burning down your competitor's adult book store. What's the matter with you anyway?"

"Look, Turk, I got the feeling the last time we met that you were thinking about taking my projects away from me. It would be pretty easy to do. They're in your name and your name only."

"I admit I've thought about it. You're so damn tied up legally, you're not interested in the real estate business anymore anyway. That's evident. All you care about is staying out of prison. I can't say that I blame you. But there's another way out of this you know."

"How so?"

"Buy me out and take all that damn cash you got stashed away in that safe in there and pay off the first mortgages and take title to the properties in your name. I'll go back to Florida and you'll have your projects."

"It's not that damn easy and you know it, Turk. I tried that once and Decker fucked me. What makes you think it would be any different this time?"

"You agree to pay off the mortgages and give me three million for my interest. I'll finish what we've got under construction and you go on about trying to stay out of prison."

"I simply don't have that kind of cash, Turk."

"I don't believe you. I know what you take in and I know what you've spent over the last couple of years. You're obviously stashing money away in case you do go to prison. You've probably got more than you need right now. Don't bullshit me, Niko."

"I'm not bullshitting you, Turk. My damn legal fees are running a quarter of a million a month. I've hired the best damn team of lawyers in the nation. They're not cheap, you know."

"Okay, so what do we do? You want me out of the way. You want your projects back. And your time and resources are being taken up with staying out of prison. Having someone burn down our buildings, quite frankly is a stupid idea. How in hell can anyone burn down projects of that size without it coming back to haunt you? Come with the cash."

"I can't do that."

"Then this meeting is over. Do what you gotta do, Niko, and

I'll do what I have to."

"What do you mean by that statement? Sounds like a threat to me."

"It's no threat, Niko. I'll tell you to your face. I'm going to take over our projects unless you come with the cash. After your legal battles are over, if you want them back all you got to do is pony up."

"What assurances do I have you'll keep that bargain?"

"You don't. You'll have to trust me, Niko. You'll have to trust me."

"Trust is bullshit; cash is king."

"My sentiments exactly, Niko. I'm glad we understand one another. See ya."

"I'd be careful, Turk."

"I will Niko. You need to be careful, too. You might end up in prison before you know it." Niko slammed the door on his way out. Turk took a deep breath and wondered how he was going to extract himself from this mess. A mess he'd created by getting involved with this element in the first place.

* * *

Not even Bobby Lee Cook, the famous Georgia lawyer, could keep Niko from going to prison. Niko was found guilty of arson and conspiring to kill a competitor. Sentencing was scheduled to be announced in thirty days. Bond was denied and Niko was locked up, pending his appeal. Overton had turned State's witness and testified against Niko in return for a suspended sentence.

Turk finished and refinanced the apartments, shopping center, and industrial projects. He secured permanent loans and took title to the properties. He had an unwritten agreement with Cory, who was running Niko's various businesses. As soon as Niko paid Turk three million and paid off the mortgages, the properties were his. Turk didn't see that happening; the State of Georgia had put Niko away, and the Feds were next in line. The authorities transferred Niko to a Connecticut jail to await trial for interstate transportation of pornography in that State.

Niko continued his appeal with the law firm of Bobby Lee Cook. He felt it was only a matter of time before he would be out on bail. But that simply wasn't the case. He was bound over and bail was denied; a new trial was about to take place. Cory was on her way to Connecticut to meet with Niko to see what options were left for him. She stopped off in New York to meet and give assurances to their mob connections that she could handle Niko's porno business on the East Coast.

* * *

Turk's, wife, Karen, had been patient during this whole process of Turk's coming to Atlanta and taking over Niko's real estate projects. She spent a lot of time with Jason, which Turk didn't have time to do. He was constantly apologizing for his absence. But finally, Karen had had enough of his excuses.

"Turk, we need to take a break and talk. We haven't been together as a couple for almost a year now. I've stepped back and let you get on with your business. I know you've been under a lot of pressure but it's time you became a father to Jason and a husband to me again."

Turk was taken by surprise. "You haven't said a word until now. Why all of a sudden?" He had been so involved; he'd damn near forgotten he had a wife and son. He really felt that what he was doing, he was doing for them. Selfish on his part, he thought.

"Like I said, I was giving you time and bridging the gap for you. It's time we discussed our future. I want to know where Jason and I fit into your plans."

"You know damn well where you fit, Karen. You guys mean

everything to me. I'm doing this for us as a family."

"Awe, come on, Turk. Who do you think you're kidding?"

"Look, I've quit drinking. I don't gamble or run around, and I take good care of you financially. What more do you want?"

"You think that makes for a healthy relationship? You give us money, you not drinking and gambling. That's your definition of a good husband and father? Really!"

That was what Turk thought being a good husband was all about. He knew he should spend more time with Karen and Jason, but his business wouldn't allow that. After all, he was working for their future. Didn't she see that? "Well, it's a pretty good start. What more do you expect of me? I think I'm a good husband."

"No doubt you mean well, Turk, but your definition of a good husband and father just isn't the same as mine. You need to think about it a little more. Jason and I have made plans to move back to our condo on the beach in St. Pete as soon as he finishes this school year."

"You've got to be kidding me. How long have you been planning this?"

"I've been thinking about it for some time now."

"When does Jason get out of school?"

"See, that's a perfect example of what I'm talking about. You have no idea when he starts school or finishes, do you? You used to be involved in his school activities. You haven't been for a damn year."

"No, I assumed you knew and I didn't need to."

"What about my health? When is the last time you paid any attention to that?"

"Christ, I've invested hundreds of thousands of dollars to deal with your heath. Is there something you're not telling me?"

"You've been so damn tied up with Niko's business you haven't paid any attention to what's going on around you. Turk, I need more treatment. I'm going back to Florida where I can get it. You stay here and take care of business. Jason and I will be there when you get your shit together."

"Me, get my shit together? I thought I had! I'm committed to our relationship. I'm committed to raising Jason. I've changed my habits. What else do I have to do, for crissakes?"

"You figure that out, Turk. You'll see what I mean. Jason's school year is over in three weeks. I've already made plans to go back to Florida. We'll talk more. Right now I need some rest."

"Why didn't you tell me your MS was acting up again?"

"You have enough to worry about without worrying about my MS. Let's leave it there for now, Turk. I'm going to take a nap."

He thought things were good. Karen's MS was in remission. He'd quit drinking, running around, and gambling. He knew he needed to spend more time with Jason, like he used to. But hell, he had to make a living. Damn, all of a sudden he wanted a drink.

CHAPTER—18

It was foggy, wet and cold when Cory landed at LaGuardia airport in New York. Deon rented a car for them and they headed for Trenton, New Jersey, where they were to meet one of Niko's East Coast partners. After that meeting, they were going on to Warsaw, Connecticut, to visit Niko, and make plans for running Niko's many businesses should he fail to get out on bail, which according to his lawyers, seemed likely.

The nondescript building looked like an unlikely place for a family operated restaurant. Rain was coming down. The fog was settling in over the harbor, the light was poor and the meeting Cory and Deon was about to attend was suspect. The element they were about to meet were high up on the illegitimate scale. The mob wanted to know how Niko could run his pornography business from prison. They didn't like all the publicity Niko was getting. In short, they wanted answers and assurances that their cut of the pornography business would continue uninterrupted.

Deon went in first. He looked around and saw two men sitting in a booth and two men sitting at the counter. He recognized one of the men in the booth. He only knew his nickname, which was Stubs, a name given him in high school because of his short arms. The other man in the booth was an older, harmless looking gentleman. The two men at the counter were obviously there for his protection. Deon approached them, and asked, "Is this where we meet?"

Stubs nodded and asked, "Where's the broad?"

"Cory is in the car? I'll go get 'the broad.' Do I have your word this meet is okay? No funny business?"

"No funny business. You won't have to get her. She's right behind you." Deon turned to see Cory being escorted in by two more very big men. "Let's go in the back where we can talk." Stubs and the older gentlemen got up and headed for the back room.

Deon was leery about this meeting, but felt helpless. He motioned for Cory, and they followed the two men.

Stubs turned and said, "We hear Niko is going away for a long time. Who's gonna run the show?"

"I am," Cory said.

"You? Come on now. What makes you think you can run Niko's operation?"

"I've been running it for some time, and I will continue to."

"What if we don't think you can?"

"It doesn't matter what you think. As long as you get your cut, what do you care?"

"Suppose we want a bigger cut?"

"What makes you think you're entitled to a bigger cut?"

"Niko's people are turning against him. How long do you think you can keep his operation going, being a woman and all?"

"You're referring to Overton turning State witness, right?"

"Sure, the word on the street is he'll be taking over, after he buries Niko."

"Okay, I've had enough of this shit! No one is taking over, including you. Your deal is the same deal Niko cut with you, no more, no less. I'm getting out of here. So don't fuck with me, understand?"

Stubs started to laugh and said, "Pretty pants, just what are you going to do about it? We can do you both in right here and throw you to the fishes; no one would be the wiser. So don't go being a smart ass with me, you little bitch!"

The old gentleman had not been introduced, and hadn't said anything. He raised his hand. Stubs backed away, and the man said, in a quiet, civil manner, "Miss, you're pretty sure of yourself. You talk a good game. Can you back it up?"

"Have your thug here look out the door and see."

The old man stayed calm, and Stubs jumped up from his chair, and rushed to the door. Peering out, he saw his men seated at two different tables, with two men he didn't know. Another man stood at the front door; while still another was stationed right outside their door.

"Boss, looks like we gots lots of company."

The old man smiled and said, "I saw two cars pull into the parking lot just as we came in here. I thought you might have some back-up. You might be able to handle Niko's affairs after all. Do I have your assurance our deal is still in place, and we won't have any trouble from the Feds, or this Overton guy?"

"I'll take care of Overton. I don't have any control over the Feds. You *will* continue to get your cut. Niko will be out on bail soon. It will be business as usual in a few weeks," said Cory.

"I hope so, for his sake. But my sources tell me he's in for the long haul. Good luck, lady. I presume this meeting is over."

"It is. I didn't get your name."

"Ask Niko. He knows who I am. Good night, Cory."

Deon was smiling as he left the back room until he entered the diner. His men were on the floor with their arms and legs spread. The old man turned and said, "You weren't quite as prepared as you planned, Cory. Don't fuck with me either. As I said, good night."

Between the damp, bone-chilling evening, and what she had just gone through, Cory was cold and angry. Deon had set up this meeting and it could have turned out badly for both of them. She thought he was more capable. She would have to be even more careful in the future. "Deon, you screwed up! We could have been killed!"

"I could have handled them, Cory. I could."

"That's bullshit and you know it. Send the rest of your crew back to Atlanta. We have to meet Niko in the morning. We've still got a three-hour drive ahead of us."

* * *

"How are they treating you, Niko?" Cory asked.

"Like any other damn jail. Believe it or not, prison treats you better than being in a county jail. How'd your meeting go with Trafficante?"

"So that's who that was." Trafficante was the boss of the New York Mob. "I figured as much. It was nerve-racking to say the least. We weren't very well prepared. Deon didn't do a very good job."

"You were okay. He just wanted to meet you to see what you were made of."

"You mean to tell me you knew what was going on all along, and you didn't tell me?" Cory was mad as hell, and hissing so loud at Niko, a jail guard asked if everything was okay. She dismissed him with a wave of the hand, and continued her tirade. "Niko, how can you be so goddamn devious and not tell me?"

"Come on, baby. You handled it. Nothing was going to happen to you. Like I said, they wanted to see what you were made of. I couldn't have told you. "

"You damn sure could have, Niko. What's wrong with you anyway? Setting me up like that."

"I'm sorry. I knew you could handle it. Enough of this...we've got a lot to discuss while we have the chance." The opportunity to meet with a confidante wasn't allowed in prison. You weren't supposed to do business. Being in a county jail, Niko took liberties that weren't usually afforded other inmates. He was paying off the night jailers.

"All right Niko, but I don't pretend to like what you did." Cory knew she couldn't push Niko any further.

"What are we going to do about that turncoat, Overton?'

"We probably shouldn't do anything. The Feds will be keeping a close eye on him."

"Shit, he's trying to take over the West Coast operation, and he's working on taking over a portion of our business in the Carolinas and Kentucky. He has to be stopped, and the only way to be sure is to whack him."

"Niko, what are you thinking? We can't do that. We shouldn't even be talking about it," Cory said, looking around to see if anyone was listening. When she had visited Niko while he was in the Atlanta Pen, a prison guard was right next to them to insure that they didn't talk business. Cory professed to be his girlfriend. The only other people who could visit Niko were his immediate family members and his attorneys.

"I got these guys under control. We can discuss anything. We have to do something about that little traitor bastard. He's going to be testifying for the State at my next trial."

"Your lawyers say they can handle him in court, and not to do anything to him. If *we do*, the authorities will surely know you had something to do with it. They say lay off Overton. He'll hang himself in the end."

"Just how is he going to hang himself, tell me?" Niko wasn't convinced.

"As close as the Feds are watching him, they'll have to bust him for trying to take over part of our business. We don't think he can operate without the Feds being aware of it. If the Feds allowed Overton to operate any of our businesses while you're on trial, our lawyers claim they can stop him from testifying. They think they can anyway."

"I don't know if I want to risk that." Niko had become more paranoid with each incarceration. This was his fifth.

"Look, Niko, you need to listen to our lawyers. You really do."

"Okay, okay, being locked up changes a guy, you know."

"I can understand that. Let's get on with business." Cory felt sorry for Niko. He was a changed man. He was still recovering from almost being killed. He could barely walk. But she felt part of his disability was for show. He had worked very hard at his rehabilitation, but prisoners with a disability were afforded more perks.

"My lawyers tell me I need to move my cash. The Feds will likely seize my office building, under the RICO Act. You'll need the combination to the safe. Can you memorize it?"

"I already have. I know the combination."

Surprised, Niko asked, "How'd you get it?"

"Donatelli gave it to me."

"You mean he's had the combination all this time?"

"He has. He had the safe installed."

"Overton told me I should have let him change the combination." *That was one time I should have listened to the little prick.*

"Look, Niko, don't be so damn paranoid; no one has gotten into your safe. You should worry more about that locksmith, Overton, than about Turk."

"While we're talking about Turk, what do we do about him?"

"What do you mean?"

"After he found out I wanted Overton to burn our projects, he told me flat out he was taking my real estate projects."

"He also told you when you paid off the mortgages, and paid him three million; he would deed them back to you. I think he'll keep his word, don't you?"

"Cory, I hardly trust anyone anymore," a saddened Niko replied.

"Come on, Niko. You'll be out of here soon." Cory saw a side of Niko she'd only seen a couple of times. He looked tired and beaten, not his optimistic self.

They discussed paying Turk three million and asking him to stay on for a year. Then they decided that they didn't need to do that. Turk would probably keep his end of the deal anyway. Niko told Cory where to stash the cash. He had about ten million in the safe, and a bag full of diamonds, worth another fifteen million. They discussed his trial, his health, his rehabilitation, and him still trying to go legitimate by selling off the porno business. He'd already conveyed the Fox Theater to the Atlanta Art Department and his mansion to a non-profit benefiting gifted student's advanced studies, none of these gifts seemed to help his plight. Cory and Niko talked into the night, when finally the jailer came, and said, "Mr. Pappas, my shift is up. You have about fifteen more minutes before my replacement gets here."

"Okay, Neil, thanks."

"How'd you get to him, Niko?"

"Easy. Never underestimate the power of cash. Cory, you'll

wait for me, won't you?"

"Of course, I will, Niko." Cory was surprised. This the most interest he'd shown in her since they first met. They embraced, and Cory left, wondering, was Niko showing her interest because of what she was doing for him, or was it how he really felt? She needed to sort out her true feelings for Niko

* * *

"Cory, you were in there for six damn hours. I thought they'd put you in jail, too." Deon had been sitting in the car listening to the radio.

"That long, huh? It didn't seem like it."

"What now, Cory?"

"We need to get back to Atlanta. We've got a lot of work to do. Niko's lawyers will be here tomorrow to visit him. We won't come back here for three weeks, until just before his trial starts."

CHAPTER–19

"Did you get them settled in, Digger?" Turk asked. Digger had just returned after driving Karen and Jason back to St. Pete.

"Yes, the trip was a smooth one, considering the shape Karen is in."

"What do you mean?"

"She was having a hard time getting around. I had to carry her into the condo. Isn't there something you can do, Turk?"

"I had no idea her MS was acting up again until she told me last week. I must have had my head in the sand." Turk was truly troubled by his unawareness.

"Don't be too hard on yourself, boss. It's not like you haven't had your hands full this past year."

"I've really tried, Digger. I quit drinking. I quit running around. I don't go out with the boys anymore. I play golf, and that's about it. All I'm trying to do is make enough money to service my real estate debt, and support our lifestyle."

"Evidently that's not enough now days, boss. Women expect more from their men in this day and age, I guess."

"I've got to do something. I really love Karen and Jason. This MS business is such a mystery. If only there was something out there to treat it. God only knows I've tried everything. I always thought if you had enough money, you could fix anything, obviously I was wrong. I've spent hundreds-of-thousands of dollars and that hasn't done a damn thing."

"You'll do right by them, Turk. You always have. Speaking of that, what are we going to do about our projects?"

"Cory telephoned and said Niko wants to transfer the two apartment projects into his wife's name. He's trying to set her and his kids up with enough income in case he's sent off to prison. Not a bad idea. From what I hear, Niko will be in for quite some time."

"How's that going to work?"

"Cory claims she'll pay off the construction loans. I've got to come up with a number for my interest, then contract with a rental company to manage and maintain them. Niko wants me to stick around for a year to insure that the income and management is competent. The cash flow from those apartments, absent a first mortgage, will provide for his wife and kids for the rest of their lives."

"What about our airport properties?"

"He wants me keep them until his trial is over. Then I don't know what he wants to do. I really don't care. The real estate is in my name."

"What's Niko plan on doing about Overton? I can't imagine him not getting rid of Overton after he turned state's witness."

"According to Cory, there's not much he can do right now. If I was Overton, I'd quit trying to take over Niko's porno-business. Niko can still get to him, I'm sure."

"Overton is greedy, and not very smart. His drug habits might kill him."

"If drugs don't, I predict, Niko will. That's not our problem. What we have to do is get out as quickly as we can. The Feds are going to bust Niko and that will include his real estate deals. I don't know if the Racketeer Influence and Corrupt Organizations Act, referred to as the RICO Act, extends to what we're doing, but I'm sure we'll find out shortly. The GBI and the FBI are raiding his offices, and established businesses, which include his recording studios, his adult book stores, furniture business, trucking company, and his warehouses. Everything he owns, and every employee is being harassed. I don't even think Niko is aware of how much shit he's in."

"What's your plan? When will the authorities start coming after us?"

"They already have. The GBI have subpoenaed our records. I'm sure the FBI will follow with something."

"When we wrap things up here in Atlanta, are you going back to Florida?"

"I hope so, but right now we have our hands full. Niko won't be getting out anytime soon. Things will get more complicated. He's obviously making provisions for his family, so he realizes the going could be tough. I have a meeting with Cory as soon as she figures out where she'll set up her office. The Feds have already seized Niko's downtown office building."

"When did they do that?"

"Niko's lawyer turned it over to them last week. It was seized under this damn recently enacted RICO Act."

"Tell me about this RICO Act."

"As I understand it, the RICO Act is a United States federal law that provides extended criminal penalties and a civil cause for action for acts performed as part of an ongoing criminal organization."

"Nothing is ever easy for us, is it, Turk?"

"Not in the circles I seem to run in. I'm trying my hardest to stay legitimate, I really am."

* * *

Turk had built Cory a house in Sandy Springs, an exclusive North Atlanta suburb, paid for by Niko two years before. It was a big house, bigger than a single woman needed. Niko insisted on having a private entrance, and a separate office and bathroom, built in the rear of the house. This was where Cory planned on temporarily setting up shop.

Turk's appointment with Cory was scheduled for 2:00 that afternoon. He was nervous about meeting her at her house. He still had some feelings for her. He wasn't sure how she felt about him. At one time, she had said she wished Turk wasn't married. He took special care in his dress and decided to go alone. Digger wondered if that was such a good idea with Deon being ever present, but Turk insisted.

Turk pulled into the wide driveway. There he was met by what looked like a doorman, but was part of Deon's security team. After a thorough frisking for weapons, he was led to the rear of the house, where Deon occupied a small office in the back of Cory's three-car garage.

"Donatelli, we meet again."

"Probably won't be the last time, Deon. I'm here to see Cory."

"I know what you're here for, fuck-face."

"Don't be nasty Deon, don't be nasty," Turk cautioned.

"One of these days, Donatelli, I'll get you. One of these days; you can count on it."

"Come on, Deon, get over it. You know who butters your bread. You can't make a living working for anyone else; no one would hire your sorry ass. So escort me to Cory's office and shut up."

"Yeah, right, you asshole," he said in disgust, and pointed to the bungalow on the other side of the Olympic-sized pool. "Cory is expecting you."

"I know. Have a good day, Deon," Turk mocked as he headed for Cory's office.

Turk, very familiar with the layout, observed that the living room had been turned into an office. Cory was seated behind a large desk, too large for the room. As Turk approached, she said, "Nice to see you, Turk. How have you been?"

"Nice to see you, too, Cory. I'm fine under the circumstances. What about you?"

"I've had better days."

"I guess that goes for both of us, huh."

"Yes. Sorry to hear about your wife. I understand she went back to Florida."

"She did."

"Have you come up with a number?" Cory asked, not wasting any time.

"Yes. I'll release both apartment buildings to Niko's wife and kids for a million and a half as soon as Niko pays off the construction loans."

"How much are those?"

"They total three million, plus or minus ten thousand."

"That's about what we figured. How about I give you a million in cash for your interest?"

"A million-two-fifty will work."

"Okay, I can agree to that. I'll have our lawyers arrange the closing. We should be able to fund in two weeks."

"Are you sure? Can I count on that?"

"You can. You have my word." Cory's word was good enough for Turk.

"What about our other projects? What does Niko want me to

do about those?"

"Like I told you on the phone, we'll either sell them or you can hold them until Niko gets out."

"Do you think he will get out?"

"I really don't know. To be honest, Turk, I'm tired of worrying about it." Turk noticed a change in attitude. She wasn't as optimistic as she always seemed.

"You sound concerned, Cory. Are you?"

"I am. Niko isn't acting the same. The Feds are really busting our asses. Even if he wins this trial, which I don't think he will, there won't be anything left of his empire."

"All of this has got to be wearing thin with you, Cory. Are you in for the long haul?"

"I don't know how to answer that. The GBI and the FBI want to put me away, too. So far, I'm okay, but I don't know how long I will be." Cory got up, walked over, and sat down on the sofa.

"Anything I can do?" Turk asked, staring at her cleavage. Cory wasn't wearing a bra and her short mini-skit was hiked up, exposing her inner thighs. He couldn't take his eyes off her.

"Do you like what you're staring at, Turk?" Cory asked, changing the subject.

"Is it that obvious?"

"It is."

"You're a very attractive woman, Cory."

"It's been a long time since anyone paid me a compliment. You really think I'm attractive, Turk?"

"I always have. I've often thought what it would be like to be with you." Turk was getting in deeper than he wanted to. But he couldn't help himself. It had been weeks since he'd made love, and he'd always wanted Cory, but Niko was in the way. Now he wasn't. Turk was tempted, but didn't know how far

Cory would let this go.

"You *are* with me, Turk. What do you mean by that statement?"

"You know damn well what I mean, Cory." She spread her legs a little more, exposing her womanhood. She had no underpants on.

"Why don't we do something about it?" she said, getting up and smoothing her skirt.

"How the hell can we? Your monkey is standing guard outside, and besides, if Niko ever found out, we'd be in a lot more shit than we already are."

"This is a big house. Deon knows better than to come in here. He's never been inside my house. Follow me."

"What about Niko?" he asked, feeling really guilty, but following her.

'What about him? He won't know, and besides, I don't care. It's been a long time since a man has touched me. I want you to touch me, Turk," she said as she turned and entered her bedroom with Turk close behind her. "Wait right here."

Turk stood still. Cory disappeared into the bathroom area. He couldn't believe he was doing this. He'd been faithful to Karen and now he was about to backtrack into what he used to do. When Cory came back, he was determined to tell her, sorry, but he had to leave.

Soft music came drifting out of the walls. Then she appeared dressed in a skimpy, see-through nightgown. Her long red hair framed her face, and soft white shoulders. She moved slowly toward the bed, beckoning Turk to follow. He was mesmerized. He couldn't take his eyes off this long-legged beauty that he'd desired for over three years.

"Turk, make love to me. Make me feel like a woman."

"Are you sure about this, Cory?" Turk was making one last

feeble attempt to stop this seduction.

"I've never been surer. Shut up and devour me. I've wanted you for a long time. Make love to me, *now*."

Turk ripped his clothes off. Cory said, "Don't move. Stand there. I want to look at you. Make it hard for me, Turk. I want to see it hard."

Turks erection was almost instantaneous. He was well-endowed and his penis stood straight out. "Now come here and stand beside the bed," she commanded. Turk did as he was told. She stroked his manhood and began kissing the sides, just teasing him and said, "Now what do you want me to do, Turk? Tell me."

"Finish what you just started." He whispered, as she enveloped his penis. He climaxed so hard, his legs trembled.

Looking up at him, and smiling, she said, "I'm wet and ready for you."

"Put two pillows behind your head, and spread you legs," he demanded, while pulling her nightgown over her head.

He caressed her breasts. The nipples grew hard at his first touch. Turk then slid his tongue along her belly, and to the inside of her thighs, softly touching the channel with the tip of his tongue. Cory was thrashing about and moaning. He held her down while nibbling her nipples and running three fingers in and out of her juicy vagina. Cory bucked against his fingers while saying, "Oh Turk, it's been so long. Take me!"

"Not yet, Cory, not yet." Turk slid down between her legs and buried his face into her clit and sucked softly. The intensity of her climax turned Turk on even more.

He then slid up and straddled her face, allowing her his penis. She grasped it at the base and worked it in and out of her mouth with passion. Turk exploded again and weakly fell to one side.

Getting his second wind, Turk gently turned her over, pulled her to her knees and rammed his rock-hard erection home. She gasped and backed into him so hard, he thought he would fall off the bed. Cory screamed, "It feels so good; I'm coming, I'm coming, don't stop, please don't stop!" Cory shook as she climaxed. Then totally spent, she collapsed with Turk on top of her. He turned and held her in a tight embrace. She looked up at him and said, "Turk, you have no idea how much I needed that. Make love to me again." Two more hours of love making and Turk departed. He hoped Deon was none the wiser.

Turk felt awful. As much as he desired Cory, and as much as he had enjoyed making love to her, he felt just as bad. Had he blown his efforts to clean up his act? Was he now going back to what he was in the past? How was he going to justify his behavior? No one needed to know. Damn, he needed a drink.

* * *

"Turk, wake up. You must have knocked the phone off the hook. I've been trying to call you for hours. We've got some problems we need to deal with. What the hell is the matter with you anyway?" Digger asked.

"I took too many sleeping pills last night. What's wrong now?" Turk asked, as he stretched. He was glad he hadn't had that drink he remembered wanting.

"Detective's Pettit and Knight have arrested CJ."

Rubbing his eyes, he asked, "Do you know what for?"

"China Jon claims they arrested him for managing a criminal enterprise. He's scared as hell."

"I can't blame him. I don't think he's ever been arrested before. This will drive him back to his cabin in the woods, you can bet on that. Have you called our bail bondsman?"

"I have. Bail hasn't been set. Won't be until the hearing tomorrow. Look's like CJ will be in jail for tonight."

"Shit, let me make a few phone calls." Turk called Cory. She had her hands full. The GBI had arrested every one of Niko's managers. Niko's lawyers were doing all they could. It was evident to Turk that the law was intent on busting Niko. He had to move fast.

"Digger, lets get to the airport project. I'll need to secure that. I have to believe that this is just the beginning of the harassment. Between the FBI and the GBI, Niko's days in business are numbered."

"Okay, I'm ready. What else can I do?"

"Stay in contact with the lawyers on CJ's behalf. Be sure bond is posted as soon as possible. This will drive CJ over the edge."

"He'll never come out of his cabin after this," Digger said, with assurance.

"I hope that's not the case, Digger, but you might be right."

Turk had been through this before. His projects were basically stopped. That was the intent of the authorities. Jail, and harass management and the business would be interrupted to a point where it would cost more money than it was worth fighting them. Niko had crossed the line, and they were out to get him, and get him good. There wasn't much Niko could do now, but watch his empire he had built around pornography be dismantled. That was why he was moving assets and cash around. The Feds would find it, Turk had to believe.

Turk figured it was time to cut a deal and get out of Atlanta, so he called the GBI. "Is Detective Donald Knight in please?"

"He's not. Who's calling?"

"Is Carl Pettit in by chance?"

"He is. Who's calling?" an impatient operator asked.

"Donatelli." Turk answered, just as irritated.

"Donatelli who?"

"For crissakes, get Detective Pettit on the phone for me."

"Sir, I don't like your tone."

"I really don't give a shit whether you like my tone or not, get either Knight or Pettit on the damn phone, please!" The phone went silent.

"Donatelli, this is Pettit what can I do for you?"

"You know damn well what you can do for me, Detective. You arrested my right hand man and I want to get him out of jail."

"That could be a while. He's running a criminal enterprise. I don't know how a judge will view his release. He might be a menace to society."

"You damn well know he's no menace. What do I need to do?"

"You need to come in and see us, Donatelli. We told you, you shouldn't have come back to work for Niko. You might be in too deep to back out now."

"I haven't done anything illegal, and you know it."

"I'm not so sure now that the RICO Act has been passed into law."

"I've heard a lot about this so-called, RICO Act. What right does that give you to arrest innocent managers?"

"Why don't you come on in and we'll talk about it, Donatelli? It will save us from having to come and get you. We have a warrant for your arrest, too. Your sidekick, Digger, better come along with you. We want to talk to him also."

"Harassment, that's all this is, and you know it, Pettit. You got nothing."

"Maybe yes, maybe not. When are you coming in?"

"I'll be there in an hour."

"Will Digger be with you?"

"No, he's out of town. He won't be back for a few weeks."

"Where did he go?"

"If you must know, he took my wife and son back to Florida."

"That's where you should have stayed, isn't it, Donatelli?" Pettit was getting a kick out of this.

"Quit laughing, there's nothing funny about any of this, Pettit!"

"I guess that depends on which side of the law you're on, doesn't it? I expect to see you in an hour."

Turk had been through this drill before many times. He was glad Karen was in Florida. This would take him a few weeks to sort out. He needed to find out more about this RICO Act, before he met with the GBI.

As he hung up the phone, Turk turned to Digger and said, "You need to get out of Georgia. I told the detective you were in Florida with my wife and kid. Why don't you go to Miami; hide out for a while? If they arrest me, I'll need you on the outside."

"How do I contact you?" Digger asked.

"That will be difficult. See if you can find Pop. He'll be our contact. Do you think he'll be okay?"

"Pop's okay. He'll do it as long as it's not illegal. He's pretty protective over his security license."

"I know, but I think we're probably blowing this all out of proportion. This should be over in a couple of weeks. Then it will be back to business as usual."

"I hope you're right, boss. This just feels bigger this time, that's all."

"You feel it, too? We'll see, won't we?"

Turk gave Digger two hundred thousand in cash, with instructions to keep an eye on Karen and Jason and headed downtown to turn himself in to the GBI.

CHAPTER—20

It was about 3:30 when Turk arrived at the downtown Fulton County jail where the GBI field office was located. He approached the bullet proof glass wall which had a four-inch round hole in it, with a receptionist in uniform sitting behind it. Bending down so he could talk through the hole, Turk said, "My name is Turk Donatelli. I'm here to see Detective Pettit; he's expecting me."

"The receptionist looked up quickly, turned, and gave some kind of signal. Then two guards came barreling out of the glass enclosure, grabbed Turk, flung him against the wall, pulled both arms behind his back, and handcuffed him. "We have a warrant for your arrest," one of them said. Then he read Turk his rights, as they pushed him through another door, down a narrow corridor to a holding cell.

The cell would hold eight people comfortably. Turk counted at least sixteen packed into this very small cell. The stainless steel toilet was overflowing and the floor was a sticky mess of urine and slop. Drunks were lying in it. The metal benches were occupied by some very big black men. The rest of the men stood in a row facing the bars.

Trying to collect his thoughts, Turk rubbed his wrist, and moved his shoulder around. It felt like it was dislocated, or strained, probably from being slammed against the wall and violently handcuffed. Not much he could do, but wait. This was the detective's way of softening him up. Little did they know how tough Turk Donatelli was.

Three hours had passed and no one came to see him no matter how much he protested. He had managed to get a seat, and protection from the other inmates by giving up his solid gold neck chain to a very large black man, who at one time had worked on one of Turk's projects. Protection was needed. There were some tough street dudes in that cell. All by design, Turk figured. He spent the night huddled on this metal bench under the protection of his recently hired bodyguard.

The next morning, after very little sleep, a cart loaded with very weak coffee approached the outside of the cell. Inmates scrambled to get in line first before the coffee was gone. The big black men didn't hurry; they just went to the front of the line as weaker men moved aside and took their time fixing their coffee. Most had extra sugar in their pocket for the occasion. Mr. Big, a nickname Turk gave his care tender, brought him back a cup of black coffee, and said, "You gonna hire me when I get out?"

"Sure, what are you in here for?"

"I beat up on my wife and son. They turned me in, they did. I can git out in ninety days if I got me a job. You hire me then?"

"Of course I will, Mr. Big. I'll give you my number. You just call me when you get out." Turk had no intention of honoring his request. Survival was the name of the game in this cell.

"Thank you, suh'. I'll be holden' you to that, I will."

"Hey guard, when do I get to use a telephone?" Turk yelled.

"What's the matter, Donatelli? You trying to get out of here or something?" He answered, laughing as he turned his back and went to the next cell with his deplorable coffee.

Turk had had enough. He said to Mr. Big, "I'm going to cause a stink. Cover my backside, okay?" He stepped toward the bars, and yelled out as loud as he could, "Guard, I need help! Guard, I need help!" No one responded. "Okay, Mr. Big, how can I get the guards attention? I need to use a telephone."

"What's it worth to you? Evathing gots a price in here, you know."

Turk thought for a minute, and said, "Mr. Big, see this watch? It's worth a lot. Will that be enough?"

"Yes suh. That will do it."

"This is how it works. You get the guard's attention. I get him to let me use the phone and you get the watch. Okay."

"I'll get the guard here. All I can do is get you out of here to some place else. Getting to a phone is your business, not mine. Give me the watch."

"Don't you trust me, Mr. Big?"

"Trust is bullshit."

"I've heard that before," Turk said, as he handed him the watch.

Mr. Big turned around and hit the guy next to him square in the face. Blood spattered all over Turk, and half the cell. No sooner had Mr. Big hit the man then there was complete chaos. Mr. Big had Turk's back. Inmates were falling all around him. Three guards rushed to the cell, afraid to open it until another six arrived. Then they started expelling the ones that weren't fighting and handcuffing the ones that were. Turk managed to step to one side while this was going on. All this accomplished was a transfer to an even dirtier cell without the presence of Mr. Big...or his watch. Now Turk was in a world of shit; the inmates knew he was the one who had started the chaos.

As the inmates were closing in on him, he saw Detectives Knight and Pettit approaching the cell with big shit-eating grins on their faces, Pettit said, "Enjoying your stay with us, Donatelli?"

"Get me the hell out of here, Pettit," Turk said, through clenched teeth. The guard opened the cell at Knight's instruction. Knight and Pettit led Turk back to a small room with a table and three chairs. He was told to sit down; that they would be right back.

The detectives made Turk wait four hours, sitting on a metal chair in a damp, dimly-lit room. Turk was about to doze off when the door burst open and there stood Pettit and Knight. Pettit held a steaming cup of coffee in hand. Turk could smell the coffee and figured it was for him. Not the case.

"Okay, Donatelli. Have you enjoyed the last two days?"

"What happened to my rights? I want to call my lawyer. You have no right to keep me in here, no right at all."

"This is the South, Donatelli. We do things a little different here than you Yankees do."

"I'll see to it you don't get away with this, you wait and see."

"Okay, let's cut the shit. We want you to testify against Pappas. You agree and we'll forget the charges against you."

"Just what are those charges?" Turk still had no idea what he was in jail for.

"Your 'racketeering activity' as defined by the RCIO Act."

"RICO Act, my ass. I'm tired of hearing about this damn RICO Act. I want a lawyer. You have no right to deny me a lawyer."

"Look, Donatelli, Niko is done, finished. We want you to turn State witness."

"You look, Detective. I haven't done a damn thing illegal. I don't have any idea what Niko is involved in. I run a real estate operation. I have no desire or intention of saying anything without a lawyer present. So you might as well put me back in that cell and press charges because I'm not saying another word."

"You're making another wrong decision, Donatelli. We're going to make your existence in Atlanta unbearable. One last time...help us convict Niko and we'll leave you alone."

Turk didn't respond. The detectives summoned the guard and he was led back to the hall where he was allowed to make a collect phone call. He called Cory, no answer. He called Niko's law firm and was told lawyers were in the building and he should be getting out shortly. "Sit tight." He was escorted back to the holding cell. Mr. Big was still there. Three hours later, Turk was released to his attorneys on one-hundred-thousand dollar bond.

"Before I tell you about my treatment after and during my arrest, tell me, just what in hell is this RICO bullshit?" Turk asked Bert Stein, the lawyer he was provided by the law firm representing Niko.

"In your case, Turk, the GBI figures if they threaten you with a RICO indictment, they can get you to plead guilty to a lesser charge, in part because the seizure of assets would make it difficult for you to pay a defense attorney. Despite its harsh provisions, a RICO-related charge is considered easy to prove in court, as it focuses on patterns of behavior as opposed to criminal acts. Does that make any sense to you?" Stein was a young lawyer and seemed to stumble over his words.

"I still don't understand. Why haven't I heard about this RICO Act before and how can they come after my assets? I didn't do anything."

"The RICO Act is relatively new. It became law in 1968, I

believe. If the authorities can prove assets were derived from money considered illegal gains, those assets can be seized."

"You mean our real estate properties I've developed with Niko can be taken?"

"Maybe, Turk. They've already seized his downtown office building. I'm sure you're aware of that, aren't you?"

"I am aware, but I didn't understand how they could. Can you legal beagles get around this RICO Act?"

"We feel we can. Most of Niko's assets were the product of legal profits. Any asset he may have acquired with money made from pornography might be suspect."

"Bert, you say suspect. Is there a chance we can keep our real estate I'm working on?"

"Yes, a good chance."

"How so?"

"Niko did one thing that may save his assets." The lawyer chuckled. "No pun intended. Get it? Asset, ass?"

Turk failed to see the humor. "What did he do?" he asked, showing his distain.

Bert, gaining his composure, continued, "Niko paid taxes on all the money he garnered from his pornography business, or so he claims."

"Paying taxes does all that?"

"No, no, there's more to it than that. We have to prove that pornography isn't an illegal enterprise. We've been fighting for that in court for Niko for years. We think we'll win that battle."

"Yeah, in the meantime, he goes broke because the authorities are arresting and harassing all of his legitimate businesses."

"That's their intent."

"Okay, Bert, what do you suggest I do?"

"I can't tell you what to do, Turk. Cory is in charge. She'll advise you. We'll take care of your indictment; the DA will drop it. They got nothing. All they're hoping to do is scare you into testifying against Niko. That's all."

"*That's all*, Bert? Isn't that enough?" Turk said, thinking this young lawyer had a lot to learn.

* * *

"Karen, why didn't you tell me the MS symptoms had gotten worse?"

"I didn't want to bother you, Turk."

"How are you feeling now?"

"I'm in bed most of the time. I get outside once in a while, but I don't have much energy, I tire easily."

"How's Jason doing?"

"Oh, he's fine Turk. He loves the beach. He's playing with his friends on the beach all day long."

"How's the caregiver we hired doing?"

"Okay, I guess. I don't like to think of me needing a caregiver. Can't we just call her our housekeeper?"

"Sure, honey. I'm sorry."

"There's nothing to be sorry about. When are you coming home?"

"I can't leave Atlanta right now."

"Can't you come home for the weekend? We haven't seen you in months. I miss you terribly, and I know Jason does, too."

"I can't right now, baby. I wish I could, though, I miss you guys, too." Turk hoped she wouldn't press him further. He couldn't leave the State of Georgia until the indictment was cleared. He didn't want to worry her any more than she already was. Stress caused her MS symptoms to get worse.

"There's something you're not telling me, Turk Donatelli. What is it?"

Laughing, Turk asked, "How can you tell?"

"You'd jump on a plane and come and see us if something wasn't terribly wrong. What have you gotten yourself into, Turk?"

"Nothing I can't handle, honey. The GBI wants me to stick around and not leave Atlanta, that's all."

"That's all you say. What has Pappas done now?"

"Why do you think it has anything to do with Pappas?"

"Come on, Turk. Don't play games with me. He's in some kind of shit, isn't he? And you're being dragged into it. I told you to stay away from Niko; that he was trouble."

"Right again. Karen, this will all blow over soon. I'll be home before you know it."

"Yeah, okay if you say so." Karen could tell by the tone of Turk's voice that that was the end of the conversation.

"Can I do anything for you and Jason? Do you have everything you need?"

"We're fine, Turk, Take care of business and hurry home. I love you."

"I love you too, sweetheart. Bye." Turk was very worried about Karen. He knew she was sicker than she was letting on. He also felt guilty about his liaison with Cory. Damn, he wanted a drink.

The next morning, he found his newspapers neatly stacked by the front door. When he went to get them, he noticed a car parked in the front with Pop's Security embossed on the side. There was another car at the corner of the property facing Roswell Road. A guard was standing next to his front door as well. Turk felt Digger's presence, even though he wasn't there.

He poured a cup of coffee, not really wanting to get on with his day. Opening the *Atlanta Journal*, there staring at him, the headlines read "Pappas Escapes." Turk hurriedly read the caption below the picture of Niko, stating that a guard must have left the cell door ajar and Pappas just walked out. *Wow!* Turk, thought. Niko was in some shit now.

He lifted the phone and called Cory. "I know, Turk. I just saw the paper. What in hell was Niko thinking?"

"You mean you didn't know about his plan to escape?"

"Of course not! I suspected something when he asked me to transfer assets around. He was hell-bent on taking care of his wife and sons. I felt he was up to something."

"What do we do now, Cory?"

"As much as I hate to say it, there's nothing we can do but wait, I guess."

"Do you think he'll contact either of us?"

"I have no idea, Turk. But I do know one thing, and that is we'll be contacted by the GBI and the FBI. I'm surprised we haven't been already. I really am."

"Wow! That's all I can seem to say. Between the RICO Act and now with his escaping, it looks like it's over for Niko. His businesses will surely be taken and or broken up. Shit, what do you want me to do, Cory?"

"I have no idea, Turk. Let's see what happens in the next few days and then decide."

"Okay, I suppose this ends our 'trysts'?"

"Unfortunately, it does."

"I'll talk to you tomorrow, or if anything more comes up before then. Bye."

"Yeah, okay, bye." Turk was further depressed. He needed to cut a deal with the authorities and get back to Florida and take care of Karen and Jason and leave this shit behind him. But how was he to do that? What would he do if Niko contacted him?

Turk felt that he was in a no-win situation. He called

Detective Knight and said, "I need to see you. I want to talk about a deal of some kind."

"First things first, Donatelli. Has Niko contacted you?"

"No."

"Did you know he was planning an escape?"

"Hell no!" Turk was irritated that he would even ask him that."

"Are you ready to turn State witness?"

"No, Donald. That wouldn't do you any good. I don't know any more than you guys know for crissakes, and you know it."

"Then why do you want to meet?"

"I want to go back to Florida and take care of my sick wife and my son. I'm washing my hands of Pappas. I need to come to an understanding with you and the FBI, so I can leave the State."

"I don't have time for that right now, Turk. You'll have to wait a few days, and then I should be able to come up with something. Right now, you, Cory and Vera Staidly are the folks Pappas will probably contact, and if he does, you better get on the phone to us before you get in any deeper. You do understand that don't you, Donatelli?"

"I do. Call me when you want to meet."

Turk's next call was to Bert Stein, his attorney. "Bert, where does this leave my case?"

"I don't know. Our whole law firm is trying to regroup. We don't know what to do now. I'll have to get back to you."

Turk turned on the morning news and there, plastered all over the TV, were pictures of Niko. His BIO was being dissected and theories abounded as to why he would escape if he didn't do anything wrong, like he claimed he did not. There were reports about the gifts he gave the city's Art Department and the non-profit organizations. The press and the reporters were making Niko out to be a murderer, a pornographer, and a guilty man on the run. The media was having a field day. All the while, the hundreds of employees who worked for Niko had no idea what their future held; nor did Turk for that matter.

* * *

Overton was smiling as he read the paper. The pornography business was his; it was just a matter of time. He called Naylor, "Butt-fuck, I know you can't read worth a shit, but Pappas just fucked himself good!"

"How so, boss? And I can read. I'm not stupid, you know?"

"Niko escaped from a jail in Connecticut."

"Really? How'd he do that?" Naylor was impressed. He'd only met Niko once, but he considered that to be one of the highlights of his life.

"Just up and walked out, they say. He probably paid-off a guard or two, knowing him."

"Man that guy sure knows how to live, don't he?"

"What the hell does escaping from jail have do with living, you dumb ass?"

"Escaping from jail has to be hard. I was in jail once. When they close the door, you feel so damn helpless with so much steel around you."

Overton just shook his head. He loved Naylor, but he *was* stupid. "Get the car numb-nuts; we're going for a ride." Overton wasn't sure what to do now. He was still on the West Coast; it was probably time for him to head east. If he was going to take over the porno business, he needed to cut a deal with the book store owners and quick. He would also have to go to New York and get the mob's stamp of approval. He would be the new porno king. He was excited by the prospect. So excited he wasn't aware of the car that was following him.

* * *

Niko figured if he could get rid of Overton, he could beat the murder wrap. He was the only witness. Then he would turn himself in and face the lesser charge of escape. For a measly five thousand dollars, he'd managed to bribe the night guard. All the guard had to do was jam the cell door lock, and Pappas was one door from freedom.

Niko had made plans known to no one in his organization, months prior to charges being filed against him, for the murder of an adult book store competitor, of which he claimed innocence. He'd convinced an old high school sweetheart, a prominent real estate broker practicing in Douglasville, Georgia, to cover for him should he need to go into hiding.

Niko, always meticulous, stored enough cash, vehicles, clothes, and furnished a garret over her garage. He also befriended a retired police officer, Russ O'Hare. He'd known Russ for fifteen years. Russ was on Niko's payroll while he served as a Fulton County police officer. Russ needed money and Niko needed information. Russ procured Niko a high-powered rifle with a six-power scope, equipped with a silencer, should the need for one arise.

The evening of Niko's escape was not complicated. The guard simply stuck a Pepsi can in-between the door and the casing and left it ajar. Niko waited until about midnight and walked out through the back door and drove away in a car left there by Gerri Short, the high school sweetheart.

Gerri was a pretty woman, about Niko's age, forty-four. Gerri lost her husband during the Vietnam War. He was a captain of a foot patrol, and was leading his squad into battle, when he tripped on an IID and was blown to pieces along with four other soldiers in his patrol.

Niko openly protested the war and reconnected with Gerri during the funeral services. He actually had a brief affair with her some months after, then broke it off, all the awhile setting her up in the real estate business by purchasing a REMAX franchise for her. Gerri employed thirty licensed sales people, and was a very successful businesswoman, who never fell out of love with Nickolas J. Pappas. When Niko asked her to equip her garret in case he divorced his wife, she thought nothing of it. She owed him, she loved him and she wanted to help him in any way she could. She was convinced of his innocence.

Niko drove all night and arrived early morning. He went upstairs to Gerri's garret, lay down, and went to sleep. He woke up hungry. First he had to change his appearance. He shaved off his mustache and beard. Then he dyed his hair blonde and showered. His clothes, which he had stocked months before, were hippie-style: bell-bottom-pants, and a tie dyed shirt, fashioned with a wide belt. The platform shoes just wouldn't work; one leg was much shorter than the other. He had to somehow masquerade his considerable limp. He did this simply by doubling up on shoe inserts. He topped that off with an Atlanta Braves baseball cap. Now he was ready to eat. He decided, at considerable risk, to go to one of his favorite places, the IHOP, to test his disguise. He loved their pancakes.

Niko finished up his pigs-in-a-blanket breakfast while noting all around him people he knew...none of whom recognized him. He'd passed the first test. He had plenty of cash, and he was on a mission. But first, he wanted to see his two sons. He hadn't seen them for months. They both played Little League baseball. Niko drove past the field where they were playing, parked some distance away and observed them through binoculars. His wife, Kate, was sitting in the bleachers by herself. For a moment, he felt bad for her, but he'd taken care of her future financially, so the guilt didn't last long. Niko used woman like he chewed gum, often. Once the flavor was gone it was thrown away. He followed his family home in his white four-door Chevy van. He drove on past. It was almost four o'clock and Niko needed to get to a payphone to receive a call from Deon.

"Boss, it looks like Overton and Naylor are headed back to Atlanta. What do you want me to do? Follow them?"

"You know damn well what I'd like you to do, Deon. But you've already made it clear you won't do it. I'll take care of those two."

"I'll rough them up for you, boss, but I won't kill them."

"Roughing them up isn't going to do me any good for crissakes, Deon. I need to stop Overton from testifying and that won't do it."

"I know. How do I get in touch with you?"

"You can't. The GBI and the FBI will be looking for you. Stay on the West Coast, and keep a low profile until I contact you."

"How are you going to do that?"

"Never mind how. Just stay put for a while. I've been in this booth too long. I've got to go. I'll find you."

Now that Niko knew Overton was on his way back to Atlanta, he had to make plans. He wasn't sure how he was going to take him out, but he knew he had to. His freedom depended on it. He wasn't about to spend the rest of his life in prison because of that little prick. He would spend a few years in jail for escape, but not for conspiracy to commit murder. All he had to do was rid the only State's witness the U.S. Attorney had and that was Overton.

CHAPTER—21

Three weeks had passed. Most of Niko's employees were either out on bail or the charges had been dropped. Turk's charge of operating a business funded by a criminal enterprise was pending, subject to a deal with the GBI. They were convinced he could be a valuable State's witness against Niko. Pettit and Knight were stringing Turk along, knowing full well they didn't have enough grounds to prosecute him. Turk knew this as well.

China Jon requested a meeting with Turk to discuss his future. His three days in jail had taken its toll. He was subject to the same conditions Turk experienced, but wasn't as fortunate to have a hulk of a man protecting him. The harassment he experienced convinced China Jon he wanted out of Turk's organization.

"Turk, I know I told you I would stay on for another six months, but I want out now. The time I spent in jail was enough for me. You can handle the pressure. I can't."

"I understand, but do me a favor, CJ. Will you please commit to stay long enough for me to go to Florida and take care of some family business? When I get back, I'll give you a parting bonus and you can go back to your cabin in the woods. Will that work?"

"My cabin would be a nice quiet and safe place for me to go. You ought to think about joining me. Events surrounding you and your business are suspect, too, you know. How long are you planning to be in Florida?"

"Depending on the GBI...I have to get their permission... probably three weeks, four at the most."

"That long, huh?" CJ was nervous about staying in Atlanta. The short time he was locked up he'd made up his mind that this was the end of him mixing with society.

"That's not long, CJ. I know you want to leave. I can appreciate that you want to leave after what you've been through, but I need someone here I can trust. That pretty much is only you, so what do you say?"

"All right, I'll stay on for thirty days and then that's it, Turk. Don't even ask me to stay any longer. Is that a deal?"

"That's a deal. I owe you one. Thanks, China Jon." Turk secretly wished he had a cabin to escape to. He now had to get the GBI to let him leave town, to say nothing about his bondsmen who had one-hundred-thousand dollars at risk. He needed to call Cory and advise her of his plans.

"Hi, Cory, got a few minutes for me?"

"It depends on what you want, Turk," she answered in way too sexy voice.

"Whoa, I don't think there will be any of that, will there?"

"Why, what do you mean, you devil, you?"

"*Me* a devil! You're the devil for even thinking about it." Turk was turned on for some reason. How he could be, with all this shit going on around him? He thought, *a dick has no conscience.*

"I'll be at the office...I mean house...most of the day. Come on over anytime." Cory was still trying to get used to having her office in her home.

"Have you heard from, you know who?" Turk asked.

"No, I take it you haven't, either."

"I haven't. I'll be over in an hour or so."

"I'll see you then. Oh, Turk I'm horny as hell. Think about that on your way here. I've got plans for you."

"You're crazy, Cory." Turk thought he was just as crazy for even thinking about sex, but damn, he was turned on by the thought of making love to Cory, with Niko on the loose.

The guards at the gate were new. Turk didn't see Deon around anywhere. They just waved him through. As he approached Cory's front door, the hair stood up on his neck. It felt like someone was watching him, but he couldn't put a finger on it. He wrote it off as being paranoid.

He opened the front door, and Cory yelled out, "Come in here, Turk. I'm in the bedroom."

"You've got to be kidding me, Cory. I'm not going in there. We can't do this now."

"If you want to talk to me, Turk, you'll have to."

"Like I said, Cory, you're a crazy woman, you are." She didn't answer. All he could hear was music. He slowly opened the bedroom door. Would Niko be there, too? Could this be a set-up? Shit, he was concerned for his safety now. Cory said, "Stand still, Turk. Stand right there." Turk was so jumpy, he hit the floor.

When he looked up, Cory was standing over him with her legs spread. All he could see was her womanhood. She was dressed in an outfit she must have taken from one of Niko's porno shops. Her see-through panties had no crotch, which he was directly under. Her long legs were sheathed in mesh stockings suspended from a garter belt; a bra made to hold up, not cover; stiletto heels, and a face mask covering her eyes only.

"Damn, you scared me, Cory," he said, as he got to his feet.

"Before we talk you're going to make love to me, Turk, maybe more than once. Get over to the bed right now. I've been thinking about fucking you for three hours."

"Now I see why you liked working for Niko."

With a coy smile, she asked, "What do you mean by that?"

"You obviously like danger and I can't think of anything else that could be more dangerous than you and me making love, while Niko probably is outside observing your every move."

"I doubt it. He knows better than to come around here. This would be the first place the law would look for him, and besides, the SOB can watch as far as I'm concerned."

"Maybe you're right or maybe you're crazy," Turk said, as he took her in his arms and carried her to the bed.

"And what does that make you, Turk? Just as crazy."

"Shut up and get down on your knees."

"Yes, master." Cory said, mockingly.

Turk was just as turned on as Cory was. The danger made his first climax more intense than he had ever experienced. He slid her around on the bed, forcefully spread her legs, and hungrily kissed her neck and tweaked her nipples. He slid his lips down her belly to the inside of her thighs, and licked the lips of her hot, wet clit. Turk wasn't finished; Cory was wild and so was he. She screamed, "Bite me and bite me hard, Turk."

Turk returned to her nipples and bit down on them firmly. She cried, "Harder, goddamn it, bite me harder!" Turk obliged.

"Now bite me lower, bite me, damn it!" Turk had never bitten a woman this hard before. He'd heard about women wanting to be hurt, but he'd never experienced it first hand.

He moved to her clit and bit down on the lips he'd so gently massaged a few minutes earlier. She started to grind her hips into his face. He could hardly breathe. He was forced to bite harder to get some relief when all she did was moan and yell out, "I'm reaching it! I'm reaching it! Bite harder!" Turk did, and Cory's climax was so strong that her body went into a rigid state and then shook violently.

Turk, needing air, raised his head just as she grabbed his shoulders, and turned him over on his back. She straddled him, took his penis in her hand, and sat down hard, plunging it deep inside her. She rode Turk like a bucking bronco until she reached another intense climax, with Turk reaching one at the same time. Then she rolled off him and lay weeping beside him.

Turk, trying to catch his breath and wondering what she was crying about, asked, "Cory, did I hurt you?"

"Hurt me? Hardly, Turk. I've never let another man see this side of me. I'm so ashamed." She turned her back to him.

Rolling her over and taking her into his arms, Turk said, "Cory, you were wonderful; don't be ashamed. You know what you like."

"Will I ever find a man who understands me, Turk?"

This was deeper than Turk wanted to get. He liked Cory a lot, but he was in love with Karen. He was in over his head, and realized he would have to deal with more than Niko. All he could think to say was, "Cory, you'll find the right man, you will." Evidently, that wasn't the right thing to say. She jumped out of bed and said, "You bastard!" and ran to the bathroom crying. "I thought I meant more to you than that."

Turk went to the door and said, "Come on, Cory. Come out; we need to talk."

"Get out of here, Turk. I don't want to talk right now. I don't want to see you, either."

It finally dawned on Turk that Cory's feelings for him were more than his for her. Why wasn't he aware of that before now? His pecker got him in more trouble than his drinking and gambling ever did. He pleaded with Cory to come out of the bathroom, but to no avail.

"Cory, I'm going to St. Pete for a couple of weeks, if the GBI will let me out of the state. Is there anything I need to do for you before I go?" He wished she'd come out of the damn bathroom so they could talk.

Still sobbing, she said, "Go, Turk, go and leave me alone. I'm sure that what I just demanded of you won't go any further, will it?"

"No it won't, Cory. You're a good person. What can I say to make you feel better?"

"Nothing, Turk. Just go. Please just leave. We'll talk when you get back." He cautiously left her house, looking over his shoulder. He felt used, and he felt he had betrayed his family. The guilt he was feeling was overwhelming. He needed a drink.

* * *

Turk's flight into Tampa was rough. Tampa is the lightning capital of the world. The storm they flew through was rocking the plane up and down, left and right. The plane fell five-thousand feet. After gaining control, the pilot came on the intercom and announced, "Ladies and gentlemen, sorry about that. The worst is over, but it will be bumpy the rest of the way. The storm is too big for us to go around. Be sure your seatbelt is fastened securely. We'll be landing in thirty minutes."

This flight, the GBI, the FBI, his business, his infidelities, his yearning for a drink and Karen's MS was driving Turk to the brink. It seemed his world was closing in on him, and closing in fast and furious. Maybe Karen could bring some sanity to the craziness going on around him. He felt so damn guilty for his recent conduct, that he was sick to his stomach, or was it the awful flight that made him queasy? Turk caught a cab to their condo on St. Pete beach.

When he arrived about 3:00, Karen wasn't around, the caregiver was gone, and Jason must have been outside playing. He went upstairs to the master suite to wash up, and change clothes. Karen was sleeping, curled up in a ball in the middle of their bed. She looked so peaceful. He didn't want to disturb her, so he quietly crept downstairs, being careful not to wake her. He sat out on the patio, on the beach, thinking about the good times Karen, and he had, drinking a Scotch, discussing family affairs, and waiting for the sun to set. The sun always set in the same place with the same intensity. It looked as though the ocean ate it up every day, and released it every morning. An infinite cycle, it seemed.

He heard someone come through the front door. It was the caregiver. Lilly was fifty-five years old, divorced, overweight, and a devout Catholic. She slid open the patio door and said, "Welcome to St. Pete, Mr. Donatelli. It must have been a rough flight with the storm that just passed through here. Was it?"

"It was. Hi, Lilly. You're even prettier than the last time I saw you."

Blushing, she said, "You're a flirt, Mr. Donatelli, a flirt, I tell you."

Smiling right along with her, Turk said, "As soon as you put those groceries away, why don't you join me, and bring me up-to-date on this family of mine?"

"I'll be glad to, just give me a minute." Lilly was relieved that Turk was home. She worried a lot about Karen. She wasn't talking right.

Turk was thinking about his problems in Atlanta, and about the drink he knew he shouldn't have, when Lilly returned and took a seat next to him. "Sir, Miss Karen has taken a turn for the worse, I'm afraid. I pray for her every day...I do."

This added to Turk's angst. "Describe *worse* for me, Lilly, and for crissakes, call me Turk."

"I don't think that's proper, Mr. Donatelli."

"What isn't proper, calling me Turk, or defining *worse*?" Turk was growing impatient.

"You cussing, and me calling you Turk," she said firmly.

"Okay, whatever. Lilly, why do you think Karen is *worse*?"

"Oh, lots of things. It's not just me. The doctors tell me so."

Turk was growing weary of this back and forth talk and said, "Come on, Lilly, tell me what's going on."

"Don't get short with me, sir. I'm just saying."

"Saying what?" Turk asked, trying to mask his lack of patience.

"Ms. Karen hasn't gotten out of bed in the last four weeks. She wants to die, she says."

"She wants to what?" Turk exclaimed, as he jumped out of his chair.

"She doesn't feel like she wants to live this way. She cries all the time...she does."

"Have you told the doctor this?"

"No, I don't feel right about doing that...I don't"

"Did she go into detail as to why she doesn't want to live anymore?" Turk knew the answer to that question. He wished he hadn't asked her.

"No, I'm supposing it's the disease."

"What about Jason? Does he know about this crazy talk?"

"Heavens no, Mr. Donatelli, of course not. Jason can't know."

"He must know. She's crying all the time."

"Sir, I don't like talking about this. I can't take care of

someone that doesn't want to live. She wants to die...she does."

"Okay, Lilly, I understand how you feel. Why don't you take a few weeks off and I'll talk to Karen and straighten this out. I don't want you to quit."

"I don't want to, either, but it's all Miss Karen talks about. I think you might have a hard time convincing her any different."

"Here comes Jason now. Thanks, Lilly. Take a few weeks off and please reconsider, will you?"

"I will. I have a few things left to do in the house. Thanks for coming home, Mr. Donatelli, they both missed you very much... they did."

That last comment pulled at Turk's heart. He was full of guilt for a lot of things, but why hadn't he been aware of what was going on with Karen, why? Jason came bounding over the seawall. "Turk, you're home, you're home! What did you bring me?" Without fail when he went out of town, Turk always brought something home for Jason, since Jason was a little boy. He was now almost twelve and Turk still looked forward to surprising him.

"It's where I always leave it, on the dining room table. Go get it, and come back out here, and see me."

Rushing inside, Jason grabbed the bag, ran back to the patio, and sat next to Turk. Opening the package revealed a state-of-the-art tape recorder-radio combination. It was the best Sony made, and it was light, and compact. The last one Turk bought Jason was heavy and bulky. This recorder had a dozen more features than the old one. Jason was beside himself, and excitedly said, "Turk, you always know what I want." He started reading the operating manual, which he would read cover-to-cover several times. Jason would be able to do whatever that machine was meant to do, and probably some things Sony didn't know it could do.

While Jason was stuffing the batteries into the back of his recorder, Turk asked, "How's your mom. Is she doing okay?"

Turning from happy kid, to solemn, Jason said, "I don't see her much anymore. She stays in bed all the time. I'm worried about my mom. She cries all the time." Tears started to form.

Turk pulled his chair closer, and put his arms around the boy and said, "Son, I'll take care of your mom. Don't you worry. I'll take care of her. We'll figure something out. Don't you worry so much. I'm home now." Turk's guts were killing him. Here was this eleven-year-old-boy, whom he loved, worried about his mother; whom he also loved, and he had been thinking about a damn drink, and worried about his business, and being unfaithful. What an asshole he was! He needed to do something about it, *and now.*

Looking up at Turk, tears running down his cheeks, Jason said, "I'm so glad you're home, Turk. I feel safe when you're home. Will my mom get better?"

Holding back his own tears, he answered quietly, "Jason, she'll get better, I promise." A promise Turk knew he probably couldn't keep, which made him feel even worse.

"Can I go show my friends my new Sony?" he asked, wiping away his tears.

"You sure can. I'll rustle up some dinner. I'll leave yours on the counter. Try not to be too late, okay?"

Throwing his arms around Turk, Jason said, "I love you." And then ran off down the beach with his new Sony.

Turk broke down and cried. His head on his knees, he said out loud, "Why me? Why me? What can I do?" Feeling a hand on his shoulder, Lilly said, "You can pray, Mr. Donatelli, you can pray." He'd forgotten she was still there. He looked up at her, his eyes full of tears and said, "I'll do that, Lilly. Thanks and good night."

Opening the refrigerator, Turk found some center-cut pork chops. A container of cottage cheese, a can of pineapple and some shredded cheddar. A bag of boiled five-minute rice would round-out the meal. A box of double-fudge brownie mix would make the condo smell good, and make Jason happy. Turk pan-fried the chops, scooped the cottage cheese onto a bed of lettuce, topped it with chunks of pineapple, and sprinkled cheddar over it. He greased a glass baking pan, mixed up the brownie mix and set the timer. He knew Jason would be late coming back, so he put the food on his plate, and covered it in foil.

Turk plucked a few flowers from the neighbor's small garden patch. He found a small vase and set them in water. He rolled two large joints and plated Karen's food. He arranged the serving tray and carried her dinner upstairs.

Karen was sitting up. She figured Lilly was preparing her dinner. Surprised by Turk's presence, she cried out, "Oh, Turk, I'm so glad you're home. I missed you so much!"

Turk placed the tray on the nightstand, and sat down on the edge of the bed. Holding Karen in his arms, he said, "I missed you, too, baby. How about you smoke a joint and eat some dinner?"

"Just hold me, Turk, just hold me." Turk pulled her close to his shoulder, and she cried and cried and cried. When she finally stopped crying, the food was cold and Turk's arm had fallen asleep. She looked up, teary-eyed and said, "I'm sorry, Turk."

"Don't be sorry, baby. Why don't you eat something?"

"By now dinner must be cold. Light up a joint for me so I can stop shaking. Then I might eat a bite or two,"

Turk lit the joint, and handed it to her. She struggled to put the joint to her lips, unable to hold her hands still. He reached for the joint, placed it to her lips, and said, "Honey, when did this shaking start?"

"A few weeks ago. I can hardly scratch my nose. Some days I can't," she answered as she took two more deep hits. Marijuana was the only thing that seemed to have any positive affect on her symptoms.

"Karen, can we talk about this?"

"What do you mean Turk?"

"About this MS, and how sick you really are."

"Honey, I'm not going to kid you. It's over for me. The disease is going to kill me."

"Aren't you jumping the gun here, Karen? There are a lot of things we can still do, I'm sure."

"Help me downstairs, and you can warm up that dinner you prepared. We can watch the sunset together. Want to?"

"Just like old times, huh?"

"Yeah, Turk, just like old times, without the alcohol. You'll have to carry me."

Turk was stunned that the disease had progressed to the point of Karen not being able to walk. Digger had warned him. Turk cradled her in his arms, and carried her to the patio without saying a word. He went back upstairs, retrieved her dinner, and placed it in the oven alongside Jason's.

"Karen, what does Dr. Lake say about your condition? Is this the MS raising its ugly head, and then going away?" He would get a firsthand report the following day from Dr. Lake.

Muffling a cry, she said, "Unfortunately, he has diagnosed my MS as Progressive, meaning it's only a matter of time, and it will kill me." She burst into tears.

"Come on, Karen, Jason will be here any minute. You don't want him to see you crying, do you?"

"My life is over. I don't want to live this way, Turk. I *can't* live this way." Karen, said, crying even louder.

Growing impatient, and worried the neighbors would think he was beating his wife. He said, "For crissakes, Karen, can't you stop crying long enough for us to talk about this?"

"You don't get it! I want to die! I want you to help me! I don't want to live, period!"

Not accustomed to giving up, Turk couldn't comprehend why she was acting this way. Her life might not be the best from this point on, but there were walking aids, wheelchairs, and they could afford the help necessary for her to enjoy what time she had left. "That's crazy talk, baby. What about Jason? He needs you. I need you. There has to be something we can do."

"I'm no good to you. I'm no good to Jason. I want out, I tell you, I want out!"

Turk didn't know how to deal with Karen. She was bright, she was young, and she was beautiful. He just didn't understand. He hoped Dr. Lake would give him some insight as what to do. But in the meantime, he needed to get Karen back upstairs before Jason saw her like this.

"Honey, I don't want Jason to see you like this. I'm going to carry you back upstairs. You can smoke another joint and I'll get your dinner for you."

"I'll smoke that joint, but I don't want any damn dinner," she said, angrily, further confusing Turk. A minute ago, she was crying hysterically. Now she was angry. He carried her to their bed. By the time she'd finished smoking the joint, she relaxed enough, so that Turk went downstairs.

The GBI had only given Turk a week to get his affairs in order, and then they expected him back in Atlanta. His bail bondsmen wouldn't release him. He claimed the one-hundred-thousand dollar bail would break him if something happened, and Turk didn't return as agreed. So Turk posted a cash bond, so he could get out of Atlanta and travel to Tampa. How in hell was he going to deal with the GBI and Karen, too?

Jason came running in and said, "This is the coolest thing ever, Turk. Want to hear me announcing a football game?"

"Sure." Turk was still in deep thought. Jason flicked on his recorder and sure enough, he had organized a pretend game. The Miami Dolphins beat the Buffalo Bills, twenty-one to fourteen. His friends supplied the cheering in the background and Jason provided the play by play announcements.

"That's real good, Jason. You've got quite an imagination, son. Good job."

"Thanks, what's for dinner? I'm hungry."

"You're always hungry. Pork chops and brownies. Sit right there at the counter, I'll get it for you."

"I love pork chops. After I eat, can I go out and play?"

"Sure, just stay on the beach where I can see you."

"That's what I thought you'd say. My friends are going to meet me out front. Thanks." Jason devoured his dinner and bounced down the steps to the beach running. Turk could see his friends merging toward him. Another pretend football game was probably in the making.

Turk went back upstairs and Karen was asleep. He pulled the covers up, and looked down at her, wondering how he was going to beat this dreadful disease, Multiple Sclerosis. He didn't want to lose Karen; all very selfish, he thought. He then went outside and watched Jason and his friends play real football.

CHAPTER—22

Karen refused to let Turk get one of his high school friends to sit with her while he went about taking care of some business, and meeting with Dr. Lake. Indignant, Karen claimed, "Turk, I really don't need a sitter." Lilly was on a long over due two week vacation.

"I'd be more comfortable if you had one." Turk countered.

Sarcastically, Karen parried, "It's not always about you Turk..."

Giving in, Turk said, "I was just trying to help." He drove Jason to his grandmother's house, and left Karen alone, figuring he wouldn't be gone that long, and she'd be okay.

"How have you been, Turk?" Dr. Lake asked. "It's been a while."

"Things could be better, but at least I have my health."

"I'm sure you're here to talk about Karen."

"I am. All she seems to do is cry. Is that a symptom of the disease?"

"We're not sure. Depression is. That must be why she's crying. You say she cries continually?"

"Since I've been home, she's cried ninety-five percent of the time, and she wants to die."

"How do you mean she wants to die? What makes you think that?"

"She tells the caregiver she wants to die. She tells me she wants to die. She wants me to assist her. I have no idea what to do."

"This isn't unusual. Karen is very smart. She realizes that she will be confined to a wheelchair, and possibly confined to bed for the rest of her life. She probably can't face that. She needs to see a psychiatrist. You'll need some help too. A person with your personality won't be able to cope with a person just giving up. Her MS is at a stage where it will only get worse," Dr. Lake stated in a very calculated way.

"So you're saying, Doctor, she's going to be an invalid for the rest of her life?"

"Unfortunately, Turk, she will be."

"Nothing we can do?" Turk felt like he'd been hit with a hammer. This was all so much to deal with and he only had five days to do it in.

"You both can make the most of it with some professional help. That's your only avenue."

"She won't agree to see a psychiatrist, with or without me."

"Turk, I don't want to sound callus, but I can't do any more than I've already done. I've prescribed her medication to deal with the depression and to help her sleep. I understand her rigidity is lessened by smoking marijuana. There has been some research that claims some success with MS patients smoking marijuana, but it is illegal and I can't recommend it."

"You might not be able to recommend it, and I'm no doctor, but I'll tell you this, it's the only goddamn thing that seems to help her," Turk claimed, visibly shaken.

"Turk, I'll continue to see Karen, but there's not much more I can do. Is there anything else you want to discuss?"

"No, Dr. Lake, there isn't. I've got a lot to deal with. Thanks."

As Turk was driving back to the beach, he wondered how he was going to get back to Atlanta in the time the GBI allotted. How was he going to deal with Karen when he managed to go back? How long would it take him to wind down his business affairs in Atlanta? Where was Niko? And then there was the problem of dealing with Jason. How would he break the news to him and how would he take care of him? Karen was washing her hands of that responsibility, and his father wouldn't do a damn thing. Turk was in a world of shit.

Turk never ran from problems. He knew only one way to deal with tough issues, hit them head on and hard. The first thing he would do was get someone to stay with Karen, full-time. He knew Lilly wouldn't be able to do it, or wouldn't do it as long as Karen didn't want to live and cried all day. It would take a person with a strong sense of duty and compassion. Karen wouldn't be easy to deal with. *Whom could he get?* he asked himself, as he waited for the drawbridge to unfold over the Indian Rocks inland waterway. Maybe there was an in-home care service; something like that. Then, of course, he would have to find a place for Jason...he couldn't take him back to Atlanta; it would be too dangerous. Deep in thought, he pulled into his condo and went upstairs to check on Karen, thinking she might have some ideas.

As soon as Turk entered the bedroom, he could tell something was terribly wrong. On the floor were two empty pill bottles, and Karen's arm and head were hanging over the side of the bed, over a pool of vomit. Turk knew immediately she had overdosed. He turned Karen over and laid her face up on the bed. She was still breathing, but was unconscious. He called the operator, and asked her to send an ambulance. Without thinking, he grabbed the pot, the pipes, and ash tray and hid them in a dresser drawer.

The hospital was only five minutes from the beach. Turk could hear the siren wailing. He rushed downstairs and opened the front door. He'd no sooner returned to the bedroom, when two medics with a gurney rushed upstairs, and gently pushed Turk to one side. They methodically administered oxygen. They gave her a shot of something, loaded Karen onto the gurney, and were out of there in less than ten minutes.

One of the medics asked, "Sir, do you know where the hospital is?"

"I do," Turk replied.

"I think we got here in time…she should be okay. Please go to administration and fill out some paperwork." That was it, nothing more.

"I will." Turk said, in a trance-like state. He collapsed into a chair next to the bed, thinking, *What will I do? What can I do? What will I tell Jason?*

* * *

Staring through another four-inch hole in a glass wall, a woman in administration said, "Mr. Donatelli, your wife is okay, and resting. The attending physician will be out to talk to you. Please take a seat in the waiting area. Before you leave, please come back and see me. We have some paperwork we need to finish."

Turk wondered if this glass cage was bullet proof also, reliving his jail house experience, and answered, "Yes, ma'am. I will…thanks."

Turk was thumbing through a *Sports Illustrated* magazine, not reading it, just going through the motions, still in a semi-daze, when a young ER physician approached him, and asked,

"Are you Mr. Donatelli?"

"Yes."

"Let's go to my office where we can talk. Please follow me."

"Mr. Donatelli, your wife overdosed on her prescribed medications."

"I know. She tried to commit suicide, didn't she?"

"I can't say that. We pumped her stomach. She will be fine. She can be released tomorrow, depending on what the authorities have to say."

"What do you mean *authorities*...what authorities? This is no one's business but ours."

"We have to report any overdose to the Pinellas Police Department. There's a detective waiting to see you."

"Christ, which is exactly what I don't need." Turk, mumbled.

"What'd you say?"

"Do you need me for anything else?" Turk asked, not wanting to repeat what he'd just said.

"No, like I said, your wife will be fine." Turk didn't hear him. He was on his way to see the detective.

"Mr. Donatelli, why do you think your wife tried to commit suicide?'

"Detective, I don't know that she did. It could have been an accidental overdose, you know."

"We both know better, Mr. Donatelli. Were you two having domestic problems?"

"For crissakes no, detective. We get along fine. Look, I need to go take care of our son. Will this take long?"

"We're not going to sign a release until we're sure she'll be okay, and not try this again."

"I appreciate your concern, detective, but is it really any of Pinellas County's business?"

"You're making my job difficult, Mr. Donatelli. Anytime we

feel there's been an attempted suicide, we have to fill out this report. We realize it may be difficult to talk about, but all we're concerned about is your wife, please understand," he said, showing Turk a two page list.

"I'm sorry, I do understand. Fire away. I'll answer all the questions listed on that sheet, best I can."

Turk found that this wasn't the end of the questioning. The authorities were still going to talk to the neighbors, her doctors, and her immediate family to be sure she received the treatment she warranted. Turk felt this was an invasion of his privacy, but he also knew they were trying to help. He wondered how deep they would dig into his background. He had a good reputation in St. Pete; not so in Atlanta.

* * *

Turk had two days to wrap up his affairs in St. Pete. He'd hired a full time nurse. He contacted Digger and made arrangements for him to stay at the condo while Turk went back to Atlanta. Digger was the only one Turk knew who was strong enough of character to handle Karen in a crisis and to be sure the nurse just didn't up and quit.

Turk talked Jason's grandmother on his dad's side into caring for Jason until school resumed in six weeks. Jason knew his mom was sick and needed care. He didn't need to know the details.

Turk met with his bankers to insure that his considerable real estate holdings were in order and his loans were extended. Karen was still adamant about him helping her commit suicide. She cried continually. The crying was driving Turk nuts. Nothing anyone could say or do stopped her from crying. He would be glad to get away from it for a while, but he also felt very guilty about feeling that way. He was three days late getting back to Atlanta.

As Turk stepped off the plane, two Fulton County sheriffs were waiting for him. They read him his rights, loaded him into the back of their Ford cruiser and delivered him to the Fulton County jail. By now, Turk was accustomed to this kind of treatment. He was put into another holding cell. The other inmates in that cell meant nothing to Turk. He wasn't afraid of what they might do; in fact, he put the fear in most of them. He retreated to a corner near the end of the metal bench and said, "Move over mate, I'm sitting down."

The black man looked up at him and said, "You white honky. What makes you think I'm going to move for your white ass?"

Turk grabbed him by the throat, and said, "Don't fuck with me today. I got nothing to lose. Slide the fuck over or get up before I fucking choke you to death."

The inmate clearly didn't want any part of Turk, nor did anyone else in that cell. Not only did he get up and move; the guy next to him cleared out as well. Turk sat there for another three hours, and finally his name was called. He knew the drill. He would be escorted handcuffed, and in leg irons, to either Knight's office or Pettit's, where he would be grilled about Niko, and his so-called criminal enterprises.

"Do you like it here, Donatelli?" Detective Pettit asked.

"Come on, Pettit, what now? I haven't done a thing to deserve this continual harassment, and that's all it is. When are you guys going to stop this shit?"

"You didn't live up to your end of our agreement. You're three days late getting back to Atlanta. So we thought we would bring you to *our house*. We have some questions for you, Donatelli."

"You don't have to arrest me every damn time you want to ask me a question." Turk was seething.

Laughing, Pettit said, "Better us than the FBI."

"Come on, what do want? I've got things I've got to do."

"Have you heard from Niko?"

"No, I haven't, and I don't expect to."

"You're screwing his girlfriend. Niko might not like that."

That explained what Turk felt on his last visit to Cory's office. He knew something, or someone was watching him. The GBI had staked out her house. He guessed he really knew that. Why danger was so intriguing to him, he'd never figured out.

"Get your nuts off watching, did you, Pettit?"

"Don't be a wise ass, Donatelli. You're in no position to be spouting off."

"Look, I don't like getting personal with you assholes, but let me tell you something. My wife just tried to commit suicide. I've got an eleven-year-old-son I need to care for. I'm going to wrap up my operation here in Atlanta, and I'm going back to Florida as soon as I can. So let me the frig out of here so I can do just that."

"I'm sorry to hear about your wife, Turk. I have a son of my own, so I do sympathize, but it's not going to be easy for you to leave Atlanta with as much unfinished business as you have left here," Pettit said, using his first name for the first time.

Detective Knight hadn't said a word until now, "Turk, we hope you can do that. You're in deeper than you think. Our sources tell us Niko's partner is in town, and is going to take over your business, along with Niko's. We've lost contact with him. We need him. He's our only State's witness against Niko."

"He's hooked on drugs and he's not very smart. All he knows is muscle."

"Muscle seems to work in his field," Detective Knight surmised.

"How do you know he's turned on you guys?"

"We can't find him and we aren't able to contact him. Our

sources have him taking over a few of Niko's porno shops. If you have any idea how we can get to him, we need to know. Do you?"

"I don't. The last time I heard, he was on the West Coast somewhere."

"Look, Turk. We need your help. We'll stop harassing you if you're serious about leaving Niko's employment...are you?" Pettit and Knight seemed sincere.

"Okay, guys. First, I don't work for Niko. I'm a real estate developer. But I plan on severing my relationship as quickly as possible. You can count on that."

"Okay, can we trust you to tell us if Niko or Overton contact you?"

"You can. So do we have a deal?"

"We do. You're free to go. Again, we are sorry to hear about you wife, Turk. We knew she wasn't well."

Turk couldn't believe that the GBI, and the FBI, for that matter, would drop the criminal charges against Overton in return for testifying against Niko. Overton was really free to do whatever he needed to do to gain Niko's businesses without worrying about the authorities. In hindsight, they had to regret making the deal they struck with Overton.

Turk went back to his big empty house in North Atlanta. Pop's Security still had men stationed around the perimeter and at the front door. Turk thanked the guard and headed for his well-stocked bar. He needed a drink badly. This would be his first in over a year. Pouring three fingers of Scotch, a splash of water and three ice cubes, he settled down next to his Olympic-sized pool and pondered his precarious situation, when the phone rang.

"Hi, Turk. I'm glad you're back. We need to talk," Cory said.

"I didn't think you wanted to talk to me, Cory."

"Come on, Turk. I was too emotional that day. I'm over it and over you, too."

"Really. When do you want to meet?" She didn't sound too convincing to Turk.

"Both our houses are staked out by the GBI and the damn FBI as far as I can tell. I'll meet you at Friday's in an hour."

"Okay, which Friday's? The one located at I-285 and Roswell Road?"

"That's the one. I'll be there in an hour."

Turk swirled the three ice cubes around in his drink until they disappeared. He set the drink down without taking a sip. He'd passed that temptation. He went to his bedroom master bath, splashed some water on his face, brushed his teeth and combed his hair, slipped on a pair of tan slacks, a polo shirt and a pair of brown penny loafers. He noted the bags under his eyes. He was tired, not having had much sleep in the past week. As soon as his meeting was over with Cory, he planned on taking a sleeping pill, maybe two, and catching up on some needed rest.

"You're late. What took you so long?" Cory asked.

"I had to look good for you, Cory." Turk said, as he looked down at her exposed cleavage.

"What are you looking at now, Turk?"

"Your breasts, Cory, your breasts, that's what I'm looking at." She was a very attractive package and Turk couldn't help but want some more of her. His feelings made him feel guilty.

"Forget it, Turk. We've got some serious shit to talk about." She liked Turk looking at her. She *liked Turk*.

"Before we talk, let me ask you...were you followed here?"

"I was. The GBI follows me everywhere I go. I'm getting used to it."

"I was too. You heard from Niko?"

"Not directly, but I've heard from him through Vera." Niko had conveyed ownership of his adult bookstores and his warehouse operation to Vera Staidly, in hopes of convincing the authorities that he was disassociating himself from the porno industry.

"What's that have to do with me?"

"Vera wants you and me to run Niko's businesses, all of them."

"We can't do that, Cory. They'll lock us up sooner or later."

"Vera offered us two million in cash, that's one for you, Turk, and one for me."

"Wow! Let's say for conversation's sake that we consider the offer. What exactly would we be running?"

"The lawyers tell me that the pornography business is legal now. His recording studios and his other businesses are all legit companies. So in essence, we wouldn't be breaking any laws. We'd be okay."

"I think that's a pipe dream of his. Niko is hoping he'll come out of this somehow and his businesses will be intact and it would be business as usual for him, I bet."

"Why do you think it's a pipe dream, Turk?"

"Simple, the RICO Act will do him in."

"The lawyers think they can beat the RICO Act."

"I think the lawyers are just going to drain what cash Niko's businesses have left and then they'll be gone, along with his money and his businesses. That's what I think."

"How so?"

"My understanding of the RICO Act is that any business funded by a criminal enterprise is subject to be seized by the Feds."

"Again, the lawyers claim that the RICO act is unconstitutional."

"Okay, go with that. Why are you working out of your house, and the GBI is occupying Niko's ten-story office building in downtown Atlanta?"

"Niko turned that building over to them before the lawyers had a chance to thoroughly research the recently enacted RICO Act. Niko also thought it would keep him out of prison if he didn't fight the seizure."

"Okay, I see you're not convinced. Let's do this. We'll analyze each business, get a legal opinion, and then go to the authorities, reveal our plans and see what they say."

"Turk, you've got to be kidding me. Go to the authorities... why?"

"Simple. Do you want to run these businesses looking over your shoulder every minute?"

"Of course not, but telling the law what we're going to do might not be good business."

"It's the only way I'll have anything to do with it."

"All right, let's analyze the businesses over the next few weeks and see if there isn't a deal in there somewhere. I'd like a million dollars, wouldn't you?"

"I would, but not at the expense of going to jail."

"I have to agree."

"Let me ask you something. What about Overton? The GBI tells me he's taking over Niko's porno business. What do we do about him?"

"Vera's aware of Overton. She doesn't seem to be concerned about him. She controls over 400 stores. What few he may be able to take over won't put a dent in the cash flow, she claims."

"I think she needs to be a little more concerned than that. Even though Overton is low-ranking as far as the mob is concerned, they'd rather deal with him than some dike loyal to Niko."

"Why?"

"Overton has always wanted to be the head dog, the big cheese, and he's got just enough knowledge and just enough balls to try and take over Niko's business."

"I know he's trying, but I don't think he'll succeed. Vera will to see to it that he doesn't, I believe. And besides, the mob is probably getting the same cut. Vera wouldn't change that deal."

"We'll see, won't we? Let's talk about us."

"What about us, Turk?"

"I think I know how you feel about me. I know how I feel about you. Can we be lovers?"

"I don't know. I'll have to think about it."

"Fair enough, think about it. I need a few days to think this through. My first thought is that as much as I would like a million in cash, it's not going to work."

"Okay, then you call me when you're ready to discuss this opportunity some more."

"I will, Cory. I'll walk you to your car."

"No, don't do that, Turk. I'll be fine."

Turk felt something was up. There was something Cory wasn't telling him, or something Cory was afraid of, and he felt he needed to be careful, very careful.

* * *

A good night's sleep took care of the bags under Turk's eyes. Jimmy was due to pick him up any moment. First, he'd inspect his projects and then he needed to meet with China Jon. Turk still had to find a replacement for CJ. He would be very hard to replace. He was thinking about creating two positions, one for the airport project mall and one for the industrial park.

Finishing his inspection, Turk headed for CJ's office. Brenda, CJ's assistant, greeted him with a cup of strong black coffee, just the way Turk liked it, and rambled, "CJ isn't here yet and he hasn't called. He's never late. He's always here before I get here, Mr. Donatelli."

"Have you called his apartment?"

"I have, there's no answer," Brenda said, concern written all over her face.

"Brenda, have CJ call me when he gets in. I'll be in my office." Turk felt something was seriously wrong. He hurried out of the office and said to Jimmy, "I've changed my mind. Let's get on over to CJ's apartment and fast."

"Okay, what's up, boss?"

"I got a feeling something isn't right. CJ hasn't showed up for work. Get a move on!"

Twenty minutes later, they pulled into Riverbend, the apartment complex CJ lived in. Lined up in front of his building were four police cars, an emergency vehicle and an ambulance. Turk flew out of the back seat and up the stairs to CJ's apartment, only to be stopped by a policeman.

"Sir, this is a crime scene. You need to go back downstairs."

"Officer, I need to see who is hurt!" Turk said, struggling with the officer who was holding him back.

"You can't go in there. You'll have to wait," the officer said, forcing Turk back down the stairs.

"Officer, my guy didn't show up for work this morning, and he's a close friend. I need to see if it's him that's hurt, please," Turk, begged.

"Sir, I'm not going to tell you again! Get back downstairs or I'll have to arrest you. Now!"

Backing away, trying to see inside China Jon's apartment, Turk saw Pettit through the apartment window. Turk screamed, "Officer, I see Detective Pettit in there. Tell him Donatelli is out here and wants to see him."

"Look, I've had enough of you, mister! I told you to get back downstairs and I mean it!"

"Fuck you! I'm going in." Turk ducked under the officers outstretched arm and burst into the apartment. Detective Pettit turned and immediately recognized Turk, and said, pointing to CJ's body lying lifeless on the floor. "He's one of your workers, isn't he, Turk?"

"Oh my God, it's China Jon." Turk started toward him only to be held back by Pettit.

"Stay back! Forensic isn't finished. When you thought things couldn't get any worse, right, Turk?"

"How'd he die, detective?"

"It looks like he was strangled, after being cut up."

"Cut up, cut where?" Turk couldn't see any cuts.

"There are two deep cuts on the other side of his face, running from his ear to his chin. That didn't kill him. Someone choked him to death. It looks like he put up quite a struggle."

"It was Overton, that bastard...I'll get him!" Turk said, without thinking.

"Overton, you say? How do you figure?" Pettit asked.

"Those two cuts are his calling card."

"How do you know that, Turk?"

"I just know. Overton cut someone else who works for me the same way."

"Okay, Donatelli. We're going to need to talk some more. I'll finish up here and then meet you downtown."

"I'll need a few hours, Pettit. CJ was my very best friend...a great guy. Did you know that?"

"No, I didn't Turk. I'm sorry to hear that. See me sometime this afternoon, not tomorrow...this afternoon, Turk. You got it?"

"Yeah, I got it, detective...this afternoon." Turk was in a daze, thinking, *Can things get any worse?* And he had even been contemplating staying involved with Niko. *Surprising what a million dollars will make you do. I'm one sick puppy.*

Turk got back into the car, and Jimmy asked, "Is that China Jon's apartment, boss?"

"It *was*, Jimmy."

"I'm sorry, boss...I know he was your best friend. He loved you like a brother. He told me so. Where do we go from here?"

"Let's get back to the job site and fast, Jimmy. I've got another gut feeling something is wrong."

As soon as they exited the freeway, Turk could see smoke, lots of it. It was coming from their partially constructed mall. Fire trucks were everywhere. Hoses were running across parking lots; ladders were in the air; police cars and emergency vehicles with sirens blazing were arriving.

"Jimmy, go around back to our offices. We should be able to gain access through that gate." Turk was running on adrenalin. His world was literally coming apart.

Turk approached the doublewide trailers that served as the onsite construction office, where China Jon had worked. He rushed inside, and stopped in his tracks. There, lying head down on her desk, in a pool of blood, was Brenda. Two deep cuts sliced from her ear to her chin were evident.

Turk screamed, "You son-of-a-bitch, Overton, I'll get you if it's the last thing I do." Jimmy was standing behind Turk with his head over a trash can, vomiting. Turk rushed out of the office and went looking for a policeman. Overton had somehow managed to place a tractor-trailer full of fuel in the middle of the mall. Probably blew it up with explosives.

Turk found a police officer and directed him to the trailers where Brenda was. He also asked him to call Pettit on his radio and get him over there, as quickly as possible. Just as he was saying that the gas lines blew sky-high. The second floor of the mall collapsed shortly after that. Turk had to get away. The entire mall was destroyed.

* * *

"Turk, wake up," Cory said, shaking him. "For crissakes wake up, Turk!"

Rising up on one elbow, fully clothed, and looking around, Turk said, "How'd I get here?"

"Jimmy brought you," Cory answered.

"How long have I been here?"

"All night. You were out cold as soon as you lay down."

"Was I drunk?" Turk didn't feel hung over.

"No, as near as I could tell, you were in a state of shock. After all that's happened to you, I can understand why."

"Shit, I was supposed to go downtown to Petites office. I've got to call them." Turk was starting to remember the tragic events of the previous day.

"No need to do that. Detective Pettit and Knight are waiting to see you in my living room."

"Tell them I'll be right out. I need to wash up. I smell like smoke and I feel like shit."

"Making the GBI wait might not be a good idea."

"They'll wait, trust me. I won't be long"

Turk felt safe in a shower. The shower walls made him feel secure. The sound of the water drowned out his thoughts. He wished he could stay in there forever. Finally drying off, he put on the same clothes that he wore yesterday, still smelling of smoke, and entered Cory's make-shift office, her living room.

"Hello, guys. Sorry about yesterday. The events must have knocked me out."

"Turk, where can we talk in private?" Pettit asked, nodding his head toward Cory.

Before Turk could answer, Cory said, "I've got some business to attend to. Lock the door on the way out, or tell security to." She had an appointment with Niko's lawyers.

"Thanks, Cory. I'll call you later," Turk said while taking a seat on the couch.

Detective Knight sat next to Turk, and Pettit sat in a chair next to the couch. Knight spoke first. "Turk, you think Overton is responsible for your friend's and his secretary's death?"

"I'd bet my life on it."

"What makes you so sure?"

"The two deep cuts on CJ's face. You saw the same cuts on his secretary's face."

"We need more than that, Turk. What else you got?"

"He burned my damn shopping center down, too."

"Again what proof do you have that he did?"

"That's his forte...burning down buildings. You know that guys, right? Even though, I didn't think he was smart enough to pull off destroying my mall."

"Where do you think Overton is hiding out?"

"I have no idea, but I'll find the bastard."

"That's our job. If your assessment is right, you're probably next on his list. You and Digger beat him up pretty bad last year. He's probably got it in for you two. By the way, where is Digger?"

"Like I told you, he's in Florida somewhere, I think."

"Donatelli, when are you going to start telling us the truth? We know he's at your condo looking after your wife. Why do you continue to play games with us?" Pettit asked.

"Probably because of the way you two have been treating me. I don't know, self preservation, I guess."

"You claim you want out of Niko's operation. Your best friend is dead. Your mall has been burned to the ground. You've transferred ownership of the apartments to Niko's wife.

The Feds have seized Niko's downtown office building. Your ailing wife is in Florida. You need to get your act together and help us find Niko and Overton," Detective Knight said.

Taking a moment to reflect and to digest what Knight just said, wondering where and how they got their information, Turk said, "I can't add anything to that. You know what's going on better than I do. I don't have any idea where Niko or Overton could be. As thorough as you guys are, you'll find them."

"I hope we find them before they find you, Turk. Are you sure you don't have something else going on with Niko's operation we need to know about? We're not going to be able to keep the FBI off your ass much longer. You need to give us something; come clean if you will," Pettit claimed.

"What makes you think I have more?"

"Well, do you?" Pettit asked.

The only thing that they weren't aware of was the latest offer. Should he tell them about that? Turk took a minute to answer and said, "Cory and I have been offered a million dollars each to continue running the businesses Niko has left."

"Now we're getting somewhere. Just how are you to be paid this million dollars, and by whom, Niko?" Knight asked.

"No, I told you I haven't had any contact with Niko, nor do I know anyone that has. Vera Staidly offered the deal to us, in cash."

"She's the one Niko transferred ownership of his adult bookstores to, isn't she?" Knight continued questioning Turk.

"Yes and his warehouse operations."

"What about his other businesses?"

"His recording studios, his trucking business, and record business are still managed by Cory."

"What is it you and Cory have that Vera Staidly can't do?"

"Vera is strictly adult books stores. Cory is trucking and the other so-called legitimate businesses, and I'm the real estate guy. There's something else going on here. Vera hates me."

"How does she feel about Cory?"

"Cory used to work for her. I think they get along fine."

"Did she accept the offer?"

"No, I don't think so, though she might have and not told me about it"

"How'd you leave it?" Knight queried.

"I told Cory I needed to assess each business to insure that I wouldn't be doing anything that would land me in jail."

"And what was her response?" Pettit asked.

"She kind of agreed."

"Kind of agreed? What do you mean by that?"

"I think there's probably more to it. I think Cory is still loyal to Niko."

"Were you leaning toward accepting the offer?"

"A million in cash is hard to turn down. I'm seriously considering it."

"That would be a mistake, don't you think?"

"The lawyers tell me the porno industry is pretty much legal right now. After all, women are burning their bras and having sex in public. I believe the rest of Niko's businesses are legitimate."

"You're kidding yourself, Turk. It maybe quasi legal now, but it wasn't when Niko built his smut empire. All his other businesses were a product of an illegal one. The RICO Act will sink all of his enterprises, trust me."

"Niko's lawyers tell me they think they can beat the RICO Act."

"Yeah, and they thought they could keep Niko out of jail, too. So, could they? NO! And that's where you're going to end up,

Donatelli, if you don't cooperate with us."

"How do you figure?"

"The FBI is about to take over handling you. If you don't cooperate, they'll nail you to the cross, believe me. You don't want to mess with the Feds. You'll end up going away for a long time. Then what will you do?"

Turk was getting the message. He needed to cut some kind of deal and bail out. "I guess you're right. What do you want from me?"

"Are you willing to work with us?"

"It depends on what you want me to do?"

"Don't do anything right now. We need to discuss Vera's offer with the Feds. They might want you to accept the million dollars and continue working with Cory. We'll get back to you."

"When you say Feds do you mean the FBI?"

"Yes...and the States Attorney's office."

"I don't like this much, you know. I could end up dead or in jail."

"We can keep you out of jail and we'll continue to try and look out for you."

"You've been on my ass for a year now. When will I hear back from you? I'm supposed to get with Cory later this week."

"We'll get back to you in a few days. Now get out of here and get some rest, Turk. You look like shit," Knight offered.

"You might take your own advice. You guys don't look so goddamn good, either."

CHAPTER—23

The detectives left. Cory, back from her appointment, was standing just outside the living room patio door. Turk wondered how much she'd heard and whether or not the room was wired. Damn, he was getting paranoid.

Turk motioned to her to come in. "What did the GBI agents have to say, Turk?"

"The same shit as always. They think you and I know where Niko is. They're not convinced Overton had anything to do with CJ's murder, and burning down the shopping center. They want more proof."

"Who do they think did it?"

"They don't know, but you can bet they think Niko had something to do with it. Do you think he did?"

"No…no…Niko wouldn't do anything like that…would he?"

"How can we be sure, Cory?"

"I'm sure, I am."

"Okay, but I have my doubts. Cory, I've had enough of this day. I'm going to get Jimmy to take me back to my office. Then I've got to return a bunch of phone calls. The insurance company wants to interview me; and according to the GBI detectives, the FBI wants to talk to me. I've got burned down buildings and dead employees. It will take me a week to sort through all this shit. I'll get back to you as soon as I can."

"We need to give Vera an answer soon, Turk. She can't wait a week."

"She'll damn sure have to. You handle her."

"I'll try. If I have a problem, I'll call you. Let me know if I can do anything for you, Turk."

"I will."

* * *

Turk didn't see any sense in continuing to use payphones to call Digger. The FBI obviously had his home phone tapped. The GBI knew where Digger was; if they'd wanted to pick him up, they could have.

"Digger, how's Karen doing?"

"She doing the best she can under her circumstance. The question should be, how are *you* doing? The news accounts reported by the *Atlanta Journal* sure as hell put you in a bad light. Do you think it's Overton or Niko who's after your ass?"

"Digger, I don't know for sure…probably Overton. Cory tells me she's sure it isn't Niko's doings. So much shit is coming down around me, I'm not sure of anything anymore. Have you got things under control there?"

"Yeah… I've hired two caregivers splitting time to take care of Karen."

"Can they handle her?"

"They probably can't, but my girlfriend can."

"I didn't know you had a girlfriend."

"I met her in Miami a few years ago."

"What's she like? What does she do?"

"She's Cuban, great looking, and a damn good cook."

"You say you've known her a couple of years?"

"I actually knew her before that. She was an acquaintance of my best friend, Leggs." Leggs was killed in Miami. He worked security for Turk. His death was reported by the Dade County Narcotic Squad as a drug deal gone bad. Digger felt it was Sammy Lorenzo's doings. Sammy was an under boss of the Miami Beach mob.

"How does she get along with Karen?"

"As good as anyone can. Karen cries all day long. She wants to die. I can't convince her any different."

"Okay, before you put me through to her, I need to call Jason's grandmother, and see how he's doing. Then I'll call you back, and talk to Karen."

"Turk, she insists she won't talk to anyone, not even you."

"I'll be damned. Okay, make arrangements to get to Atlanta as soon as you can. I'll send Jimmy to pick you up at the airport."

"Okay, but what about the GBI? Won't they arrest me?"

"I've taken care of that. I'll tell you about it when you get here."

"If you say so, boss. I'll be there as quickly as I can."

Turk's next call was to Jason's grandmother. "Betsey, how are you doing?"

"I'm doing fine, Turk."

"How's Jason?"

"He's good, but he really wants to see his mother. He wants to know where you are. What do I tell him?"

"Betsey, tell him I'll be home soon. And for heaven sakes, talk to your son, Darrell. After all, he is Jason's dad."

"My son doesn't listen to anything I say."

"All right, I'll call him. Let me speak with Jason."

"He's not here. He's doing his homework with a friend. You

want me to have him call you?"

"No, Betsey, I'll call back. Give him a hug for me and tell him I'll call soon."

"Okay, Turk. What about Karen? How is she?"

"I think she's feeling a little better. She needs more time, that's all." Turk was lying.

"I hope so, Turk. Jason will have to be in school in a few weeks. I won't be able to handle that, you know. I'm too old to be on the road." Betsey was approaching her ninety-first birthday.

"I know, Betsey. I'll call you...bye." The whole family on Jason's dad's side couldn't get out of their own damn way as far as Turk was concerned. He'd call Darrell to see if he could help.

"Darrell, Turk calling. I need your help."

Indignant, Darrell barked, "What gives you the right to ask for my help?" Turk had made it clear on numerous occasions that he felt Darrell was a worthless dad. Darrell would make a date with Jason and then not show up. He signed Jason up for Pop Warner football and never attended a game. He seldom paid his court-ordered child support or ever sent Jason a birthday card. Turk tolerated the way Darrell neglected his son for Karen's sake, maintaining that having two dads was good for Jason.

"Cut the shit, Darrell! You know damn well I think you shirk your duties as a father, but that said, I need you to enroll Jason in school and care for him until Karen is back on her feet."

"Why can't you do it? My wife is jealous of him, you know."

"I'm in Atlanta and have some unfinished business to attend to. Grow some balls and tell your wife tough shit—get over it."

"If what I've read is true, you're about finished in Atlanta. My wife is God fearing. I can't talk to her that way," Darrell mocked.

"Darrell, we don't need to get into a pissing contest. Will you take care of our son until I can make other arrangements or not?"

"What do I tell Jason this is all about?"

"Tell him the truth. His mom is sick, and she needs time to get better, and I've got pressing business to attend to in Atlanta. Or lie. You're pretty damn good at that, too." Turk couldn't help but get the last dig in.

"My wife is pregnant with our second child. If I take Jason in, I won't be able to do it for very long."

"How long can you?"

"Three months at most."

"Okay, I'll make my plans accordingly. Oh, and Darrell, you better treat him right. If I hear of any mistreatment by you or your new wife, I'll come down on your ass." When Jason had visited Darrell during the summer school break, his wife was working the boy to death, mowing the lawn, weeding the garden, and cleaning the house. They hardly ever took him anywhere or did anything with him.

"You want me to take care of Jason, and now you're threatening me!" Darrell knew that he better do as Turk asked or he'd get the shit kicked out of him. Turk had done it once before. He'd had it coming.

"I'll send Jason some money and I'll be checking on him and *you*. It's going to kill me to say this, but thank you, Darrell. Bye."

* * *

"Turk, this is the local FBI Director, Agent Buck Morley. Buck, meet Turk Donatelli," Detective Knight said, making the introductions.

"Do I call you Buck or Agent Morley?" Turk asked, extending his hand.

"It doesn't matter to me…either one. Can I call you Turk?"

"Please do." Buck had a firm handshake while looking Turk square in the eyes. There was something about him that Turk liked.

"Detective Knight and Pettit briefed me on the deal that was offered to you. A million bucks in this day and age is a lot of money. What made you want to cooperate with us, Turk?"

"When I got involved in Niko's Atlanta businesses a few years ago, I was handling his real estate deals. Over time, these projects, through my own stupidity, have turned into what you guys call criminal enterprises. Whether I agree with that assessment or not, really doesn't make any difference…does it?"

"No it doesn't. Pornography is illegal, pure and simple."

"I obviously don't agree with that for the same reasons Niko has spelled out publically, and in court many times. But like you just said, Buck, it doesn't matter how I feel. What does the FBI want me to do?"

"We want you to accept the offer made to you."

"You mean take the million, and join Cory in running Niko's empire, or what's left of it?"

"Yes, that's what we want you to do," Buck was quick to state.

"I've got a lot on my plate, Buck. I have a very sick wife I need to care for. I have a young son to raise. I have a shopping center to rebuild and Overton is killing off my people. How can I be any good to the FBI?"

"Quite frankly, Turk, we want Niko. He's made a fool of us. We find him and the rest will be easy."

"What about Overton?"

"We're not worried about him. We'll get him. He's not very smart. It's Niko we want."

"And you think I can help?"

"If you accept Cory Doran's offer, in time Niko will surely show himself. When he does, you let us know and the rest of your problems are history."

"It was Vera Staidly who made the offer, not Cory," Turk corrected.

"We believe Vera is taking instructions from Cory."

"I didn't get that impression. How do you figure?"

"That's not important. What is important is, having someone inside to feed us information so we can get to Niko. We figure you can help us do that."

"If I do, what do I get in return?"

"We'll keep you from going to prison."

"You mean you will indemnify me from any and all involvement in his so-called criminal enterprises?" Turk knew he was in way in over his head now. Between the FBI and the GBI, he didn't stand a chance. He needed to cooperate and get the hell out of Atlanta, if he could.

"That's what we mean. There will be certain conditions that will apply."

"Here we go, Buck. Those conditions will kill me."

"Look, Turk, this isn't your first run-in with the law. We're aware of your past Miami Beach Mob connections and you busting that building inspector. You've been as damn near that element as can be. You've crossed the line this time and we're offering you a way out."

"It doesn't look like I have any choice, does it?"

"You always have choices...it's just that some are better than others."

"I've heard that before. I want to bring Digger to Atlanta. I need him around me for protection; protection the FBI or the GBI won't be able to offer."

"Don't under estimate us, Turk, but if you'll feel more comfortable with your man around, we don't have a problem with that."

"I'll need to go to Florida and deal with family issues."

"Okay, just keep us informed."

"What about my Atlanta real estate? Am I going to be able to keep ownership of that?"

"Come on, Turk, you know better. The State or the Feds will end up with most of the real estate, including Niko's other enterprises."

"What about the construction loans I've guaranteed personally? How do I deal with those?"

"That, you need to work out. You'll get an insurance settlement and you'll have a million in cash. Won't that cover your debt?"

"I don't know. It's pretty generous of the FBI to let me keep the million, though."

"We didn't say you could keep it, Turk. We said you could use it to clean up the debt. If you don't use it for that purpose, it will be forfeited along with the rest of Niko's holdings."

"Do I need a lawyer to write all this up?"

"That's your decision."

"In the past, the States Attorney's office wrote up a letter of indemnification. Can't we do the same in this case?"

"We have to do that anyway, Turk. It's being prepared as we speak."

"Pretty damn sure of yourself weren't you, Buck?"

"We want Niko, and you're going to help us get him."

"I suppose. Get me that letter and let's get on with it."

* * *

Niko pulled into Wendy's and parked in front of the payphone booth. It was approaching the time to call Vera

Staidly. Vera, concealed in the back of one of her delivery trucks, was driven to a designated payphone waiting for Niko's call. She had no idea where he was hiding out. She'd received her instructions written on a note pad she found on her desk, with dates, and times to be at certain phone locations to receive calls from Niko.

* * *

Niko asked, "Vera, do you know where Overton is?"

"I have no idea. How are you, Niko?"

"I'm fine. Did you offer Turk and Cory our deal?"

"I did."

"Did they accept?"

"Cory has, Turk hasn't...at least, not yet."

"Does Cory think he will?"

"She thinks he probably will."

"How's our cash flow?"

"It could be better, Niko. Overton has interrupted some of it."

"What do you mean...interrupted?"

"He's collecting the revenue from four of what he claims are his stores."

"That little bastard...I'll deal with him as soon as we figure out where he is."

"I'm working on it."

"Good. I've got plenty of cash. You need to get some to my family."

"I've done that. I understand Turk transferred ownership of the apartments to your wife."

"He did after I paid the asshole over a million dollars. I hope I can clear up my mess before the Feds take those too."

"How are you planning on doing that, Niko?"

"I've got to take care of Overton, and then I'll turn myself in."

"You think that will work?"

"For crissakes, Vera, I wouldn't be doing it if I didn't think so."

"Okay, okay, Niko. I've got the FBI and the GBI all over my ass. They arrest me and my managers once a damn week. What am I supposed to do about that?"

"Isn't that what I'm paying those damn lawyers for?"

"They say they need to talk to you, Niko. Will you talk to them?"

"I can't right now. Tell them I'll make contact when it's time to turn myself in."

"All right, I will. Be careful, Niko. I worry, you know."

"Don't worry, Vera. I'll be fine. Just find out where Overton is before the law finds him. I'll call you the day after tomorrow. You still have my instructions, don't you?"

"Of course I do."

* * *

In two days, Turk reached an agreement with the insurance company. They agreed to pay off his construction loans to the banks for the vertical construction only. He still had to deal with the mortgage on the land and the infrastructure. The clean-up was well under way. The only thing salvaged was the concrete foundation and some underground utilities. The city of Atlanta wanted him to rebuild. Turk was weighing his options.

The States Attorney and the FBI had written a letter of indemnification for Turk that had him handcuffed. The basic agreement stated that if Turk did what they asked him to do, and told them everything he knew, he would not be prosecuted for anything he might have done. Any breach of those terms meant that Turk would be charged with aiding a criminal enterprise. What real estate holdings he had left would be seized, thanks to the RICO Act.

* * *

Turk had a meeting set with Cory for 1:00 that afternoon. Jimmy had picked up Digger the day before at the airport.

"Digger, it's time we headed for Cory's place."

"Ok, boss. I'll bring the car around. Will Deon be there when we arrive?"

"I don't know for sure. He wasn't there the last time I met with Cory. We'll find out, won't we?"

"We will," Digger said, with a slight grin.

"Don't go tangling touchholes with him, Digger. Remember we're on the side of the law now."

"That doesn't stop me from wanting to beat up on him again."

"I know, Digger, but please restrain yourself." Turk felt Digger wouldn't do anything out of line. He knew what was at stake for both of them...FREEDOM.

Waiting at the entry to Cory's driveway was Deon and one other security guard. Turk rolled down the window and said, "What do we owe this pleasure to, Deon?"

"Don't be a wise ass, Donatelli, Cory is waiting for you. Your goon here will have to wait outside." Digger bristled at that comment.

"Be careful, Deon. You know what happened to you the last time you mixed it up with Digger, don't you?"

"He was lucky. It wouldn't be the same outcome today."

"You two don't need to provide those FBI agents across the street with any entertainment, do you?" Turk asked, laughing.

"I'd like to," Deon sneered. "Get on out of here, Turk. Digger, you need to stay in the car."

Cory was waiting for Turk. She was dressed so damn sexy

that Turk did a double take, and said, "Cory, why are you dressed like that?"

"Like what? Don't you like the way I'm dressed, Turk?" she asked very seductively.

"You look like a high-class hooker. You got plans or something?"

"I plan on sealing our deal, Turk."

"How do you know I've accepted the deal offered?"

"You need the million in cash, that's why."

"Okay, I'll go with that...now what?"

"Now we need to officially seal it." Cory said, as she reached behind her and let her red hair fall to her chest.

"Oh no, not now Cory...the goddamn FBI is right across the street! You're as crazy as a shit-house rat."

"Oh yes, now, Turk. I want you right now, and you know how I like it." Turk looked around. Cory had drawn all the drapes.

"We can't do it right here in your living room, can we?"

"No one will see us." Cory was now peeling away her blouse. Her small, but taut breasts stood straight out.

Turk was turned on, and said, as he stripped off his clothes, "You bitch. Is this part of the deal?"

"It is and it will be, Turk. Now spank me, and spank me hard!" she said while taking off her skirt. She now stood naked in high heels, garter belt and net stockings.

Turk, still sitting down was looking at her waist. He reached behind her and grabbed the cheeks of her butt, and pulled her toward him, burying his face in her vulva. He bit down on the lips surrounding her clit and threw her onto the couch. He then slid up to her erect nipples and bit down on one then the other. Cory cried out, "Harder, Turk harder!"

Turk wasn't accustomed to masochistic love making, but it

was turning him on. He turned her over and slapped her buttocks until they were red. Cory was squirming about in his lap. Turk could feel her love juices flowing down his leg. He grabbed her hair and flipped her over, forcing her down to his erection. He penetrated her mouth while holding the back of her head. He then stood and worked his penis in and out until he exploded, still holding the back of her head. He pulled out and Cory gasped for air. Turk turned her over, and pushed her head into the back of the couch and inserted three fingers, while pinching her breasts. He worked his hand around until he had four fingers inserted while his other hand continued to twist her nipples. Cory screamed out, "Fuck me now, Turk, fuck me!"

Turk withdrew his fingers and said, "Not yet, Cory. I'm going to tease you now. I'm going to make you beg for it." He flipped her over on her back, grabbed both her cheeks and brought his face full-force on the lips of her vulva and sucked. He felt her clit get hard and he bit down on it. Cory screamed and bucked hard. "Do it now, Turk. Please fuck me now!"

Turk flipped her over again and rammed home his throbbing penis. He grabbed her waist with one hand and her hair with the other and pulled her toward him, violently penetrating her deeper. They both reached a powerful climax and collapsed on the couch.

A few minutes passed, and Cory said, "You've learned a few tricks since our last encounter. You know how to please me now, Turk. Welcome aboard...this seals the deal. By the way, I have this on film."

"You bitch! Did Niko put you up to this?"

"Let's just say it's my insurance policy that you will continue to work with me, and by the way, service me."

"This might backfire on you, Cory. What if Niko gets a

copy?"

"I'm not worried, Turk. Should you be?" There was something in her tone that concerned Turk. He would be extra careful around her from this point on.

* * *

Now that Niko felt he had Turk under control, Cory and Deon could steer his other businesses away from Overton's grasp, while Turk was cleaning up his real estate deals. All he needed to do now was find Overton and dispose of him.

Soon after Niko escaped from prison, he was immediately placed on the "FBI's Ten Most Wanted" list. Word got to the FBI that Niko had contacted old associates in the mob, and arranged for a contract to be put on Overton's life as revenge for his betrayal. Overton became one of the most sought-after gangsters in America, as word spread to every wiseguy and gunman that an "open contract" had been placed on him—in other words, no specific hitman was tasked with the job; whoever could prove they killed Overton would receive a substantial reward.

Overton turned State's witness after he was arrested during a routine traffic stop; Naylor ran a stop sign. Overton was screaming at Naylor, "You goddamn fool! We've got guns and drugs in this goddamn car and you run a fucking stop sign! You're a fucking idiot, Naylor, a fucking idiot!"

As the police officer approached the car, Overton was sliding the guns and drugs under the seat. The officer noticed the flurry of activity in the front seat, and said to Naylor, "You just ran a stop sign, sir. May I see your license, registration and proof of insurance?" A routine request when stopped for any traffic violation.

As Naylor fumbled for those, he said, "Officer, I didn't mean to, I really didn't. I thought I stopped, I really did."

The alert officer noted how nervous Naylor was and said, "Step out of the car, please...both of you."

"Why, officer? We haven't done nothing. Here's my license and stuff," Naylor stammered. He was so nervous; he dropped them on the ground.

The officer suspected that they were hiding something, so he ordered, "Both of you get out of the car and put your hands on the trunk where I can see them." As Overton and Naylor complied, the officer radioed for back-up. He could hear Overton still cussing out Naylor. "Naylor, I'm fucking going to kill you when this is over! You're the biggest fucking idiot in the world!"

After searching the car, the officers found a small cache of guns, an ounce of marijuana, some amphetamines and a small bag of what looked like heroin. Overton and Naylor were booked on charges of possession of stolen weapons, transporting stolen property across state lines, and possession of illegal drugs. Conviction meant a long stretch in federal prison. Sensing a potential breakthrough in their investigation of Pappas, the FBI got involved, offering Overton leniency in exchange for his help in bringing down Niko. Believing that he was too low-ranking to expect much assistance from the mob, Overton agreed to turn state's evidence.

During the next year, Overton helped the FBI in building charges against Pappas, and claimed in a sworn affidavit that Pappas had given him an order to set fire to Nat Ballard's adult book store. He further revealed that he was acting as a backup when Pappas murdered Leroy Gates, an adult book store manager just for asking for a pay raise. The FBI also learned from Overton, in exchange for complete freedom, about crimes never linked to Pappas, including the bombing of one of Niko's competitors, and his extortion of a small-time pornographer in

Arizona.

Nicholas J. Pappas was convicted of conspiracy to commit arson and distribution of obscene materials; Overton personally testified against his former partner. Pappas was sentenced to six years and six months in prison. While appealing, and out on bail, Pappas received word that the IRS had teamed up with the FBI to investigate him for fraud. Pappas was indicted in South Carolina on racketeering and transporting pornography across State lines, thanks largely in part to Overton's testimony.

CHAPTER—24

"Cory, do we rebuild the shopping center or do we wait?" Turk asked.

"Niko...I mean...I think we should wait." A slip by Cory just reinforced Turk's suspicions that she was somehow in communication with Niko. He let the comment slide.

"That's fine with me. I'll need another million-three to clean up the debt. Can you arrange for that?"

"I'll get with Vera and see what I can do."

"After I pay off the loans, who do you want me to transfer the title to?" This was a leading question the FBI had programmed Turk to ask.

"First, let me see if I can get the money and then I'll let you know who we want to hold title." Cory was stalling for time; she needed to find out from Niko. She wasn't in direct contact with Niko. She received her orders from Vera and sometimes Deon. She still didn't know Niko's whereabouts.

"Cory, let me ask you something. Where do you think Niko is hiding out?" Another question Turk was instructed to ask. The FBI wired Turk just about every morning before he left his house, with questions to ask, depending on whom he met with. Turk's biggest worry was being frisked by Deon, or Cory asking him to make love to her. He was in a constant state of alert. The pressure he felt was starting to wear him down.

"I've told you a dozen times, Turk, I have no idea where Niko is. Why do you keep asking me?"

"Don't kid me, Cory. I think you know damn well where he is." Another scripted response posed by the FBI.

"I don't. But I ask you again. Why do you want to know?"

"It would be a lot easier for us to do our job if we could somehow have direct contact with Niko." Yet another stupid scripted remark. The FBI had idiots working for them too.

"Drop it, Turk. We don't need to know." Cory was growing impatient with Turk's digging questions.

"Okay, okay. What else do we need to do?"

"You need to complete the clean up of the shopping center site and finish the construction of the last four buildings in the industrial park. How long will that take?"

"The clean up will be finished in another couple of months. The industrial park will take another six to eight months. What about you? What are you going to be doing?"

"Mostly, I'll be meeting with Niko's lawyers. Vera seems to have her end of it covered."

"Just what is her end of it?"

"For crissakes, Turk, you're asking a lot of needless damn questions. What's got into you anyway?"

"I'm just trying to protect my ass. I don't want to end up in jail." Turk felt he better stop questioning Cory for now.

"I've told you a million times, you're just a real estate developer. You have nothing to worry about."

"Yeah...right. Look, I've got to make a trip to Florida. Are you good with that?"

"How long are you going to be gone?"

"I don't know for sure. A week or two, I suppose."

"When would you leave?"

"I'd planned on flying out of here the day after tomorrow."

"All right, but you'll have to do one thing before you go, Turk." The sound of Cory's voice and her seductive look told Turk what that would be.

Worried that she would want to be serviced, and discover the tape recorder, Turk said, "Sorry, not today, Cory, but I'll see you at ten in the morning. Until then, think about what I'm going to do to you." So as not to add to her film collection of them making love, Turk was going to force her into her rather large closet to be mauled over and made love to.

"I'll be ready, Turk. I'll have a surprise for you. Be prepared."

"Hell, Cory, I don't need any more surprises. I might have a heart attack!"

"I think you might be able to handle what I have in store for you, Turk. See you tomorrow morning…bye," she said, as she licked her lips and flashed him a sexy look.

Turk could hardly control his desires in spite of the ever-present danger. "Tomorrow it is. See ya."

* * *

"What do you think is going on with Cory, Turk.?" Agent Morley asked.

"I think she's communicating with Niko."

"Do you feel she's having direct contact or through an intermediary?"

"Your guess is as good as mine. You've listened to the tapes, haven't you?"

"We have. We caught her slip just like I'm sure you did. We need to find out before you leave for Florida. How do you suppose we do that?"

"I'd shadow Vera and Deon."

"We're doing that."

"I figured you were. I think Cory is taking directions from Vera. I don't think Cory has direct contact with Niko. Maybe Deon Gates is playing a part as well."

"What makes you think that?"

"Deon appeared out of nowhere. He was gone for a few weeks. He's as close to Niko as Cory is; not as close as Vera, but close."

"Damn it, we've got to locate Niko!" Agent Morley said in desperation.

"He'll turn up, Buck. He'll turn up," Turk said, sensing Buck's frustration.

"What makes you so damn sure, Turk?"

"It's Niko's nature. He loves the spotlight. He wants Overton more than the FBI does. You find Overton, shadow him for a while, and Niko will show up."

"You might have something there. We think we know where Overton may be. With Overton out of the way, Niko could beat the charges against him now, with the exception of the escape charges. He'd be out in three to five years easy. Okay, go to Florida, but stay in contact."

* * *

Overton owned an old farm house in rural Roswell. The city of Roswell was located just outside of North Atlanta between Alpharetta and Sandy Springs. He'd purchased the house when he got into selling drugs in large quantities to support his own habit five years before. It was a secluded location. A half-mile-long dirt road led to the little farm house. There were three outbuildings that Overton used to store stolen cars, drugs, and goods stolen from high-jacked trailer trucks.

Overton went to a great deal of expense to conceal his farm.

There were no utility bills. The buildings were powered by a series of gas generators. Water was supplied by a deep well. Sewer was supplied by a septic tank system. He kept traffic going in and out to a minimum, mostly accessed late at night with the lights turned off. The windows were covered with blackout shades. He was very selective about whom he let come and go. Overton and Naylor had committed several murders of Niko's competitors on the farm. Their remains were dunked into a vat of acid.

Cliff Overton now controlled about fifty of the four hundred stores under Vera Staidly's watch. The money was collected by a runner, who, in turn, would meet Naylor, who then would convey the cash to Overton. He would bundle the mob's cut and send another runner to New York with it. The mob didn't really care who they got the money from, Vera or Overton. It made no difference as long as they got their cut. Niko was aware of what was going on, and the effort to find Overton was increased.

* * *

"Deon, are you sure you've checked everywhere?" Niko asked.

"I've checked every place Overton has ever been known to frequent. I've beat up ten book store operators and they all claim Overton's hired muscle collects the money. They have no idea where he is or what to do. They're as tired of the suspense as we are."

"He can't stay undercover forever. Between us, we should be able to figure out where the hell he is, don't you think?"

"You'd think."

"How's Cory doing?"

"I think she's doing Turk."

"I know she is. He's tough to control. Do you think he's

really on our side?"

"Boss, you know damn well I don't."

"Don't worry about him. Turk should be finished with my projects in a few months and then I'll turn you loose on him."

"I can't wait...the sooner the better."

"Here's a list of what I want Cory and Vera to do. I've written it in a half assed code. I don't have a lot to do during the day," Niko said, chuckling.

"You doing okay boss...you need anything?"

"I'm fine. I got everything I need, except Overton."

"We'll find him, boss...we will."

"I hope so for my sake. I've got to get out of here before someone recognizes me."

Deon and Niko left the Pancake House parking lot.

* * *

Turk's trip to Florida convinced him he needed to bail out as quickly as he could. Karen was getting sicker and Jason needed his attention and care. Karen would not talk about anything other than that she wanted Turk to help her commit suicide. She wouldn't discuss Jason or their relationship; she simply didn't want to live anymore. She had zero desire to live. Turk could not convince her any differently nor could the psychiatrist.

Turk met with her doctors and all they offered was that patients inflicted with MS become depressed. Turk could understand depressed, but he couldn't understand nor would he accept suicide. His brother committed suicide when he was twenty-one. He would care for Karen as long as he could. Jason was another matter. He'd have to learn to be a mother and a father; something he didn't know if he could do.

Even more distraught than when he had left, the flight back to Atlanta was short. Digger met him at the gate with more bad news. "Turk, your house has been burned to the ground."

"You've got to be shitting me, Digger. When did this happen?"

"Last night."

"With all the damn security, the GBI and the FBI, how in hell did someone get in there and burn the damn house down?"

"I guess because you were gone, the GBI and the FBI, pulled off their watch. Pop's two guards were shot in the back of the head."

"Well, ain't this some shit? When will it ever end?"

"It's got to be Overton, don't you think?"

"Christ, who else could it be?"

"I don't know...could it be Niko who's doing this?"

"I don't see why he would, do you?"

"It's a good way to get rid of you and to divert attention from him. I don't know, I'm just guessing."

"This is so unreal. I should have listened to Karen a long time ago. What an asshole I am."

"I wouldn't be so hard on yourself, boss. You were doing what you felt was best at the time. We all make mistakes."

"Yeah, you're right there, Digger. I just seem to make bigger ones."

"The FBI wants me to drive you to their office. I promised them I would to save you the embarrassment of them waiting for you at the airport. You good with that?"

"It doesn't look like I have any choice does it? Let's go."

* * *

"Turk, you need to start pressing Cory harder. We need to get Niko and stop this destruction," Agent Morley said.

"Just how do you suppose I do that, Buck? I've done everything you've asked me to do."

"We know damn well you're screwing Cory. You should be

able to get some kind of hint where Niko could be. We don't think you're trying hard enough, Turk. You know the consequences if you don't step it up." Buck was as agitated as Turk. He'd gotten orders from the top to pressure Turk Donatelli more. He felt sorry for him.

"Consequences, my ass! What more can I do? You tell me and I'll do it."

"When's the last time you talked to Cory?"

"Just before I left."

"Not while you were in Florida?"

"Buck, you know damn well I haven't talked to her. The FBI has every damn phone in this town tapped. Come on now."

"Ok, you go meet with her and press for some information about Niko's whereabouts. You've got to give us something, Turk. I can't protect you forever, you know."

"You're not doing a very good job now, are you?"

"You're still alive, aren't you? You could be dead." Buck didn't like treating Turk this way. But his bosses were desperate for some answers.

"Yeah, no thanks to you," Turk said sarcastically.

"Go see Cory and report back to me."

"Do you mind if I find a goddamn place to stay first? You seem to forget between my wife, my business, and now my house...I'm done here in Atlanta. I'm about to leave town whether the FBI likes it or not."

"You do that and you'll go to jail. Need I say more, Donatelli?" Buck was as desperate as Turk. They had to locate Niko.

"You've said quite enough, Buck. And I've had about all I can take. It's about over for me. I'll give it one more attempt." Turk was resigned to help. But how could he?

* * *

"How was your trip, Turk?" Cory asked.

"Okay, under the circumstances, I guess."

"Turk, Vera has the money to pay off the balance of the loan on the shopping center."

"That's good news. Who do I transfer ownership to?" Maybe Turk was closer to getting out of Atlanta than he had thought he was.

"The lawyers are drawing up the papers now. They should be ready in a few days."

"What about the industrial park? How do we handle that project?"

"The same way…Vera will pay those construction loans off as well."

"Isn't Niko concerned about the RICO Act? He's putting out all this money and in the end; the Fed's will seize his assets."

"The lawyers tell us different."

"So you *are* in contact with Niko? He's still calling the shots, isn't he?"

"I'm telling you one more time. I've had no contact with Niko, and if I did, what concern is it of yours?"

"I don't want to go to prison, that's my concern. You're getting your instructions from someone other than Vera, I know that."

"Turk, what more do you want for crissakes?"

"Well, for one, you haven't even mentioned my damn house burning down. Do you know who did that?"

"You know I don't…probably, Overton's gang."

"Cory, you better be leveling with me. If I find out you're bullshitting me, there will be hell to pay."

"Why would I bullshit you, Turk?"

"To protect Niko, that's why?"

"You think I still have feelings for Niko, the way I've been fucking you? How can you think that?"

"He's probably in on it, too."

"What do you mean by that remark?"

"I think he put you up to it. He probably thinks that you screwing me will keep me around longer. Shit, I don't know."

"You're right, you don't know. You need to get to the lawyer's office and finish the transfer of the real estate. Then the only thing you have left to do is finish the four buildings in our industrial park. Then you can go back to Florida."

"Pretty callus, Cory. What about us?" Turk mocked.

"There's no us anymore, Turk." As much as she cared for Turk, Niko had made it clear that their romance, if it could be called that, was over.

"It's that easy for you, huh?"

"That easy, Turk. It was fun, but it's over between us."

Turk sensed a sound of regret in Cory's voice. "I should be able to wrap up the construction in another two months. Then I suppose I'm unemployed. Is that right?"

"That's right, Turk. From now on, you'll report to me through Deon." Niko also made it clear that there would be limited contact between Cory and Deon.

"That will be the day. I simply won't do that. I'll finish what I have to finish, but I'm not going to deal with Deon."

"You'll just have to. I've got work to do. Goodbye." Cory was sad to see their affair end. She really cared for Turk.

Turk left, shaking his head, wondering what was going to happen next. "Digger, we need to find Niko."

"Shit, Turk, if the FBI can't find him, how are we going to?"

"Niko is somehow communicating with Vera, and Deon. The FBI and the GBI have followed them day and night. But somehow, Niko is getting to them. We need to figure out how."

"I want you to tail Deon for a while and see if you can figure out how Niko and he are communicating."

"What about you? What if Overton comes after you?"

"As many agents that are on my ass, I should be okay. I'm going to book into the Royal Coach hotel for now. I'll be careful."

"I've got some ideas I want to check out anyway. I'll leave you off at the Royal Coach." Digger was concerned for Turk. He wanted them to get out of Atlanta before one of them turned up dead.

CHAPTER—25

Niko watched the grey squirrels scurry about the hardwoods gathering their winter stock. The ground cover was damp. The sun was just breaking its way through the tree tops. This was his third day setting up his station. He could view Overton's front door from his perch. His leg and hip throbbed. An impatient man, Niko wasn't having any luck locating Overton. No one had entered or exited the farm. Maybe Overton wasn't going to show.

Deon, through one of the downtown drug dealers, got word that Overton and Naylor could be hiding out there. Why Deon hadn't thought of that earlier was a mystery. Deon remembered when Overton bought that farm five years ago. He reported the possibility to Niko, and Niko, in turn, set up vigilance on a ridge overlooking the complex of buildings.

Toting, his 30-0-06 rifle, water, and other provisions a half-mile through the woods was difficult for Niko. What kept him going was his determination to kill Overton so he would escape going to prison for life. He hurt so much after each trip into the woods that he had to take extra pain medication. The pills made him fall asleep one afternoon. He didn't know what woke him up, but he shook his head, and below, he observed some activity. It was getting dark and hard to make out who was entering the farm house, but there were two men visible. He trained the six-power scope on them, but couldn't make out who they were, just as they disappeared into the barn.

Niko was wide awake now. The adrenalin made him forget some of his pain. He sat in a prone position hoping to see Overton in his scope. After about thirty minutes, he realized that his perch on the ridge just wasn't going to work. There were simply too many trees in the way for a clear shot, and if he missed, he might not get another opportunity. He needed to rethink his plan. Niko was encouraged by the activity below, even though he didn't know who it was. But he had to believe that Overton and Naylor would show themselves sooner or later. He would keep his watch for now.

"Gerri, did Russ get me the shotgun?" Niko asked. Russ O'Hare was the retired police officer in Niko's pocket.

"Yeah...what do you need with a shotgun, Niko?" Gerri, his high school sweetheart, was worried about Niko.

"I need it for my own protection, Gerri. You don't need to know."

"Will I see you tonight?" Gerri had only slept with Niko twice since his escape. She was blinded by her love for him.

"Yes, I'll see you tonight. Bring the shotgun with you."

"I can't wait!" Gerri was happy with anticipation.

* * *

Gerri knocked lightly on the garret's entry door. Niko peered through the peep hole and seeing her, opened the door, put his arms around her and said, "Gerri, I've missed our time together."

"I've been waiting for this for weeks now."

"Waiting for what, Gerri?"

"Wanting you to make love to me, Niko."

Gerri was medium height, pretty, slightly overweight, middle-aged; a woman with a pent-up desire for her old classmate. She wasn't Niko's type. He liked his women young, and beautiful, but he also knew how important Gerri was for his freedom. He would make love to her this evening as he would many more evenings to come to insure her allegiance.

Taking the double-barrel shotgun from her hands and a box of double-odd-buck ammunition from the other, he placed them on the kitchen table and led her to the bedroom. Niko wasn't much of a lover. He was much more interested in his own gratification than his partner's. It was pretty much all about Niko. He never really worked at satisfying his women. Most were intoxicated by his reputation, money and power.

"Gerri, take your clothes off!" Niko demanded. That was about as romantic as he would get.

Seductively peeling off her clothes, Gerri stood naked in the dim light. Niko sat on the edge of the bed and motioned her to come to him. He put his arms around her and pushed her to her knees. The years had taken a toll on Gerri. Her breasts sagged, her stomach stuck out, and her thighs were thick. But she was experienced and she brought Niko to a climax in short order. He, in turn, gently raised her to the bed, laid her on her back, and penetrated her. He started to pump and then the pain was too much for Niko; he made no apologizes. He rolled over on his back and said, "Gerri, you'll have to get on top." The trips into the woods had taken their toll on Niko.

Gerri straddled Niko, and guided him into her. Niko wasn't large, but Gerri was so much in love that any kind of contact was all she needed. She started rocking up and down and Niko was in so much pain, he went limp. He said, "I'm sorry, Gerri. I hurt too much."

Gerri rolled over and said, "Niko, I understand. I'm sorry"

"Don't be sorry, Gerri. Why don't you masturbate? I'll watch. I want to see you reach a climax."

"Are you sure, Niko? I've never done it while a man watched."

"I'm sure, Gerri. It would please me," Niko said, as he reached over, and opened the dresser drawer, bringing out an eight inch dildo.

"I've never...I've never...." Gerri said.

"Come on, Gerri, you'll like it. Slide up in the bed and I'll make you feel good." One of his turn-ons was masturbating women. He knew all the right spots to bring them to a climax.

Gerri slid up. Niko placed two pillows behind her back and said, "Now spread your legs, Gerri...spread them wide."

Niko was getting hard again. He slid the tool into her vagina and worked it back and forth at the same time he massaged her breasts. Gerri started to moan; she liked what was happening. She lost her inhibitions and began to thrust her hips up and down as Niko pressed the tool deep into her. She screamed as she reached a climax and Niko rolled over and she rose and guided his penis into her. She was totally satisfied as Niko knew she would be.

* * *

Deon parked his car in front of the warehouse. Vera was waiting for him in her office.

"You think you've located Overton, Deon?" Vera asked.

"I think so. I don't know if Niko has seen him yet or not. I'll know after my meeting today. Is everything set?"

"Yeah, you'll go out concealed in the back of the sixth delivery truck this morning. I'll give you instructions just before you leave. You have to meet him in person this time. I've parked two cars at two different locations. Be sure you're not tailed. You know you'll probably be followed when you leave here."

"I'm not worried about losing a tail. I can handle that, but why am I meeting Niko in person? Isn't that being a little reckless?"

"He wants to talk to you personally. I've got a duffel bag full of cash to deliver to him."

"What else do we have to discuss?"

"Here's a list of book store owners who are under Overton's control."

"So, what do you want me to do about that?"

"Burn them out."

"Simple as that, burn them out?"

"Yeah."

"What's in it for me?"

"Fifty grand in cash for each one burned to the ground."

Looking at the list, Deon said, "Wow, that's a lot of stores. If Niko finds Overton, all this won't be necessary, will it?"

"That's what I said, but Niko wants to let Overton know he's still in the game. I think his emotions are getting to him. I really don't think it's necessary, either, but Niko is the boss."

"I'll start in South Carolina. The Feds will know what's going on. It won't be easy to avoid them."

"They won't care. The more stores that are destroyed, the better they'll like it."

"How do you figure that?"

"Think about it, Deon. Porno shops being shut down in the Bible belt...the locals will love it and the Feds will, too."

"I guess you're right, I've never thought about that much." Vera knew that Deon wasn't the sharpest tool in the shed. He never seemed to think much about anything. But, they'd worked together for over ten years so she had a soft spot for him.

"Your transport is ready. Deliver this to Niko and tell him good luck for me. Be careful, Deon."

After exchanging modes of transportation three times, and some pretty nifty driving, Deon felt assured that he wasn't being followed, so he pulled into Wick's Lumber parking lot. Niko was waiting for him. Deon slid into the front seat and said, "Good to see you, Niko. How are you doing?"

"It's damn good to see you, too, Deon. Things are getting a little crowded. I'd like to be able to move around a little more. But I'm stuck until I find that goddamn Overton."

"He's not at the farm house?" Deon asked, as he handed Niko the duffel bag stuffed with cash.

"I don't think so, not yet anyway." Opening the bag and tossing Deon a bundle of one hundred dollar bills, he said, "Here's some walking around money. Did Vera tell you what I want done?"

"Yeah...I'll start in South Carolina," he said, as he tucked the ten-thousand dollars under his waistband.

"Good. After you burn a few stores, the owners will get the message and stop dealing with Overton's gang. Beating them up didn't seem to help. What do you think?"

"I think the owners and operators are in a tough spot. It's either Overton on their asses or you. What we have to do is find Overton."

"No shit. Tell me something I don't know."

"Vera said you had another mission for me."

"I do. As soon as I take care of Overton, I want you to take care of Donatelli."

"You mean beat him up?"

"No, I mean kill him."

"*Why?*"

"Let's just say he's fucking with a part of me I don't like him fucking with, and leave it at that." Niko had assigned Cory to seduce Turk, under the premise it might help his organization. Now that she had, Niko despised Turk and wanted revenge.

"I thought something like that was going on," Deon said, almost as an after-thought.

"What do you mean by that, Deon?"

"Is Turk screwing Cory?"

"Do you know that he is? How do you know? Have you seen them?" Niko was on the edge of his seat, staring at Deon. Niko felt a loss of respect. He didn't want anyone to know that his woman was sleeping with anyone but him.

"No, boss, I haven't, but from what you said, I thought, I thought..." Deon stammered, realizing a little late that Niko didn't want to admit or even suggest that Turk was screwing Cory.

Breathing hard, trying to contain his temper, Niko said, "Deon, just take care of Turk, as soon as I take care of Overton."

Changing the train of thought, Deon said, "We've got to find him first."

"I think he'll show up at the farm. It's just a matter of time."

"Are you sure about taking out Donatelli?"

"In a few weeks, he won't be any use to me. I can't stand the thought of him fucking my woman. He has to go."

"What's in it for me, Niko? I'm not sure I want to cross that line. This is murder, you know."

Reaching into his bag of cash, Niko handed Deon another fifty-thousand dollars and said, "You make the hit and there's another fifty in cash waiting for you."

"Crossing that line won't be so bad after all." Deon shivered as he stuffed the five bundles of one-hundred dollar bills into his shirt.

"All right, you got your cash and your orders. I'll see you in a few weeks."

"You got it, boss." Deon couldn't help but think that Niko was losing it. Needless burning of his stores, and as much as he disliked Donatelli, he didn't see seeking revenge for screwing his woman. Niko wasn't thinking as clearly as Deon was accustomed to him doing. "Vera says hi. Be careful, Niko, there's a lot of folks looking for you."

"Rest assured I'll be careful. They can look all they want just as long as they don't find me before I find Overton."

* * *

Niko was hungry for pancakes. He stopped off at the International House of Pancakes and ordered some buttermilk pancakes, Vermont syrup and sausage patties. He didn't see Turk Donatelli seated in the back booth.

"Digger, don't turn around. I'm going to the men's room. Leave the money covering the check on the table, go out the back door, get the car and pick me up in the rear of the restaurant. I think I recognize Niko in the booth up front." Turk was taking deep breaths, not believing his eyes.

"Are you sure?" Digger asked.

"Get out of here as quietly as you can, now!" Turk insisted.

Turk went directly to the men's room, careful not to turn toward Niko. He splashed some water on his face, not wanting to think it was really Niko, but knowing full well it was. Regardless of the beard and the weight Niko had put on, Turk recognized the coal black eyes; those couldn't be disguised. Turk went out the front door to the rear, where Digger was waiting for him.

"Are you sure it's Niko, Turk?"

"I'm pretty sure. We'll know when he comes out. I'll bet he'll limp."

"Yeah, you're right...it would be hard for Niko to get around without limping after his accident. I'm sure rehabilitation has been put on hold, don't you think?" Digger said, trying to add a little humor.

Turk was deep in thought. What would *he* do with this information? Would he tell the FBI? What would he do?

"As soon as he comes out, let's follow him and see where he's hiding out."

"That won't be easy, Turk. He'll be damn cautious. He's probably paranoid as hell right now."

"Let's try anyway."

They sat there for another thirty minutes observing the front door. Neither one of them thought to cover the back door. Niko had exited and was gone.

"Shit, how stupid of us, Digger. He's obviously gone out the back."

"Turk, are you sure it was Niko?"

"I'm not one-hundred percent sure, but sure enough that I would bet my life on it."

"That's pretty damn sure, boss. What do we do now?"

"We know that Niko likes pancakes. You'll stake out this place every morning until he comes back for more. This means he's in the area, probably in the city of Marietta.

"What about you? Who will protect your ass?"

"I'll get Jimmy to drive me around. There are enough GBI and FBI agents following me most of the time, so I should be okay. I really don't give a shit anyway." Turk was in so deep, he was beyond caring. He just wanted to bring an end to this nightmare.

"Okay, I guess." Digger didn't like hearing Turk talk like

that. He knew he had a lot of pressure on him and felt it wasn't fair. His wife, his son, his business...they were all in disarray. Digger loved Turk like a brother and didn't like seeing him in anguish.

"Take me back to the hotel, Digger. I'm tired all of a sudden." Turk decided not to tell FBI Agent Morley about sighting, Niko. He wanted to get his business completed first. The most important was paying off the construction loans he signed for personally. If the FBI found out he'd sighted Niko, he'd be in a world of shit. Right now, Turk felt he needed to protect his own interests. He'd take his chances.

CHAPTER—26

Overton and Naylor had been working out of a series of rented apartments in Douglasville, Georgia. They spent a few weeks at a time at each. Overton didn't trust Naylor to drive anymore. The last time he drove they ended up in jail. He'd brought key employees and muscle from the West Coast with him. They were eating up a lot of cash, and Niko's campaign of burning down the book stores he controlled was making Overton look bad. Not only that, his cash flow was interrupted. He knew that Niko was behind the operation. He needed to find Niko and locate Deon. If he got rid of them, he felt he could easily handle Vera Staidly and Cory Doran. They'd have no choice but to go to work for him.

Niko wanted to take out Overton. Overton wanted to take out Niko. Deon was laying in wait to take out Donatelli. Digger had staked out the IHOP in order to locate Niko. The FBI and the GBI were tailing both Turk and Digger, along with Vera Staidly and Cory Doran. It would only be a matter of time until all of these individuals would collide in a violent fashion, each hoping it would be the other.

"Naylor, we're going to start working out of my farm in Roswell."

"Hey, that's a good idea," Naylor agreed with everything Overton said. He didn't have an opinion of his own, and if he did, he knew better than to voice it.

"First thing I got to do is get me some drugs. I'm about out."

"I'll go fetch them...you want the same amount?"

"I got us a plan, numb nuts. Let's lure Fritz to the farm house and take his drugs." Naylor didn't like being called numb nuts. Fritz was the biggest supplier of drugs in the city of Atlanta.

"Why you call me numb nuts?"

"For crissakes, Naylor, don't be so goddamn sensitive. You know I love yah."

"But you're always calling me names. I'm part of this operation, too, you know." Naylor just wanted to feel needed. He wanted to be recognized for his role in Overton's amateurish play at becoming the new porno-king.

"You are and I couldn't get along without you, Naylor, you know that." Overton knew all he had to do was throw Naylor a compliment and he'd be fine.

"I know, but I just wish you would treat me better...that's all."

"I'll try. I don't mean nothing by it. Make contact with Fritz; tell him we need a shipment of drugs to take to the West Coast. He'll ask you how large. Tell him two-hundred-thousand dollars worth."

Naylor now satisfied his boss had recognized him, asked, "Same mix as before?"

"No weed...a mix of cocaine, heroin and speed. Tell him he'll have to deliver it personally. If he asks why, tell him we can't let just anybody know our location."

"What if he won't come?" Naylor asked.

"I bet two-hundred thousand big ones he'll come. He wouldn't trust that amount of money to any of his street dealers...you can bet on that. Now git on out of here."

"Where you going to be?"

"I'll go open up the farm. Meet me there."

Overton nervously drove the half mile dirt road to his farm house. It had been two years since he had been there. He felt uneasy going there again. He pushed the garage door opener wondering if the batteries were still good. With a lot of creaks and groans, it opened. He looked the generators over as if he knew all about them. The only thing he did know was that they ran on propane gas. He flicked the battery-operated switch and it came to life with a loud humming sound. He hated doing this work. He wished Naylor would hurry up and get there.

Overton went around to the back of the main house after inspecting the out-buildings; nothing seemed out of order. Working his way around to the front entry, he sensed that something was wrong. The walkway leaves and debris had been disturbed by something or someone. He thought it might be squirrels or some forest creature, but he pulled his pistol as he approached the front door.

Being a locksmith, it took only a glance to see that the lock was broken. Someone had been there, or was there. He opened the door cautiously. Seeing or hearing nothing, he flicked on the light switch. Then he heard what he thought was the back door slamming. Overton turned and hurried back outside when he saw a figure running away. Without thinking, he fired his pistol, knocking the man down. The man continued to crawl. Overton, cursing himself for being so damn trigger happy, stood over a bearded, shoddily dressed, homeless man and said, "This just isn't your day." The helpless man tried to cover his face as Overton shot him twice in the neck.

Overton left him lying there. He would have Naylor dispose of the body when he got back. He continued the inspection of the house. The homesteader had made a mess of the place. His considerable liquor supply had been consumed and the empty bottles were strewn everywhere. It looked like this guy had some help. There was evidence of two people being there. This concerned Overton; if there was another person and he came back, he would have to kill him, too. Maybe staying here wasn't the thing to do after all.

* * *

Niko couldn't believe his luck. He had planned on abandoning this perch after today. He'd almost shot the man Overton had just murdered before he realized the man was a wayward vagrant enjoying his find at Overton's expense. Niko, in considerable pain, worked his way back to his van. He'd continue his watch tomorrow and make final plans for the execution of Overton.

* * *

Overton felt uneasy. As he surveyed the mess left by the man he'd just shot, he said out loud, "The bastard got what he deserved. I ought to go shoot him again." While waiting for Naylor, he weighed the pros and cons of making this his headquarters, just as Naylor drove up.

"Are you sure no one followed you, numb nuts?" he asked, wishing he'd not said that. "Erase, erase, buddy...I didn't mean that. Did you make a deal with Fritz?"

"I did. He'll be here today or tomorrow with the drugs. He said he didn't have that much on hand and it would take him a day or two to re-supply," Naylor answered as he observed the body lying ten yards from the driveway.

Following Naylor's gaze, Overton said, "The bastard

deserved it. Help me drag him into the shed. We'll deal with his body tomorrow."

"Where did he come from?" Naylor asked as he grabbed the dead man's feet.

"He broke in, drank all of our booze, made a mess of the place, and tried to run away."

"And you shot him?" Naylor asked in disbelief.

"Yeah, what of it? He was scum," Overton answered as he helped Naylor drag him into the shed.

"Just he didn't do nothing, that's all."

"Nobody fucks with my stuff, you should know that." He didn't want to tell Naylor he had acted on impulse. He wished he hadn't, but it was too late now. It was probably the drugs. He needed a fix.

Naylor looked around the house. Shaking his head, he said, "Boss, this place is really trashed."

"No shit, tell me something I don't know." His last shot of heroin was calming him down.

"What are we going to do? We can't live in this place like this, can we?"

"We're not going to stay here. Niko and Deon know I own this place. They're bound to check it out sooner or later, probably already have. As soon as Fritz delivers the goods, we're out of here. In the meantime, let's figure out where we're going to sleep."

It was slow going. The weather had turned cold and damp. This only aggravated Niko's mending bones. But he was driven by adrenaline. He didn't want to miss this opportunity to take out Overton and Naylor. Things were finally going his way. He'd brought his rifle with the scope, but he didn't feel he was going to be able to shoot them both from this location. He'd plan on getting to them from close range, if he could.

Overton and Naylor were in and out of the house. Niko observed them through his scope. He could have taken out Naylor a couple of times, but Overton seemed jumpy. He didn't stay in one place long enough for Niko to get a good clean shot at him. Unbeknown to Niko, Overton was jumpy because of his increased amphetamine use. Then all of a sudden, Niko watched as they backed their car out of the barn and drove away. Cursing, Niko said, "Why didn't I try to shoot them from here? Goddamn it!" He made his way back to his van, promising he would not let another opportunity pass.

Overton and Naylor weren't gone long; they went to the Food Lion for some groceries, beer, and cigarettes. When they got back to the farm, they dismembered the vagrant's body and buried the remains, with one hundred pounds of lime in the back pasture. This wasn't the first murder they had to deal with and it probably wouldn't be the last they figured.

Overton was high on drugs. Naylor was trying to read a book, *Black Beauty*. He liked horses. He'd made up his mind to educate himself. He was tired of being called stupid. His father called him stupid from as far back as he could remember.

Overton didn't move when someone knocked at the door. He was enjoying his high and figured it was Fritz delivering the drugs. He said, "Naylor, see who that is, and be damn careful. Fritz might have brought some muscle with him."

"Why don't you get it? I'm reading."

"You can hardly read, you asshole." Overton said as he went to the door. "A lot of good reading will do you, numb nuts."

Overton couldn't identify who was knocking at the door, so he opened it a crack very carefully with his pistol in hand. Niko busted through, knocking Overton to the floor. Naylor jumped out of his chair and Niko fired one round of his double barrel shotgun and blew Naylor completely over the table. He then turned toward Overton, who was fumbling for his gun, and put his foot on his throat. With the barrel of his shotgun, Niko flicked away the pistol and backed away, keeping Overton in his sights.

"At long last, I got your ass, Overton."

Creeping backwards on his hands and knees and looking up at Niko, Overton said, "Come on, Niko, don't do it. Let's make a deal. We can make a deal," he pleaded.

"A deal, you say. You made your deal with the DA. Now you need to make a deal with your maker. You're going to die, Overton, and slowly."

"Please, Niko, please don't kill me. I'll do anything. Don't kill me!" he begged.

"Oh, I'm going to kill you, Overton. But I want you to think about it, suffer over it, just like you made me suffer in jail." He reached down and handcuffed Overton to the leg of the pot-stove. They were the handcuffs Niko pulled from his sex shop, and were meant to be used for bondage.

Niko was ready to pull the trigger when someone knocked on the front door. He turned quickly, opened the door, and shot Fritz in the face. As Fritz went tumbling down in a heap on the front stoop, Overton tried to break loose from the stove. Niko was reloading his double-barrel shotgun with number-two buckshot. He shot Overton in the upper thigh and said, "Feel the pain...you bastard. That is what I've been living with since you ran me off that goddamn mountain, you prick of misery." Niko didn't see Naylor moving ever so slightly.

Overton was just feeling the pain and begged, "Don't do this to me, Niko. I can make it right. I can make it right."

"Make it right, my ass. The only way you can make it right is by dying, you scum bag!" Niko needed to get this over with and out of there. He shot Overton in the face. It would be difficult to identify him. Niko reloaded, stepped over Fritz, and made his way to his van parked a couple of hundred yards down the drive. Naylor, barely conscious started crawling toward the door blood streaming from his chest.

* * *

A distant neighbor had heard shots and called the police to investigate. Niko just barely made it out before a police cruiser pulled up in front of the farm house to investigate the neighbor's complaint. It didn't take the officer long to see the body on the front stoop, and to radio for an ambulance, and help. He made his way inside where Naylor, in a pool of blood, had dragged himself to the front door. He whispered just before he passed out, "It was Pappas. It was Pappas who done it." The officer had no idea whom he was talking about at the time.

"Will he live?" FBI agent Buck Morley, asked the attending ER physician, flashing his badge

"I think so, but he's in critical condition. He lost a lot of blood."

"Can I question him?"

"Not right now. He's heavily sedated, Detective."

"When will I be able to see him, Doctor?"

"You can probably question him tomorrow morning. That is, if he makes it through the night."

"What are his odds, fifty-fifty?" Buck asked, trying to assess his chances of interrogating Naylor.

"I don't make any predictions. My staff and I have done the best we can. His chances are fair, that's all I can say. Please excuse me, Detective. Another ambulance just pulled up." The emergency room physician hurried away, leaving Buck Morley wondering what to do next.

* * *

"Turk, Buck here. We need to talk."

"I'm booked at the Royal Coach…room 303, Detective. Come on over."

"I'll be there in ten minutes."

Buck explained to Turk what had just happened, and said, "I think you might be next."

"What makes you think that?"

"My gut, Turk, my gut."

"I'll say to you the same thing you always say to me, Buck. I need more than that. I need proof."

"This was Niko's doing. Overton murdered a homeless man, and probably a drug dealer, too. Niko murdered Overton and as far as he's knows, Naylor. You're next, trust me."

"How do you figure?"

"One of my agents that are looking out for you observed Deon tailing you. He's also inquired about what room you're staying in. Why else would he do that, if it wasn't to get to you?"

"First, your agent isn't looking out for me, Buck. Don't bullshit me. He was following me because none of you trust me."

"Okay, okay so what? I need for you to meet with Cory as soon as possible and see if she can shed any light on where this fucking Niko is. We've got to find him! Turk, you need to press harder."

"Buck, I'm telling you, I don't think she knows. I do think Vera knows. What about Deon? Have you talked to him?"

"We have. Deon doesn't tell us, shit. We haul Vera in every damn week. She doesn't say a word; she just asks for her attorney. We stay away from Cory, hoping you can come up with something."

"What do you want me to tell Cory this meeting is all about?

Remember, she told me I have to deal with Deon and that she won't see me anymore."

"That's your damn problem, Turk. You got more bullshit than anyone I know. Figure out how and get back to me. Niko will get to you first if you don't."

"I think I saw Niko last week." Turk decided to come clean.

"You what...you *think* you saw Niko and you didn't inform me?"

"Digger and I were having pancakes at the IHOP in Marietta. I saw a man sitting in a booth with a beard, wearing an Atlanta Braves hat, trying to hide his cold black eyes. I'm pretty sure it was Niko."

Gathering his composure, Buck asked, "Then what did you do?"

"Digger and I sat outside the IHOP waiting for him to come out."

"And?"

"He didn't. He must have gone out the back door. We never saw him again."

"So that's why Digger has stationed himself at the IHOP. We wondered what he was doing. What is the matter with you, Turk? Haven't you realized you're one step away from a prison term...or being killed, and you keep screwing around with us? I thought you were smarter than that."

"I've obviously made the wrong decision. I'm just trying to protect my own interest, that's all."

"Trying to protect your own interest...by not telling us about sighting Niko? How would that help you, for crissakes?"

"I figured in order for me to pay off the construction loans I'm still responsible for on the Industrial Park, Niko needed to be free. Otherwise, you arrest him and I'm out a lot of money. That's why."

"All right, look. You're in serious trouble with the FBI right now, Turk. I'm going to have to arrest you for your indiscretion. Get your things and let's go."

"What do you mean? You're going to arrest me for not telling you I think I saw Niko?"

"You got that right, Turk. I can't cover for you any longer. You've lied to us one too many times. Come on, before I have to handcuff you and read you your rights." Buck wanted to scare Turk into cooperating at a higher level and he was succeeding.

"Man, how can you arrest me for that, Buck?" Turk was truly nervous and very concerned. This was the first time he felt he'd stepped over the line. Was he going to be able to save his ass and pull out of this one?

"What good are you to us? You lie and mislead us. We don't need to be second-guessing you every time you tell us something. Come on, let's go!" Buck was really upset with Turk and he knew it.

* * *

Niko washed the splattered blood from his forearms. He was still shaking from the evening's events. He felt a huge sense of relief, though, now that Overton and his sidekick were out of the way. With no one to testify against him, it was time to contact his lawyers and make arrangements to turn him into the authorities. He flicked on the TV to catch the evening news.

The news reporter, reporting from the farm house, with yellow tape surrounding the blood-soaked ground behind him, announced, "So far, the authorities have found two dead men, and one critically wounded man. The local Roswell police, the GBI and the FBI are investigating further. From our account, it seems like a drug deal gone sour. A large amount of drugs were found in one of the confiscated cars. Two-hundred and fifty thousand dollars in cash was found inside the house. We'll bring more news later in the broadcast...back to you, Ted."

Niko turned off the TV. He felt sick, thinking Naylor must not have died. How could he survive a shotgun blast to the chest? The *Black Beauty* novel absorbed most of the buckshot and had saved Naylor's life. Niko chastised himself for not checking to see if he was dead. Hopefully, Naylor would die before morning. Niko called Russ O'Hare.

"Russ, you have to do something for me."

"What is it this time, Niko?"

"I need to make sure Naylor is dead."

"I just saw the news...it was you then, wasn't it?"

"Does it matter?"

"No, I guess not. What do you want me to do?"

"Somehow get to Naylor, and finish what I started."

"I can't do that, Niko. I'm in too deep now. You get caught, I'm done. I'll be in prison for the rest of my life. Leave it alone."

"Leave it alone, shit! You're turning against me, too, huh?"

"Take it anyway you want to, Niko, I'm done helping you. It's only a matter of time and the FBI will find you." Russ O'Hare had been a police officer long enough to know that Niko was done. It wasn't *if*, it was *when*. Niko wasn't thinking right anymore.

"I'll do it myself, damn you, Russ!" Niko slammed the phone down.

On the other side of town, Deon was planning on taking out Turk that night at the Royal Coach Hotel now that Overton was out of the way. He made his way down the hall with a small suitcase in tow until he came to room 303. Looking up and down the hall, seeing no one, he removed a .22-caliber automatic luger pistol equipped with a silencer from his suitcase, inserted the key he'd gotten from a clerk he bribed, and burst through the door. Deon fired nine-shots into the bed, causing both pillows to puff with each shot. As the feathers rained down, the FBI agent said, "Drop your weapon and get on the floor with your arms spread."

Deon couldn't believe he was being arrested. How crazy was he to agree to do this. His hate for Turk Donatelli had made him do something this stupid. He dropped to the floor. There were two FBI agents in the room. Agent Morley was right: Turk was next in line. They hauled Deon to jail for further questioning.

* * *

Niko knew that if he blew out the electric transformers to the hospital's emergency room, a generator would kick in and power would be restored in less time than it took to take out the transformer. He had to do something else to gain access to Naylor's hospital room, but what? He wasn't sure which room Naylor was in. The only thing he did know was that it had to be intensive care. He sat in the hospital parking lot for three hours observing the police, the GBI and the FBI coming and going. Access to Naylor would be impossible. He headed back to his garret over the garage a dejected man.

* * *

Turk couldn't believe his eyes. Deon was being put in the holding cell across from his. He couldn't help but say, "Hey, Deon, nice to see you."

"Fuck you, Donatelli! How'd you know?"

"Know what?" Turk had no idea what he was talking about.

"You know damn well what, you prick!" Deon figured that Turk had gotten wind somehow of him being commissioned to kill him. He had no idea that it was Buck Morley who figured it out, and set him up.

"I guessed," Turk said, as the jailer unlocked the cell and said, "Follow me, Mr. Donatelli." The jailer led him to one of the interrogation rooms he'd visited a time or two in the past.

"Turk, I told you, you were next...didn't I?" Buck Morley said.

"What do you mean? Is that what Deon is doing here? Did he try to get to me?"

"Let's just say he blew a lot of holes in two pillows placed end-to-end in your hotel bed."

Turk started to shake, and said very quietly, "Buck, give me another chance. I've got to get the hell out of this town."

"Look, Turk, you're not a bad guy. You've just made some bad decisions. Don't make any more. We're going to keep you in here for your own safety for a few more days. We need to find Niko, and put a stop to this madness once and for all."

"I understand, Buck. Can't I see Digger? I need to have him make contact with my wife and kid."

"Sure, call him."

Turk did call him. He was on his way down to visit Turk in jail.

"What do you mean you know where Niko is, Digger?"

"He's hiding out in Gerri Short's garret above her garage."

"How'd you find out?"

"Remember Russ O'Hare, the police officer who Niko claimed was on his payroll before the guy retired."

"I think so; I'm not sure."

"I knew him pretty well. He contacted me and said he was sick of Niko and that he'd tell me where he was if I could get him a deal."

"How could you get him a deal? Why did he come to you? Why didn't he go direct to the GBI?"

"He figured they'd put him in jail immediately, which they probably would have. We always had a good relationship so he came to me."

"How'd he find you?"

"He contacted Pop's security, Pop contacted me, and we met of all places, the IHOP," Digger said, chuckling.

"This gives credence to the old adage, 'What goes around, comes around' doesn't it, Digger?"

"Yeah, I guess. What do we do now?"

"As soon as you leave, I'll get with Buck Morley and let the FBI deal with Niko. You've done your job. Please go to Florida and take care of Karen and Jason for me. I'll join you as soon as I can if they'll let me go."

"What about Deon? Where's he? Aren't you worried about him?"

"The FBI has him locked up."

"So it was him who caused the disturbance at the Royal Coach, I heard about!"

"Yes, but he's not your concern anymore, Digger. Get out while you can. I'll meet you in Florida. Thanks…buddy. I'd never have made it if it wasn't for you. I love you like a brother, Digger," Turk said, holding back the tears until Digger was out of sight.

Turk asked the jailer to contact Buck Morley. They escorted him back to his lone cell. He lay down on his cot and cried. The pressure he felt was enormous. More than he could bear. He was a beaten man.

"We'll get him, Turk, and as soon as we do, I'm sure the agency will let you go. But until we do, I'm going to keep you locked up."

"I understand, Buck. But let me ask you, what do you think my chances are of getting off?"

"Good, very good, especially now that you've given us Niko's location. But, Turk, you need to change your lifestyle. You've been too close to these mob elements most of your career.

You'll end up in prison or dead if you don't change your ways. That's the last piece of advice I'm going to give you. You need to take care of yourself and that family of yours."

CHAPTER—27

The FBI arrested Niko without him putting up a fight. He still claimed his innocence. Naylor recovered and turned State's evidence. Vera Staidly was arrested for running a criminal enterprise and aiding and abetting a felon. She was in the process of being released on bail. Cory Doran was out on bail with additional charges of interstate transportation of pornography pending. She continued to operate Niko's porno business. Turk managed to pay off most of his construction debts. The Feds were in the process of seizing Niko's real estate assets, which the recently enacted RICO Act allowed them to do. The FBI still hadn't dropped all Turk's charges; he was waiting for disposition of his case. He'd hired the best defense lawyer in town, Seth Stern. He was hoping he could keep his house; he would net three-hundred thousand once he sold it. But the States Attorney claimed he had built the house with money he'd received from a criminal enterprise; therefore, he wasn't entitled to keep it.

Digger was in St. Pete handling Karen's care for Turk. His girlfriend was doing a good job. Jason liked them both very much. Turk was hoping to join them in a few weeks. He'd been contacted by the New York mob; they still felt he had an interest in the adult book stores. Turk had finally arranged a meeting with Cory to see if she could convince the mob that he no longer was involved in any aspect of the porno business.

"Well, Turk, it's been quite some time since I've seen you. You look better than the last time I saw you."

"Thanks, I guess. I've gone back to running and working out. It's the only thing that keeps me sane, these days."

"Is the FBI still giving you a hard time?"

"They are, a little. How are they treating you?"

"Like a criminal."

"Well, Cory, what do you expect?"

"Pornography is basically legal now. Hell, this is the '70s."

"I think you ought to get out while you can, Cory."

"I don't know anything else, Turk, and the money is good."

"You're bright, you're beautiful, and you're young. You need to find a good man too."

"I thought I had one at one time, Cory said sadly.

"Do you mean me, Cory?"

"You know damn well how I feel about you, Turk Donatelli."

"You told me there was no *us*, remember?"

"That was just a smoke screen, Turk. Niko would have killed me if I kept seeing you."

"That's what Niko wanted to do to me. You could have warned me, you know."

"I didn't know a damn thing about his wanting you out of the way."

"Okay, all of that is over. I'm out of here in two weeks, if I can get the DA to release the charges against me. I advise you to do the same."

Getting up from her chair, she walked over to Turk and

threw herself into his arms. "Turk, can't you be with me? Aren't I enough woman for you?"

"Cory, you're more than enough woman for me, and I care for you a lot. But I have responsibilities in Florida that I have to take care of...you know that."

"Turk, please don't be offended by what I'm about to say, but Karen is sick. Your relationship with her is basically over. I know it and you know it."

"You're probably right, Cory, but I promised to take care of her and her son Jason, and I have to do just that."

"You can take care of them financially, Turk. You don't have to care for them physically."

"I do Cory, I do. I promised." Turk's mind wandered. This was his chance to prove to himself he was a changed man.

Snuggling closer, Cory whispered, "Will you make love to me, one last time?"

Unable to resist Cory's advances, Turk said, "Why will this be the last time?"

Surprised, and delighted, Cory said, "Oh Turk, you're so bad."

* * *

Niko was being held in the Fulton County jail waiting his arraignment. He'd been there for two months now. He was allowed to exercise and to rehabilitate his broken bones. He mingled with other inmates. Jail is where your reputation or your brute strength allows you freedom or serfdom. Niko's reputation was one of smut and money. In order to carve out a secure position in the jail population and to enjoy complete protection, he confided in two fellow inmates that he had indeed murdered those men. He went into detail, more detail than he should have to insure his position as a tough guy. In this case, Niko's machismo cooked his goose.

One of the inmates Niko confided in, Sean, was an FBI-planted informant looking for any kind of information to help reduce his pending drug-trafficking sentence. Sean knew that what Niko had revealed to him was not only worthy of a reduced sentence, but it might get him off entirely. He requested an audience with the warden. After a week of negotiation with the FBI, the DA, and the GBI, they made a deal with Sean. In return for his testimony against Niko, after the trial he would get time served, and be released. Between Naylor's testimony, and Sean's, Niko stood to be convicted on murder charges, running criminal enterprises, and a sundry of other charges. His sentence would probably be twenty-five years to life. His councilor was Bobby Lee Cook, the famous lawyer who previously represented crooked bankers, murderers, moonshiners and celebrities.

* * *

The Atlanta Penitentiary prison guard emptied Cory's purse on a table and thoroughly inventoried the contents. She said, "Miss Doran, please sign here. You can pick up your purse on your way out."

Cory had been through this process many times before at the Fulton County jail. Waiting for further instructions, she said, "Yes, ma'am."

"Please stand over there and put your hands on the wall." The guard said, motioning to the painted footprints on the floor and the painted handprints on the wall. She frisked Cory expertly, and said, "Please go into the room on your right and take off your clothes…knock on the door when you're done."

Irritated by this invasion, Cory protested, "I've never had to strip before. Why now?"

"Lady, if you want to visit your boyfriend, get in there and strip. I don't have all day."

The strip-search was totally out of line, and Cory knew it. She would be talking to Niko through plate glass. This procedure was meant to let her know who was in charge. Niko was a high-profile case and she was a high-profile visitor. Cory wanted to strike out at the guard, but didn't, and said as she walked toward the room, "You and I both know that this is not necessary."

Strip-search over, Cory got dressed again and was led through three more heavy metal doors. The clanging and the echoes bouncing off tall, austere concrete walls were frightening. The dank smell and the stark white-washed walls closed in on her. The County Jail was more inviting than the Atlanta Pen. Another guard pointed to more painted footprints worn bare from traffic, and said, "A light over booth number eight will come on when inmate Pappas arrives."

Nickolas J. Pappas, clothed in ill-fitting prison garb, hobbled in, chained at the ankles to the stool in booth number eight. He pushed the button signaling he had arrived. Cory made her way to an uncomfortable stool, lifted the phone, and said, "Niko, I don't like this place," all the while noting how defenseless he looked. He'd lost the power he used to emanate. At that moment, Cory's feelings for Niko changed from, love, and respect to just plain feeling sorry for him.

"*You* don't like it! How do you think I feel for crissakes?"

"I'm sorry, Niko. I just meant that the treatment is different than it was in the County Jail. How are you doing?"

"My lawyer, Bobby Lee Cook, says he might be able to arrange bail, but it's doubtful because of my escape. I had to pay the bastard a million dollar retainer to take my case, and that's just a down payment. My defense will cost me five-million or more."

"He's the best, probably one of the best defense attorneys, in the country. What does he say about your case?"

"It doesn't look good as long as Naylor and that damn jailhouse snitch turned states witness exist."

"How's your leg and hip, honey?" Cory asked, feeling the honey label was hollow. Her feelings were now almost non-existent for Niko.

"Oh, a guard wheels me into therapy every day. I have to exercise in these damn ankle bracelets. It's not like I'm going to run off, for crissakes."

"Am I going to be dealing with Bobby Lee Cook?" Cory asked, wanting to get this visit over with.

"No, I'll deal directly with Cook. That's the way he wants it. You'll be dealing with the same group of lawyers we've been dealing with before. We meet two or three times a week."

"That makes sense. I'll meet with them as soon as I leave here."

Moving closer to the glass separating them, Niko said, "Our time is almost up." Hesitating and looking directly into Cory's eyes, he continued, and asked, "Are you still seeing Turk?"

"No, of course not, honey. I only saw him because you wanted me to. I don't even like him. Why do you ask?"

"You're my woman, right, Cory?"

"I am, Niko. Can we talk about business?" She wanted to change the subject. Her romantic feelings for Niko were now extinguished.

"Not really. They monitor our phone conversations." Cory was holding a phone and looking through plate glass. Niko held one, too, staring back at her. This was his only connection to the outside other than through his attorneys.

"I know the drill. They don't want you running your business from prison. What do you want me to do, Niko?" Cory did feel sorry for him. He did look helpless; a look that Niko didn't wear well.

"As you know, I'm appealing my case. Bail is out of the question. We'll have to communicate through my attorneys."

"What about New York?" she asked. New York was their code for the mob.

"Nothing will change; assure them of that." Niko hoped the mob would see that Cory could run his adult businesses, and they would continue to get their cut.

"What assurance?" Cory asked, knowing full well that the mob didn't like dealing with a woman.

"See Vera...she'll give you a duffel bag." Niko felt a million in cash would ease the mob's itch to take over his business.

"She's in jail right now." Vera had been picked up by the FBI just a few days before.

"Our lawyers are posting bail. She should be out by tomorrow."

"I'll follow up."

"I'm relying on you, Cory. You're all I got right now." Niko needed her and needed her badly. He would cultivate additional people resources through his attorneys, but right now, Cory *was* all he had. He was suspect of putting this much power and control into the hands of an associate, especially a woman associate.

"You can count on me. I'll be there for you, Niko. I know it must be hell in there."

"It's not so bad. Our lawyers think I have a chance of a reduced sentence on appeal. You'll wait for me, won't you, Cory?" Niko was desperate, lonely and trying to be optimistic. His wife had filed for a divorce.

"Of course I will, Niko." Cory had never seen Niko look so helpless. Her feelings for him now were just monetary. She questioned what she ever saw in this man now that he was behind bars. Cory kindled thoughts of taking over what was left of Niko's porno empire.

"I meet with my lawyers tomorrow. They'll be in contact with you. I'll see you next week for sure, goodbye, baby." The guard led Niko back to his cell.

On the way back to her home office, Cory weighed the advantages of continuing to work for Niko or leaving the porno-business behind. Niko could still reach out and get her if he wanted to. It would take time for the New York mob to take over the porno industry. They may not even try. Adult book stores were going up on every corner. But there was still a tremendous amount of money to be made. Cory needed to fly to New York and meet with the Gambino family to see what their level of interest was. She would try and talk Turk into going with her.

* * *

"Turk, I've got to go to New York. Will you go with me?"

"You know damn well I can't do that. I haven't even settled the score here with the FBI. I told you I was finished with this business. Besides, Niko tried to have me killed. Why would I even want to?" Turk couldn't believe Cory had even asked him.

"I just thought about the last time we were together. You said that wouldn't be the last time."

"I meant making love to you. My life is in ruins. My desire for you is the animal coming out of me. I don't seem to have any control over my sexual urges, and especially when it comes to you."

"So that's all I mean to you, is to get your nuts off, you bastard!" Cory could go into a fit of rage quicker than anyone Turk knew.

"Awe, come on, Cory. You'll never leave Niko and you know it."

"Maybe not, but that doesn't mean I don't have feelings for you." Cory needed Turk to make an impression on the mob should she try to take over Niko's business.

"Think about what you're saying and what you're doing. You're just like Niko. The only difference is you're female."

"And just what do you mean by that remark, Turk?" she asked, indignantly.

"He treats woman the way you treat men. As long as they're doing what you want them to do, everything is okay. But as soon as they start thinking on their own, you get pissed. Doesn't that remind you of the way Niko operates?"

"You're going to New York with me! You can't refuse me!" Cory screamed into the phone, and hung up.

Turk held the receiver in front of him and wondered just what Cory could do to make him change his mind; not much he figured. Did she have designs on taking over Niko's business? He pondered. His next call was to Digger in St. Pete.

"Digger, how's Karen doing?"

"Same old…same old. She cries continually and just doesn't want to go on living."

"I've got to do something about that. How's Jason?"

"Jason is fine. He misses you and worries about his mom, but all and all, he's doing okay. What about you? How are you doing?"

"I'm still waiting for the DA to dismiss charges against me. Cory wants me to go to New York with her to meet the mob. Everything is about the same."

"What does Cory want with you in New York?"

"Something to do with what's left of Niko's porno empire, I don't really know. I didn't ask her. I just said no. She might have designs on his business for all I know."

"Hell, what Niko used to sell is legal now. I don't know if the

Mob would want any of his business. He can't have much of an operation left, can he?"

"I think there's more to Niko's business than Cory's letting on. He's still grossing a couple million a month. Niko is still in control...for how long is anybody's guess. He's talked about a lot."

"Who's talking about him?"

"Buck Morley for one. There's something the FBI still wants out of Niko and his operation. I think they want to break Niko and close him down. He's been an embarrassment to them since his escape. I believe this is more about revenge than pornography."

"Yeah, you're right there. The FBI doesn't like to be embarrassed. Niko made them look pretty bad. What else can you offer the FBI, Turk?"

"They've got everything out of me they're going to. I've got nothing else to share with them."

Changing the subject, Digger asked, "How's your health?"

"It could be better, I'm exercising a lot. I'm not eating very well. I've got most of my construction debt taken care of here in Atlanta, but I still worry about my Florida real estate debt. The DA didn't leave me enough assets to deal with that. I can barely afford Karen's treatments."

"Finances are that bad, huh?"

"I'm not broke by any means, but if the DA doesn't let me out of here pretty soon, I'll go broke. I've already turned over my Florida real estate developments to the banks in lieu of foreclosure."

"Is there anything I can do, Turk?"

"Yeah, keep doing what you're doing. I don't know how I would deal with Karen and Jason without your help."

"You don't need to worry about that. I'll handle things here until you get back. Now, you take care of yourself, understand?"

"I will, Digger, and thanks for caring." Turk felt so alone. Digger was his only confidante now that China Jon was dead. Maybe CJ had the right idea; a cabin in the woods would seem like heaven right now. This gave Turk an idea.

CHAPTER—28

"We want you to go to New York with Cory, Turk," FBI agent Buck Morley said.

"Shit, that's not part of our deal, Buck. What the hell do you want me to do in New York?"

"We want to know where and who you're going to meet and what they want." Buck felt bad about having to press Turk further, but he had his orders. The DA wouldn't release Turk without a clearance from the FBI.

Furious, Turk said, "Just what do I do to get the FBI off my back?" Turk didn't feel like he was in any shape to be meeting with the damn mob, much less continuing his relationship with Cory.

"You do this and that should be it."

"What do you mean *should be*? If I'm forced to do this, will you guarantee that the charges against me will be dropped, and I'll be free to get on with my life?"

"There are no guarantees, Turk. You got yourself into this mess. Don't be blaming me."

"For crissakes, Buck, you know damn well this is above and

beyond what you expected me to do. Can't you go to bat for me?"

"I have, Turk. I may not like it any more than you do, but I have my orders. The FBI wants you to go to New York and find out what's going on. That's all I know."

"Shit, what happens if they find out I'm working for you guys? Maybe they already know."

"You'd be dead right now if they did. You always have the choice of our Witness Protection Program."

"Oh, that's encouraging. You got anything else to make me feel better? What happens to me if I refuse to go?"

"We thought you might ask that. I'm told, if you don't agree to go undercover, to read you your rights, and put you in jail again."

"Wow! Talk about taking advantage."

"Come on, Turk, get on with it. The sooner you go to New York and get back, the sooner your deal will get done, trust me."

"Trust you! I did that already and it hasn't worked. I don't even *know* if I'll make it back. You bastards are tough."

"Maybe so...will you do it?"

"I've already told Cory I wouldn't. What do I do about that?"

"You figure that out. Say you've changed your mind in the heat of passion," Buck said with a sly smile.

"Buck, that's not funny." Yet Turk couldn't help but laugh. He was in so deep now, why should he care? His future looked pretty dim anyway. Somehow, there might be some money in it for him, which he needed badly. "All right, I'll meet with Cory and get back to you." Turk resigned himself to cooperating with the FBI one more time, but this was the last time, he vowed.

Cory's instructions, received through Niko's attorneys, were to meet with the Gambino family representative in New York

City in the next two weeks and cut a new deal. The lawyers conveyed Niko's strategy to Cory. She was to wait for them to contact her. She agreed, with the stipulation that Donatelli would accompany her, under the premise that she couldn't trust anyone else. The ones she could trust in Niko's organization were all locked up.

"Cory, you know Niko's isn't going to agree to let Donatelli go with you. That will drive him crazy," Niko's lawyer declared, shaking his head.

"I don't care. Tell Niko that I'm not going to sleep with Turk. I just need someone to go with me and that someone is Donatelli; that is, unless he can figure out whom else he could send."

"The first thing he'll ask us is why Donatelli would want anything to do with him. After all, Niko tried to have him killed. This just won't work."

"We have to figure out something. I'm not going to go alone, and like I said, Turk is the only one left that I trust. Deon is still in jail. What do you expect me to do?"

"I'll tell you what you do," said Niko's lawyer. "You take Donatelli with you and we won't tell Niko unless he specifically asks if anyone went with you. He would never agree, and quite frankly, I can't understand why Turk would want to go anyway. Something suspicious is going on here."

"Turk hasn't agreed to go. He turned me down when I asked him." Not telling Niko about Turk couldn't be better for Cory. Her plan was working.

"Then why are you pushing this, Cory?"

"With all the shit I've been through with Niko and his enterprise, Turk is the only one who hasn't screwed me. No pun intended." Cory couldn't help but smile at that choice of words.

"I didn't need to hear that, Cory. Do what you've got to do to meet with the boys in New York, and get back to me so I can relay the deal to Niko…okay?"

"Okay."

Cory called Turk as soon as she got back to her office. "Turk, I need to see you."

"What do you need to see me for?" Turk asked.

"A meeting has been set for next Friday…meet me in an hour at my place." Cory said to Turk.

* * *

The guard frisked Turk. He knew he had to make some kind of deal with Cory. He might even be able to talk her into a large fee. He needed all the money he could get his hands on.

Cory greeted Turk, "Thanks for coming, Turk."

"You made it sound like I didn't have any choice. Let's get down to business." Turk was ready to cut the best deal he could for himself.

"Whoa Turk…what's your hurry?"

"I need answers. Who are we to meet and where is this rendezvous to take place?" Turk asked.

"You know damn well who we're going to meet. I'm informed we'll rendezvous at a warehouse in the Bronx. But I suspect that's a ruse."

With the location and time revealed, the FBI wanted to know the parties involved. "Okay who are we meeting with?" Turk asked.

"I'm not sure. It will be a *made* member of the Gambino family, I'm told."

"Okay, what's this meeting going to be about?"

"You're asking a lot of damn questions, Turk. Have you changed your mind and decided to go with me?" Cory was leading up to something.

"I'm trying to assess the risk. I don't want to be walking into a trap and get myself killed. I seem to be fair game lately."

"So you've decided to go with me, then?"

"I might if we can come to terms."

"And what would those terms be, Turk?"

"That depends on what role you want me to play in New York."

"You know damn well that the mob will have a hard time dealing with a woman. I want you to front the new deal being cut."

"Why would you being a woman pose a problem? Niko is still in the loop, isn't he?"

"Of course he is." Cory didn't want to reveal her true intentions just yet. She planned on making a play for Niko's empire; a very dangerous undertaking.

"What's in it for me?"

"So you're in the deal, Turk?"

"Like I said, that will depend on the terms."

"Okay, let's stop playing games. What the hell do you want?"

"For starters, before we go to New York, I want the industrial park construction loans paid off I've signed on personally."

"Okay, we were going to do that anyway. What else?" Cory was encouraged. It sounded like Turk was on the verge of agreeing to go with her.

"Whose name do I transfer the ownership to, his wife, just like I did the apartments, or Vera Staidly?"

Sensing an opportunity to advance her plans, Cory said, "Niko wants those properties transferred to me."

"Will we use the same law firm?"

"No, I'll take care of that. What else do you have in mind?" Cory had made a deal with Seth…one of Niko's fired attorneys to represent her.

Suspicious, Turk felt he knew what Cory's real intent was. He said, "I want a half-million in cash before I go to New York."

"For crissake, Turk, all I'm asking you to do is go with me. You're getting expensive."

"Look Cory, to use your words, let's be honest about your intent. I think you have bigger plans than you're letting on. But I really don't care what your plans are and I don't want to know. I want out after this trip. You pay off those loans, I'll convey ownership to whomever you designate through your attorney, and you give me a half million in cash. Then I'm done."

"I'll give you two-hundred thousand before we leave and three-hundred thousand when we arrive in New York." Turk would be done all right. Once a deal was struck with the Gambino family, he wouldn't make it back to Atlanta.

"Trust is a bitch...isn't it, Cory? I get five-hundred-thousand before I leave or I won't go."

"How do I know you won't change your mind, and run off with the money, Turk?"

"You don't, but that's the deal. Take it or leave it." If Cory only knew that he would have to accompany her whether she paid him a dime, thanks to the FBI, she'd really be pissed, Turk thought.

"You screw me, Turk, and it'll be the last time you screw anybody. You get my drift!" Cory was seething. Her lips curled and her eyes narrowed.

"I get your drift. I'll do as we have agreed. The screwing business is over, isn't it, Cory?" Turk said, smiling.

"That's not funny...you bastard."

"I think there's some irony in there somewhere."

"Enough! Okay, I'll have the money for you tomorrow. What else do we have to discuss?"

"The FBI will be all over our asses. You'll need to make the travel arrangements."

"I already have. We'll travel by car to Peachtree Airport. A private plane will be waiting for us. I'll fill you in on the details as soon as I get them."

"Okay, I guess we've got a deal then. Are we finished?"

Getting up from her desk, Cory seductively walked toward the picture window and pulled the drapes closed. With her back to Turk, she said, "Now we seal the deal, Turk. You do know how I like it."

Astonished, Turk said, "You've got to be the craziest bitch I know." He couldn't resist the lure of this very beautiful, dangerous woman. He promised himself this would be his very last indiscretion.

* * *

"Good job, Turk. We know the area where you're supposedly meeting. You won't know who you're going to meet with until you get there." FBI agent Buck Morley was happy with Turk's report. He only wished he'd wired Turk for sound.

"Buck, I have a request before I go to New York with Cory."

"I think I know what that is, Turk. You want the DA to release you from all possible criminal charges, right?"

"You got it, Buck. That's exactly what I want."

"What if I can't get that done?"

"I won't go. You guys can put me back in jail for all I care. This is my last mission. I'll be gone after this trip. I wish I could just disappear."

"Are you going to want to be in the Witness Protection Program?"

"No."

"Are you sure? Word gets out that you double-crossed Niko, you could be in danger."

"I'm sure. But I think it will be Cory's ass, not mine."

"How do you figure that?"

"Can't you see by my report that she intends on making a play for Niko's empire? She's transferring Niko's real estate into her name. She's taking me to New York, not Vera Staidly. Cory's bright, but I think it may backfire on her."

"You might be right, Turk, but she'll be in jail along with Vera Staidly as soon as she gets back from New York."

"That's your deal, Buck. All I care about is getting the hell out of this mess. Can you get that done for me?"

"I'll try."

"No trying, Buck. Either you get me cleared or I'm done."

Buck knew by the sound of Turk's voice that he meant what he said. "I'll get it done, Turk. Make plans to go to New York."

Turk's plan was starting to work. He'd have a half-million dollars in cash, which he didn't reveal to Buck, and would be absolved from all possible wrong doing. The first step had been taken for him and his family to be Vermont bound. "I'll do that...thanks, Buck."

"One more meeting and then we're done, huh?"

"It looks that way, Buck. I wish I could say this has been fun."

"You need to be very careful, Turk. You've pushed your luck to the breaking point. You need to change your ways or you'll be where Niko is, or in the ground," Buck said in earnest. He'd grown to like Turk Donatelli.

"I hear you loud and clear, Buck. I'll heed that advice. I'm plenty tired of this drama."

* * *

"Digger, how are things in St. Pete?"

"Pretty much the same. Karen still wants out of this world. After a while, you kind of wish you could help her. Jason is doing well in school. He spends the weekends with his grandmother."

"What about his dad? Does he come around?"

"I haven't seen him for weeks."

"That figures…he's a bastard."

"What about you, Turk. What's going on?"

"I'll brief you later. In the meantime, do this for me. Please prepare Karen and Jason for a quick exit. Pack a few clothes for both, along with Karen's medicines. I'll call you and tell you where and how I want them to leave St. Pete."

"Okay, boss. I'll wait for further instructions. What do I do about the condo after they leave?"

"You and your girlfriend like the beach. Be my guest."

"I don't know what you're up to, Turk. Are you sure you don't need my help?"

"No, I'm not sure, Digger, but I have a plan and I'll need to go it alone."

"Be careful, Turk. I'll get them ready to leave on short notice. Anything else you want me to do?"

"Yeah, line up a private plane for a trip to the East Coast. Find someone you know who will keep their mouth shut."

"You got it. Take care of yourself, Turk."

"I will, Digger…thanks. I'll be in touch."

CHAPTER – 29

Cory arranged for payment-in-full of all the outstanding Atlanta debts Turk was personally responsible for. Title was conveyed to an entity that Turk felt was owned and controlled by Cory, but wasn't sure. The FBI and GBI had released Turk from all potential liability subject to his trip to New York. Nickolas J. Pappas was indicted on charges of first-degree murder, money-laundering, escape from prison, racketeering, and transporting pornography across state lines, along with a litany of other charges. His chance of ever seeing the light of day was slim. The jail informant and the full recovery of Naylor who turned States witness insured that Niko would be convicted. Bail was denied. Bobby Lee Cook would appeal if Niko was convicted.

Bobby Lee Cook was a famous Summersville, Georgia, defense attorney, whose stable of clients included Tennessee banker C. H. Butcher, Jr., who had faced twenty-five counts of fraud. Bucher was acquitted on all counts. He had represented moonshiners and money launderers, bootleggers and bank fraud schemers. The Rockefellers and the Carnegies had been his clients.

Turk had read extensively about Cook's exploits over the years. One trial that kick-started Cook's career as one of the best defense attorneys in the South, to quote one news article was as follows:

The year was 1949. Bobby Lee Cook was handling one of his first-ever murder trials, defending a man on trial for murder who had called another man a "goddamn son of a bitch."

During opening statements, the prosecutor told Dade County, Georgia, jurors that while calling someone this was a bad thing, it didn't give the defendant the right to kill the man.

Slowly, Cook rose from his chair at the defense table to approach the jury. "I have a question for you," he asked the dozen in the box. "What would you have done if someone had called you a goddamn son of a bitch?"

At that moment, an older mountain man with a long beard sitting at the back of the jury box whispered just loud enough for the other jurors to hear: "Why, I would have killed the son of a bitch."

"I had an entire opening statement planned," Cook said, "but I just looked at the man, looked up at the jurors, nodded, walked back to my chair and sat down."

The next day, the jury acquitted his client.

One other such article Turk remembered reading quoted this trial. In 1951, Cook represented a man who had been arrested for moonshining by a Georgia sheriff who didn't appreciate Cook's belief that the Fourth Amendment's prohibition on illegal searches and seizures should apply in Georgia. When Cook showed up at the jail to post bail for his client, the sheriff refused to accept the money and threatened to kill the defense lawyer if he made any further attempts to have his client freed.

"You're not going to shoot me," Cook told the sheriff. "There are hundreds of Cooks who live in this county and they will hunt you down like a damn rabbit, and they will kill you."

Cook said he put the money on the table, grabbed the keys to the jail cell and started to walk his client out the door, when he heard the sheriff cock his pistol.

"Boom! The gun fires and the bullet shoots into the doorway just above my head," said Cook. "I got my client the hell out of there."

A month later, at his client's trial, Cook got his revenge. He had the sheriff on cross-examination and asked why he hadn't also arrested his client's neighbors for moonshining. When the sheriff didn't answer, Cook responded it was because the neighbors had been making secret payments to the sheriff while his client had not. Angered, the sheriff threw a Coke bottle at Cook, barely missing him.

"I walked up to the witness stand, grabbed the sheriff by the collar, pulled him down onto the floor and started whipping up on him," said Cook. "The judge was on the bench and the jury was in the box watching me whip up on him for several minutes. They all knew the sheriff was a tyrant. After a few minutes, the judge cleared his throat and said, 'Mr. Cook, I think he's had enough.'

"I pushed the sheriff back into the witness chair and finished my cross-examination," said Cook. "Damn jury was out for only a few minutes before they came back with a not guilty verdict on all counts."

Cook, who had won eighty-percent of his murder trials, said there are two things a lawyer must prove to a jury in order to win a murder case…that the victim was a bad person who deserved to be killed, and that your client was just the man for the job.

"If you prove those two things, nine times out of ten…your

client walks." Niko had hired the best defense attorney money could buy. Turk was impressed. Niko's business was being run by Cory and to some degree, Vera Staidly, who was about to be arrested again on additional charges of being an accessory to a criminal enterprise, racketeering, and money-laundering. The FBI was only waiting for Cory's return from New York to put her and Vera away.

Cory hadn't been charged with anything yet; the authorities wanted to take her down, along with her Mob connections while she was in New York. As bright as Cory was, she was blinded by greed. She thought she was above the law. Her lawyers made her feel a false sense of security. The FBI had enough evidence on tape and public records to convict her and imprison her for many years. This would be the FBI's final blow to Niko's porno-empire. They all were anxious to get it done.

Turk was flush with cash from the insurance settlement on his house and the half-million he was about to pick up from Cory. The FBI knew about the insurance settlement and was good with that. He hoped they didn't get wind of the half-million. Turk just never seemed to learn.

"Here's the cash, Turk. We leave the day after tomorrow from the Peachtree Airport. There will be a plane waiting for us," Cory informed Turk.

"I'd like to go on ahead. I'll meet you in New York." Turk had some plans and wanted to leave a day early to execute them.

"No damn way. You're leaving with me. I'm not about to let you and a half-million in cash out of my sight."

"I've been meaning to tell you, you say *damn* too much, Cory. I thought you might object. But let me tell you this. As soon as our meeting is over in New York, I'm walking out of that restaurant. My obligations will be over then."

"Let's talk about that meeting. As far as the 'family' is

concerned, we're...that's you and I...are going to run what's left of the porno business. Their cut will increase to twenty-five percent of gross receipts, no more. For that, they will supply whatever muscle we may need. You got that, Turk?"

"I got it. Who is going to do the negotiations?"

"We'll play that by ear; probably me on behalf of Niko." Turk started laughing at that comment. "What are you laughing about? This is no laughing matter."

"You're up to something, Cory. I think Niko is history. I don't even think Bobby Lee Cook can save Niko's ass. We might end up calling you the porno-queen of the south," Turk said, still laughing.

"Oh, you think that's funny?" Cory started laughing, too. She kind of liked the sound of that name.

Turning serious, Turk said, "I don't know what you're planning, and like I said before, I don't want to know. I care about you. I'm warning you. Be careful, Cory, very careful."

"I wish you cared for me, Turk." She was momentarily saddened by what she had planned for Turk. "Don't worry about me. I'd worry about my future, if I were you."

"What do you mean by that? Are you planning on something I'm not aware of?" Turk knew that Cory was capable of having him done in after this meeting. He was making provisions to insure that didn't happen. He hoped the FBI would afford him some protection.

"When we're finished making our deal, it's over and we both know that. You'll go back to Florida, tend to your sick wife and your sick responsibility to her and her son, and I'll go back to Atlanta. It's been fun, it really has."

"I guess we know where we stand. What else do we have to discuss?"

"That's it. I'll meet you at the airport at four in the morning.

Good night, Turk."

"I'll see you in the morning. Oh, one last word of advice. Before you execute your plan, really think it through. You're not in so deep you can't make a right turn and get out now while you can."

"Turk, the only plan I have is Niko's plan." She wondered what she had said or done to make Turk suspicious of her real intent, or was he just guessing? Oh well, Turk wouldn't matter in a few days. He'd be dead.

"I don't believe you, Cory. Good night."

* * *

It was a cold September morning. The fog enveloped Peachtree Airport. Turk pulled his rental car up next to Cory's BMW. The gate was still locked. He parked, grabbed his bag, and slid into the front seat. The car was warm and Cory had purchased an extra cup of hot coffee, which she handed to Turk, and said, "Just the way you like it, black."

"Thanks," Turk said. Not another word was spoken for ten minutes. The silence was loud. Cory broke it, and asked, "Are you as scared as I am, Turk?"

"I don't know if scared is the word, but concerned...I am."

"What are you concerned about?"

"Anytime you're meeting with undesirables, whom I seem to attract, there's cause for concern. The folks that are transporting us to New York could very well take us anywhere. What do they need us for?"

"I've thought about that, too. They've basically left us alone for this long. I figure they will continue to leave us alone as long as they get their cut."

"Niko was a tough deal maker. They'll want more, you know."

"That's why I'm...I mean...we'll increase their cut to twenty-five percent of the gross." Cory hoped Turk didn't pick up on her faux pas.

Turk did pick up on it, but chose to ignore it and answered, "Yeah...that will probably do it. Hey, the fog is lifting. Our plane should be here soon."

"Our plane is here. It landed last night. It's parked somewhere on the damn runway. Excuse me, runway," She said, smiling at Turk for saying *damn*. She would miss him, she thought.

"Good catch, Cory. Let's get on out of here."

The plane taxied up to the gate, and a large man lowered the stairs, looking up and down the runway, and seeing Cory and Turk, motioned to them. They quickly boarded, followed by the man and then out of the shadows came a second man. It was obvious to both of them that this second man was armed and was there to insure that things went smoothly, or at least that's what Cory and Turk hoped. The small Gulf Stream jet taxied down the runway, and with a powerful thrust, they were off to New York. Both men sat across from Cory and Turk, staring straight ahead, not saying a word. Two hours later, they landed at a small undisclosed airport just outside New York City.

A Lincoln Town car sped toward them just as they came to a stop. Two more very large men got out of the car and motioned for them to get in. There were a few words exchanged between their escorts, and the same scene was repeated. Their new escorts sat across from them, staring straight ahead also not saying a word. Both Cory and Turk were nervous. Turk had to see if he could break the silence, and said, "Where are we meeting?" No response. "Come on, guys, what the hell is going on?" Still no response. "I'm not very comfortable, guys; someone better say something," Turk said, raising his voice.

"What you gonna do, Donatelli? Shut up. We'll be there soon

enough," the man across from Turk retorted.

Cory said, "You heard the man, Turk. Shut up...we'll be there soon enough." Spoken like a trooper when Cory was shitting her pants, thought Turk. But she did sound in total control.

"We can tell who wears the pants in this operation, Donatelli, and it ain't you," the second escort said, smiling, while jabbing his partner in the ribs with his elbow.

"Why don't you both fuck off?" Turk said, figuring if they were going to hurt them they would have done it by now. It was obvious they were hired as delivery men, and they were proficient at it.

They pulled into a warehouse parking lot. The two escorts got out and one of them said, "Follow me." Turk wondered if Buck Morley was tracking them and how. These guys were very efficient.

It was cold and dark. The cloud cover engulfed the parking lot. One escort slid a large overhead door open. The sound could be described as rusty, old. The warehouse was dark with the exception of a dim light way in the back of the space. Their second escort said, in a gruff New York accent, "Are yoose armed?"

"We're not. We've already been frisked," Turk answered for both of them.

"We need to make sure, both of you lean up against the wall."

Turk panicked. The FBI had sewn something into the lining of his jacket. Unzipping his jacket, he lifted his arms high above his head, hoping this would lessen the possibility of them finding whatever it was that was in the lining. They weren't very good at frisking, Turk had been patted down many times and it was obvious to him that this guy didn't know what he was doing. Feeling a sense of relief, Turk said, "Look this has been a long trip. Can't we get on with this?"

"Shut up, and walk toward that light."

Meanwhile, in Atlanta, the GBI, the FBI and the Fulton County sheriffs departments executed a pre-planned early morning raid on twelve adult book stores and arrested the managers. Vera Staidly was taken into custody and bail was set at one million dollars. Gerri Short was arrested for aiding and abetting a fugitive from justice. The District Attorney seized what was left of Niko's real estate assets, including the apartments Turk conveyed to Niko's wife authorized by the tough RICO Act specifically written to stop racketeers from investing in legal assets. None of these activities were known to the mob members whom Cory and Turk were to meet.

Turk didn't feel right about this meeting. He'd figured that they weren't going to meet at the same restaurant. The mob was smarter than that. When Turk brought this to the attention of FBI Agent Morley, he said, "Don't worry about that Turk. We've got your back." *Easy for him to say*, thought Turk.

As they approached the dimly-lit room, Turk could make out three men, one sitting at a small table and two standing behind him. With the two men behind them and the new players, Turk was very uncomfortable. He glanced to his left and to his right, looking for an escape route if he needed one. Directly behind the table was a door. Probably the same entry these guys came in through. To Turk's left was a long hallway leading to what, he didn't know but it was wide and very dark. He might be able to sprint down that hallway to an exit. He figured that his jogging the last several months should allow him an advantage over his pursuers. Still, he felt like a trapped animal must feel; he was trapped. He hoped Buck would come through if needed.

"Have a seat." The man sitting at the table instructed. Cory and Turk complied, Cory looking as white as a sheet. Turk was determined not to show any emotion.

"Let's take care of business so we can all get out of here," the seated man said, also in a thick New York accent. This made both Cory and Turk feel a little better. At least that seemed to be an indication they were going to be able to leave.

Cory looked at Turk and Turk at Cory, Turk realizing that Cory wasn't about to start the negotiations, so he took the lead. "You know Niko is in jail. We're here to personally insure that the adult entertainment business will be run by Cory and the Atlanta staff just like it always has been."

Looking Cory and Turk up and down, the seated man said, "What's your role, Donatelli? Niko didn't say nothin' bout youse playing a part."

This took Turk by surprise. He'd overlooked the possibility of that question. During his hesitation, Cory, bridging the gap, stated, "I've offered Turk a position in our organization. He's our real estate developer. We plan on building more stores."

"You'll be lucky to keep the ones you got. No matter, what's in it for us?"

Cory continued, "We'll increase your cut to twenty-five percent."

"What makes you think a woman can continue running the 'fuck business?" the man said indignantly.

Turk responded, "How about an introduction?"

Obviously irritated, the man said, "Names don't matter. You don't need to know. How is she," pointing a stubby finger at Cory, "goin'na run Niko's operation if she can't even speak for herself?"

Placing her duffel bag on the table, Cory said with total conviction and authority, "Look, this bag contains a million dollars in cash. I've been handling Niko's affairs now for nearly two damn years, while he fights to stay out of prison. Your cut has always been delivered right on time. That will continue. Now take this million as good faith on my part and we'll increase your take to twenty-five percent, like I said." Turk was impressed; Cory was convincing.

The man looked past Cory and said to the escort, "How come you don't know what was in this bag? It could have been a goddamn bomb…you idiot." The man he addressed standing behind Cory looked down and said, "I thought it was some overnight stuff, I did."

"You ain't worth a shit, never have been. You're only here because of your damn brother," the man said, turning his attention back to Cory. "It looks like you know how to deal. If we agree to your terms, what do you expect from us?"

"I need some muscle to keep our store operators in line. Ours have either been jailed or are on the run."

The man thought for a moment, and said, "We can do that. Give us a million a month so we don't have to do any accounting and you got a deal."

Cory hesitated, choosing her words slowly and lowering her voice. "Make it a half million and you got a deal." She said this with such quiet authority, it startled Turk.

"You drive a hard bargain, lady. Five hundred ain't enough. You've got to do better."

Cory had been negotiating deals for Niko for years; she was in her element. Not hesitating or showing any fear, she quickly said, "Look, we got to get this done. This is what I've been authorized to do. You either take twenty-five percent of the gross or a half-million a month…that's it."

The man stood, put both hands on the table, and leaned toward Cory and hissed, "Okay, lady, now I'll tell you what we'll do. You'll deliver 750-thou a month and you'll agree to that or we'll come to that shithole Atlanta and take it all…how's that?"

Cory stood and faced the man. "That's too damn much. You might be able to come to Atlanta and take over the business, but the way I got it figured, you don't want to. There's too much heat there right now. You heard my deal and that's it... take it or leave it."

The man sat back down, smiling. Then turning to his bodyguards, he said, "This lady got balls. It looks like we can do business." Looking at Cory, he said, "Okay, you got a deal; that is, as long as Niko can hold onto it." Just as the man finished saying that and before Cory could respond another tall, muscular man came running across the warehouse floor and said, "Boss, something going on outside. We need to get to hell out of here! We've been set up."

Turk never saw so many guns appear so fast. All six men held their pistols and pointed them at him and Cory. The boss yelled, "Bring them with us!" They ran toward the exit behind them, dragging Cory and pushing Turk.

Turk seeing an opportunity in all the confusion, bolted for the dark alley, leading to where he did not know. Three shots ricocheted off the concrete wall as he rounded the corner. No one followed him, or at least he couldn't hear anyone behind him. He plunged ahead in the dark looking for an exit. Having built many warehouses, Turk knew there had to be a ladder along the wall somewhere leading to the roof. He ran his hands along until he felt steel stairs. He climbed those until he reached the roof, hoping the scuttle hole wouldn't be locked. It was.

Outside, the five men were surrounded by FBI agents and the local police force. They all lay on the ground with their legs and arms spread. Cory lay in a pool of blood shot through the temple.

FBI Agent Buck Morley and GBI Detective Pettit stood over

Cory's body. Buck said, "She sure was pretty. Hell of a way to end her life. She wouldn't have served more than five years in prison. A good lawyer might have got her off with probation, who knows."

Looking around, Detective Pettit said, "I wonder where Donatelli is. She was his squeeze…wasn't she?"

"She was Niko's woman. Turk did her a few times. He wouldn't admit it, but I think he really cared for her."

"If he only knew that Cory had planned on killing him before he got back to Atlanta. Hell, that's none of our concern. He's got to be around here somewhere. We've got every exit covered."

Turk was hanging onto the top rung of the ladder, trying to pry open the scuttle hole to gain access to the roof. Feeling his way around the perimeter, he found what he was looking for, a dead-bolt. He easily slid the bolt open, lifted the lid and made his way to the roof. Turk guessed the building was over one-hundred-thousand square-feet. He could see powerful spotlights emanating from the parking lot in the rear of the building and cautiously made his way to the building's edge.

Peering over the stem-wall he could see the mob members being loaded into the police van. Where was Cory? Then he saw her…his heart felt like it would burst. He could make out Cory's body being transported by a gurney to the ambulance. They were in the process of draping the body. They covered her head…Cory was murdered.

Turk screamed, "You dirty bastards…I'll get you for this…all of you!" One of the detectives turned quickly looking in his direction. Turk ducked low in hopes that the confusion masked his outburst.

He tried to choke back the tears, but couldn't. He let them flow as he realized his true feeling for Cory Moran. He'd used her and she him, but in their own way, they'd loved each other. It had been more than sex, only he'd never admitted it to her. He didn't want to admit it to himself, because it made him feel so disloyal to Karen. He was going to miss her more than he thought possible. But he muttered out loud, "Get a hold of yourself, Turk...she's gone." He vowed revenge.

Turk's past flashed before his eyes. He was determined to start a new life, a life with Karen and Jason, without any type of illegal activity. He needed to get on with his plan. But first he had to figure out how to get to Vermont and make contact with Digger.

* * *

"Pettit, let's go inside and see if we can find Turk." Buck said.

"Are we going to arrest him, Buck?" Pettit asked.

"No, Turk's dealings with us are over. This was his last assignment. He's a free man."

"Free, my ass! If the mob finds him, he'll be a dead man if they think he had anything to do with this bust. Didn't he opt for the Witness Protection Program?"

"No, he said he didn't want anything to do with that. He's got a sick wife and a kid he claims he's going to care for. I think Turk's had enough. If he can avoid the mob, I think he'll be on the straight and narrow. Let's see if we can find him."

"Why?" Pettit asked.

"I've grown to like the guy. I'd like to see if I can't talk him into our Witness Protection Program. The tracking device we sewed into his jacket should tell us where he is."

"Turk's smarter than that. You can bet he shit canned that coat."

* * *

Turk took refuge between two very large roof air handlers,

which he figured would throw off enough heat to keep him from freezing to death. He would try to get some sleep and decide out how to get to Vermont in the morning. He slid off his money belt and used it for a pillow. He wished he'd kept his jacket, but he knew that whatever the FBI sewed into it would reveal his location. He had discarded the jacket in a large trash container.

* * *

Buck found Turk's jacket, smiled, and said to Pettit, "Let's get out of here. I hope the guy makes it. Turk means well. He grew up very poor and money has had a bad influence on him."

"Yeah, like I feel sorry for him. He's lived pretty damn well. His kind don't last long." Pettit had had a longer relationship with Turk than Buck, and wasn't fond of him.

"You're biased, Pettit. Turk was one step ahead of the GBI most of the time. Get over it." They both returned to the parking lot.

The six mobsters were being held on murder and accessory to murder charges, resisting arrest, and for various weapons charges. The GBI and the FBI had made a clean sweep of Niko's adult entertainment businesses. They closed down his warehouse operation and took control of the rest of Niko's assets under the guise of the RICO Act. Bobby Lee Cook would have to work hard to save Niko from the death penalty.

CHAPTER—30

Turk was sore and stiff from his night wedged between two air handlers. He stretched, secured his money belt, wiped the sleepy seeds from his eyes, and made his way to the edge of the warehouse roof. All that was left in the parking lot was a bunch of yellow tape marking off a large pool of Cory's blood. He reiterated his vow to himself to extract revenge for Cory's murder. The mob would pay.

The place was just starting to wake up. He observed men coming to work. A fork-lift operator was transporting large boxes to a waiting trailer truck. He could hear the knocking of the diesel engine warming up ready to transport its cargo. The driver was about ready to go. Turk made his way back down the steel ladder and walked out the back door to where the trailer truck was parked. No one said a word to him. The workers just went on about their business.

Turk peeled five one hundred dollar bills from his money belt and walked over to the waiting truck driver who was standing just outside his truck, and said, "Good morning. If you don't mind me asking, where you headed?"

"What's it to you, stranger?" the truck driver responded as he shifted his hat to the back of his head.

"I'm in need of a ride, and I'm willing to pay for it."

"Where you headed?"

"Vermont."

"I'm going through Vermont on my way to Montreal. You say you're willing to pay for the ride?"

"I am, and handsomely, too." Turk answered, flashing his roll of five one-hundred dollar bills.

Eyeing the bills, the truck driver said, "Where's your shit? I'm about ready to go."

Handing the bills to the driver, Turk said, "Don't have any. I'm ready to go whenever you are."

Counting the money, the driver said, "Son, I'm buying you breakfast. Let's get on out of here."

Turk had forgotten how hungry he was. Smiling he said, "How about the House of Pancakes?"

"There's one on the way out of here, about five miles, I figure. Come on," he said, as he pocketed the five hundred. This was his lucky day. He just hoped this young man wouldn't try any funny business. He'd never been hijacked before.

Turk ordered a large stack of buttermilk pancakes, three eggs, sausage, fried potatoes and whole wheat toast. The truck driver ordered biscuits and gravy and a side of bacon. He said, "You must be mighty hungry, son."

"I am. What's your name?" Turk asked.

"My handle is Wild Bill. What's yours?"

Turk thought for a minute, and said, "Sandy."

"You got a last name?"

"Let's leave it at Sandy, if you don't mind, Wild Bill."

"What cha running from, Sandy?"

"Myself mostly, Wild Bill...myself."

"No matter. I don't need to know nothing. You ain't planning any bad shit, are you?"

"Wild Bill, you've got nothing to worry about. You leave me off in Vermont along the way and I'll give you another thousand dollars and you haven't seen me...how's that?"

"For that kind of money, I'll take you anywhere. Where do you want to go?"

"No need for you to know. You can let me off as soon as we get to Vermont."

"You got it, Sandy. You're too young to be running from the law, you know."

"Trust me, Wild Bill, I'm not running from the law. How's your breakfast?"

Wild Bill knew by Sandy's tone that this conversation was over. Wiping up the last of his gravy, he said, "Mine's pretty good. Yours must have been better." He couldn't believe Turk had eaten the whole damn breakfast.

"How long will it take us to get to Vermont, Wild Bill?"

"Not long, four hours and we should be in Brattleboro."

"That will work. Let me off at the first truck stop."

"I know where there's a good one just outside the city." Wild Bill liked Sandy.

"You mind if I nod off and try and catch a few hours sleep?"

"Don't mind a bit. I'll turn off my radio."

"Thanks, Wild Bill." Turk surface-slept for the next two hours. A deep sleep would come later, he hoped.

Turk could feel the down shifting of the big tractor trailer as Wild Bill exited Highway 95. He was familiar with the Brattleboro area, having caddied at the local country club when he was a kid.

Wild Bill pulled up to the gas pumps, and asked, "You sure you won't reconsider and let me take you to wherever you're going, Sandy," knowing full well Sandy wasn't this young man's name.

Taking out ten one-hundred dollars bills from his pouch, Turk said, "Thanks, Wild Bill. You've lived up to your end of our deal. You never saw me." Handing him the money, Turk slid out the door and disappeared into the rest station.

At a small canteen located next to the food courts, Turk bought shaving gear, a toothbrush, deodorant, and a pullover hooded sweatshirt with "Home of Ethan Allen the Green Mountain Boys" embossed on the front. He then proceeded to the men's room to shave, and wash up. Feeling refreshed, he sought out and found an auto-advertising magazine, purchased a large cup of black coffee, a cinnamon sticky-bun and took a seat and perused the used auto section, looking for a car. He found a 1959 Ford Station Wagon advertised for twenty-five-hundred dollars or best-offer.

He went to the bank of payphones and called the owner. "Sir, I'm interested in your Ford Wagon. How many miles does it have on it?"

"I've logged seventy-five thousand miles on her and she runs good. I've kept the maintenance records, I have," the enthusiastic seller chirped.

"Runs good, you say?" Turk was trying not to sound like he was in a hurry.

"Tell you what, mister. You buy it today and I'll take twenty-two hundred, in cash, that is," he said, sounding anxious to sell.

Picking up on this, Turk said, "Will you deliver it?"

"It depends on how far I've got to come."

"The truck stop on Highway 91, Exit 4."

"That ain't far. You got cash?"

"I have cash. If you can deliver the car in the next two hours,

I'll pay you three-thousand for it."

Turk heard a gasp from the seller. Then he said, "Mister, you got a deal! I'll be there in thirty minutes or less. Where will you be?"

"I'll be sitting in the rest area. What color is the car?"

"Black."

"I'll see you pull up. I'll meet you in the parking lot right out front...how's that?"

"Like I said, mister, I'll be there in short order."

In twenty minutes, Turk saw the black Ford station wagon pulling up in front of the rest stop. A Chevy pickup truck followed. He motioned to the seller, who parked in an empty spot not far from the gas pumps. The Ford was rusted out due to the salt used on the Vermont roads during the winter. Turk didn't care as long as it got him to Braintree, Vermont.

"Who's that following you?"

"My wife...I ain't walking back to my house."

"You bring a bill-of-sale?"

"Sure did."

"Sign it and we'll be done."

"How you want it made out?"

"Leave it blank, I'll fill it in."

"Okay, mister. Don't you want to test drive it?"

"You drove it here. That's good enough for me."

"You seem mighty anxious, mister."

"I got some pressing family business to attend. Here's your cash."

"You got a name?" the seller asked as he pocketed the hundred dollar bills.

"Hank."

"Here's an extra set of keys, Hank. Any trouble, you just let me know. I ain't selling you no lemon, you know."

"You look like an honest man. Thanks, I've got to get on the road." Turk folded the bill of sale and shoved it into the glove box. Looking at the gas gauge which was on empty, he bid the seller goodbye and pulled up next to the gas pumps.

"Fill her up." Turk said to the attendant. He checked the oil, and washed the windshield.

"That'll be $6.80 please. Want me to empty the ash tray?"

"No, that's it. Thanks."

Turk pulled onto the highway, bent on getting to Braintree before nightfall. As a kid, Turk hunted in the mountains surrounding this small town. Now, he would travel the back roads looking for a farm house to rent.

He pulled into the corner country store in the middle of Braintree around three o'clock that afternoon. It had been fifteen years since he'd been there. He didn't think there would be anyone there he knew. He was hungry. He bought a grape soda and a grinder and asked the clerk, "You know of any places to rent around here?"

"Sure lots of places. What you looking for?" she asked as she rung up his purchase.

"I'm thinking about a farm house with some land. I'm not sure, but I'd like a place in the country."

"Heck, mister, you're in the country. It doesn't get any more country than Braintree. The Townsend place is up for sale or rent. Won't be cheap, though. They done it all over."

"Where's it located?"

"Up on old Camp Brook Road. You know where that is?"

Turk did know, but said, "No, I'm not familiar with the area." The clerk gave him directions. He thanked her and went to his car, drank his grape soda, and relished his grinder, a Vermont staple.

The farm house was exactly what Turk was looking for. An

out-of-stater had refurbished the white colonial-style building. The sign indicated that 260 acres came with it. Turk went back to the country store. He stuffed a quarter into the payphone and said to the operator, "Collect call to St. Pete, Florida, please."

"Digger, meet me at the Albany, New York, airport on Friday. I'll be waiting. Let me talk to Karen, please." Turk didn't want to stay on the telephone too long. The FBI probably was still tracing his calls.

Relieved to talk to his friend, Digger said, "You got it, boss. Just a minute, I'll see if I can get her on the phone."

"Hi Turk, how are you?" Karen asked, sounding depressed.

"Baby, I'm fine. I've got us a nice place...just like we talked about. Jason will have to adjust but you and I can live in peace for a while and beat that damn disease, MS. You'll love it, Karen."

Perking up, Karen asked, "Are you where I think you are, Turk?" She knew better than to name the state. Maybe her dream of living out her remaining days in the quiet and solitude of rural Vermont was about to come true.

"Yes, baby. We'll plant that garden. I can't wait to see you guys. Please follow Digger's instructions and tell Jason I'll see him soon. I miss you terribly. We'll fight MS together. I'll care for you and Jason, I will."

* * *

"We're done with Turk Donatelli. No need to monitor his calls anymore." FBI Agent Buck Morley said to his subordinate. "He's free at last. Let's hope he stays that way."

* * * * * * * * * * * *

For a preview of another exciting novel, turn the page!

A Preview....

Eva Pennington...Trouble in Georgia

By Walter Luce

1968　　　　　　　　　　　　　　　　CHAPTER 1

While Eva waited at the small private landing strip next to her Henderson, North Carolina Estate, she watched a twin-engine plane land and taxi down the runway. Emerging from the plane was Dutch Unger, whom she had called immediately after her mother's passing. She ran to him, throwing herself into his arms, exclaiming, "Dutch, I've waited so long for this. I hope you still want me. I'm ready to deal with the past and move on. Don't leave me, Dutch. I need you."

It had taken Ramon months to stage Myra's death. Smiling, Ramon, the master of disguise, observed, and approved of this reunion, knowing full well that Eva would need him in the future. Her career as one of the wealthiest, most powerful bankers in the country was just beginning. Interstate banking has been recently approved by Congress.

"Eva, I'm so sorry. Is there anything I can do?" Dutch asked, as he held her tightly.

"Just hold me, Dutch, just hold me," she said, sobbing. This was totally out of character for Eva; she never cried.

"I won't let you go, Eva. I don't want to let you go." Dutch had been courting Eva for years while she built the largest banking institution in Florida. She was too busy making deals, fighting for her depositors, and her inner demons to be with him. This was his chance, or so he thought. "Are we staying here for a few days or are we going back to St. Pete?"

"I'm not sure. Let's go to the house, have a drink and talk about it. Are you good with that, Dutch?"

"I am, but I need a place for my pilot."

"I'll have my mother's driver put him up in one of our guest houses."

"That's a good idea. Where is he?"

"He just dropped me off. He can't be far," Eva said, looking around.

"I see the car, but I don't see her driver. Are you sure he's still here?"

"Where could he have gone?" Ramon was in his van on his way back to Raleigh Airport. His next stop would be his beach front condo in Cancun, Mexico. Myra would meet him there. It would take Eva time to get over her mother's staged passing. He only hoped she would forgive Myra for their deceit if she uncovered it.

"Let's see if the keys are still in it," Dutch said.

Dutch peeked through the window. The keys were in the ignition. "What kind of employee would just run off and leave the keys in the ignition? You ought to fire his ass, whoever he is." Dutch was a tough construction man. He had a hard time dealing with incompetence.

"I've got a funny feeling we won't see him again, Dutch." Eva thought the driver looked familiar when he picked her up at the airport, but she still couldn't put her finger on why. "You want me to drive?"

Dutch smiled, and said, "I remember the first time you drove me around. Do you?" He thought back to their first meeting. Eva had denied him a large apartment loan when she managed the St. Pete, Florida, Sunset Bank branch for her father, Hans. He could remember it like it was yesterday...

He had returned to his office after a meeting at her bank. Afterwards, he could not get the image of Eva out of his mind. He needed to know more about her; he wanted to possess her.

He had buzzed Sheri Wells, his executive assistant, and said over the speaker, "Sheri, please come in for a minute."

Sheri Wells was Concept Construction Company's first employee, which now employed several hundred. Sheri was the only person in his company whom Dutch trusted totally.

Note pad in hand, Sheri said, "Yes, Dutch, what do you need?"

"Sheri, remember when we applied for an apartment loan for our Cross Creek project, and it was denied by Sunset Bank? Then you made me an appointment with Miss Pennington to discuss the reasons for turning it down."

"I remember."

"Well, she stood me up. I had some harsh words for her assistant, a little pansy named Witherstone...something like that. I told him in no uncertain terms I wanted another meeting with his boss to discuss the Cross Creek loan."

Sheri interrupted and said, "That's Timmy Witherspoon, not Witherstone. He's a good guy, Dutch."

Not missing a beat, Dutch leaned back in his chair, arms folded, and continued. "Maybe he is. Anyway, on my way out of the bank, I saw this woman. I found out she's the daughter of the banking magnate, Hans Pennington."

Interrupting him again as Sheri always did when Dutch wanted some information he didn't really want to ask for, she said, "Dutch, where are you going with this? I've got work to do."

He continued, "Be patient with me, Sheri, for heavens sake. All right, I want to know more about her. Is she married? How old she is? Where she lives; anything you can find out before I meet her. Can you do that for me?"

Laughing, Sheri said, "Now that wasn't so hard was it, Dutch? You could have told me it was another woman you were after." Dutch had been seeing several beautiful women since his divorce.

"That's not it this time, Sheri." Dutch was serious. "There's something about this one I can't put my finger on. She's different. She looks powerful. She had magnetism, and she's drop-dead gorgeous."

"I've heard that before. This won't take long; anything else?" Sheri asked, amused.

"Yes, follow up with that fellow Witherstone for an appointment with Miss Pennington."

Sheri knew Dutch would never remember Timmy's name. Once Dutch called someone something, it stuck. It would always be Witherstone to him. Chuckling, she said, "His name is Witherspoon, Dutch. Got anything else?"

"That's all for now, Sheri. Just set that meeting up for me, please."

* * *

Dutch Unger was one of Sunset Bank's largest depositors. Not wanting to lose his account, Eva felt she needed to console him for turning down his loan. Anticipating this meeting, she dressed less conservative than she usually did. She knew how to use her beauty as a business tool.

Her suit was a softer blue, skirt cut high on the thigh. She wore higher heeled shoes, accentuating her shapely, long legs.

Her blouse was white silk, bow-tie gone, buttoned to expose just a peek of her breasts. Her vest was open to her waist, just short of her rounded hips. Her chestnut-colored hair fell to her shoulders, framing her beautiful face. Eva looked professional, but at the same time sexy, just the way she intended. She rose to greet Dutch Unger, and said, "Mr. Unger, I apologize for not rescheduling our appointment personally. Your business means a lot to Sunset Bank."

Bowled over by her beauty, Dutch said, "Miss Pennington, no apology necessary. I'm the one who owes your assistant an apology. I was rough on him, I think."

Eva liked what she saw. She was attracted to Dutch. She felt his manliness; she could smell it. And he exuded confidence. "Timmy can be a little sensitive," she said. "I understand you wanted to see me about your loan request being denied. Cross Creek apartments, I believe."

Dutch was on a duel mission: to get a loan from Sunset Banks for his apartment project and to seduce Eva Marie Pennington, in that order. "Miss Pennington," he answered, "I'm sure you have reviewed my file, my history with your bank, and my original loan application. So you know I'm a qualified borrower. What I'd like to know is why you turned down my loan?"

Shifting in her chair, Eva leaned back, flipping her hair. She looked directly into Dutch's eyes, trying to conceal her attraction to him, and not doing it very well. "Mr. Unger, I denied your loan request for one reason: the project's location. It's near the dump. Toy Town, I believe it's called. Your credit and reputation are excellent."

Noting what he thought was her attraction to him, Dutch said, "I think I can prove to you that this is a very desirable location for an apartment building. By the way, it's a landfill, not a dump," he gently corrected her.

Now in her best business mode, Eva said, "Mr. Unger, I've lived here all my life. I feel I know the area well. How do you think you can validate this location enough for us to loan you three-million dollars?"

Dutch was ready for this question, and asked, "Are you willing to go for a ride with me?"

Feeling this was out of the ordinary, Eva said, "Our criteria for approving a loan doesn't include getting into a stranger's car." She smiled, and was glad he asked her to go for a ride.

Growing impatient, Dutch quickly said, "Let me be perfectly clear. You tell me you're not going to make the loan because of the location. Now in order for me to convince you differently, I need to show you the property. The only way we can do that is in my car or yours. Now if for some reason you're uncomfortable with that, ask your man Witherstone out there to ride with us. I don't like to drive. You'll have to, so come on and let's go."

By now, Eva, was totally enamored with Dutch. His protest only heightened her interest, and she said, "Its Witherspoon, not Witherstone, Mr. Unger. Do we take your car or mine?"

"You're driving; let's take yours. Is Withersp-o-o-o-n coming with us?" he teased.

"I don't think he needs to come, and besides, Mr. Unger, you advised Timmy not to get his 'knickers in a knot," Eva chuckled as she stood to leave.

Dutch got the dig and said, "Lead the way. I need to get a set of plans and a sack out of my car. I'll meet you out front."

Dutch was having a hard time concentrating on giving Eva directions. Her car was a standard shift BMW. While shifting gears, her dress hiked way above the knees exposing her inner thighs. She must have noticed and said, "Mr. Unger, eyes on the road, please. What street do I turn on?" She made no attempt at adjusting her skirt.

Dutch blushed, totally caught, laughed and said, "I'm sorry. Turn left on Fourth Street. You'll see my sign on the right. Pull up there." He still looked at her legs out of the corner of his eye.

Eva was feeling more woman than banker. She liked the attention Dutch was trying not to give her. Smiling seductively, she said, "It looks like we've arrived."

Dutch, now the developer, said, "Okay, let's walk."

Eva wasn't ready for this and said, "Walk in high heels? I can't tramp through Palmettos wearing these."

Reaching into his sack, Dutch pulled out two pair of snake boots. He handed a pair to Eva. "Put these on; they should fit."

"Pretty sure of yourself, Mr. Unger, weren't you? And you knew my size?" She was impressed.

"I thought I might get your attention and Sherri knew your size. Does that surprise you?"

"It doesn't surprise me in the least. I'm beginning to expect the unexpected from you. Can we dispense with the last names?"

"I feel better already, Eva. Please call me Dutch." *Now I'm getting somewhere*, he thought.

"Dutch, it is. Now try and sell me on this location, which is downwind from a dump."

Smiling, he corrected her again, "No, Eva, it's a landfill. It *was* a dump. What you call a dump is covered with four feet of dirt being graded right now. Can you smell anything?" Now in his selling mode, Dutch didn't allow Eva to answer and continued excitedly answering his own question.

"You can't. I purchased this property five years ago. It was only a matter of time it would be ripe for development. St. Pete is developed right up to the Gulf of Mexico. This was the only property left to expand the city limits. This location is close to the entry to Tampa via the Gandy Bridge. You can see the bridge and the bay from here. Are you still with me, Eva?"

Eva and Dutch were now walking through the middle of the apartment property that used to be Toy Town landfill. Dutch thought Eva looked sexy in her snake boots; he observed her every move.

"I'm still with you, Dutch. Your apartment project doesn't make the dump...err...excuse me, landfill, go away, you know." She was having a difficult time not referring to this landfill as a dump.

"I know that, Eva, but a golf course does."

"I read about a golf course project being built on a landfill site. Cross Creek Country Club, isn't it? I never connected the location with your proposed apartment project, though I should have...how unobservant of me."

"That's the one. You'll be able to see my contractor grading the site once we get to the clearing up ahead."

Eva grasped the concept quickly. He was a damn genius. She hadn't made the connection until now. "I'm very familiar with the development of Cross Creek Country Club. It's an environmental phenomenon partially financed by the city. Now that I think of it, our banks bought a majority of the municipal bonds for this project. Dutch I don't need to see any more. You made your point. We'll reconsider your loan."

"You're not getting off that easy, Eva. Let's stop at Pippins. I'll let you buy me lunch. What do you say?"

Eva Pennington...Trouble in Georgia ...
coming this fall from Oak Tree Press....
Take advantage of the pre-publication special at
www.ShopOTPBooks.com

ABOUT THE AUTHOR

WALTER W. LUCE was born in Vermont where he still spends his summers. He has been a successful real estate developer in Florida, Georgia, and California. He lives in the Palm Springs, California area with his wife Bonnie, where he wrote his first novel of five, ***Eva Pennington.***

He is the oldest of seven. He graduated from Braintree Randolph Union High School in 1962, and attended Miami Dade Junior college after being honorably discharged from the Army in 1967.

His hobbies are writing, running and golf.